All Traitors'

Day

Jim McDermott

Abbreviations used in the text

FDGB - *Freier Deutsche Gewerkschaftsbund*: the umbrella organization representing thousands of small trades unions in the German Democratic Republic, it was a subsidiary organization of, and entirely subordinate to, the **SED**. The chairman of the **FDGB** usually sat upon the **SED**'s Politburo.

KVP – *Kasernierte VolksPolizei*: Paramilitary wing of the People's Police, based, until 1954, at the Adlershof Barracks in Berlin. Highly indoctrinated and relatively well paid, its members were ostensibly under the authority of the Ministry of the Interior (**DVdI**); however, many reported directly to **MfS**, and their units invariably acted with, and under the operational control of, Soviet military forces. **KVP** were the precursors of the East German National People's Army (**NVA**)

MfS – *Ministerium für Staatssicherheitsdienst* (often abbreviated to **SSD**): Ministry for State Security, its employees were referred to colloquially (from 1953) as *Stasi*

MGB - Ministerstvo Gosudarstvennoy Bezopasnosti SSSR: Ministry for State Security, counter-intelligence successor organization (from March 1946) to the former **NKGB**, and forerunner of **KGB**

SA – Sturmabteilung: 'Storm Detachment' – paramilitary force of the National Socialist Party during Hitler's rise to power. It was emasculated, and largely replaced by the SS, following the 1934 purge of its leader, Ernst Röhm, and his lieutenants

SED – Sozialistische Einheitspartei Deutschlands: German Socialist Unity Party, which governed the **DDR** throughout its existence.

Prologue: 7.30am, 17 June 1953

'The Government of the Democratic Republic is not in the business of assassination. Nor does it condone extra-judicial killings, even when the national interest may demand it. The moral nation must accept the risks that moral behaviour sometimes invites.'

These observations were offered in much the same way as Moses offered the new rules to his drunken, fornicating tribes. Their recipient - a slightly-built young man with a reticent air, the sort who invites no second glances – nodded seriously, though he was puzzled to discover that the Politburo had somehow shovelled together enough of its own shit to build and occupy a high ground. There may have been a memo; he hadn't seen it.

'Of course, the State has no view on the morality of suicide. Theists may disapprove, but taking one's own life has long been regarded as an act of self-control, even of nobility, when done in the service of principle.'

A penny dropped. The audience nodded again and cleared his throat. 'And accidental death?'

'Is what it is. No government can have a policy regarding fate, or ill-fortune.'

'Who's the prize-winner?'

A file was pushed across the table. The young man removed the single sheet of paper and studied it carefully. He was surprised by what he read but didn't show it. In the past year all sorts and shades of seemingly normal citizens had done abnormal things, and in the three months since the Great Man's death the world had all but inverted, making ordinary what once might have been considered singular. In these strange days a prudent man received all revelations without comment or opinion.

He placed the paper back in its file. 'How quickly is this to be done?'

'Naturally, you should confirm to your own satisfaction that he's guilty of what it implies. Once you have, don't waste any time.'

'Is it something that's to be advertised, afterwards? Or am I to be discrete?'

The other man frowned and examined the view from his third-floor window. 'What he's done – *if* he's done it - can't be hidden. The men under his immediate command will have to be told immediately, and by evening I assume that everyone in the Party will be gossiping about it. To that extent, it's going to be broadcast by default. As to making something more of it, we must be cautious. He's become a popular man – though of course, he has enemies.'

'Who doesn't?'

'Quite. We'll leave the matter open for the moment. For now, make sure that it doesn't look like what it is. If you need to contact us during the operation, speak directly to your Minister. Give the name *Josef*; he'll know what it's about. '

'Yes, Comrade Secretary.' The young man had been a child soldier during the last weeks of the war, pushed into a too-large uniform, given an hour's tuition in the mysteries of the *Panzerfaust* and then shoved towards 4th Soviet Shock Army with his platoon commander's best wishes. Nevertheless, he had acquired a great deal more experience since his personal surrender (ten minutes after receiving the shove), assembling a range of techniques whose results resembled aneurisms, strokes, stumbles under assorted means of public transport and other opaque conditions or events that invited an *inconclusive* conclusion to autopsy reports. He regarded himself as something of a specialist in the field, given that most of his colleagues employed only the obvious and plainly-advertised means of expunging enemies of the People. It was why he had been chosen for the job - a very special, sensitive job, not to be discussed or reminisced about afterwards - perhaps never to be discovered as a *job* at all.

He stood up and, not being familiar with the protocols of dealing with the highest echelons of a socialist state, offered the other man a short, shallow bow.

'Where can I find him?'

For the first time, the other man seemed less than at ease. 'We … don't know.'

'He's gone already?'

'This morning, we think, or possibly last evening. He may be *over there* as we speak.'

'Ah.' This made the task something else entirely, and he was glad now that they hadn't yet addressed the matter of remuneration. Unlike all other 'employees' of the Ministry of State Security he was not on any departmental payroll, and each of his assignments had been costed (in a most unsocialist way) with regard to its difficulties and objective. For a moment he was tempted to open the negotiation now, at the present meeting, but decided that the irony was too sweet not to relish for a little while longer. After all, this was probably going to be his best-paid work to date, and its success would be camouflaged by the confusion attending what was growing – exploding, even - into the single greatest collective negotiation in their young Republic's history.

1

For Fischer the day began as most others did, with a visit from Frau Siebert and her broken Hettich. When he unlocked the shop door a little after eight she was waiting in the porch, as patient as a tree, the item carefully wrapped - as always - in brown paper. It was a heavy thing (he had lifted it dozens of times, and could probably guess the weight to within twenty grams), but her frail frame seemed to cope admirably with the odd shape and the time she spent in its company. As with a large but benignly cancerous growth, the body had become familiar with the burden.

He took it gently from her hands and invited her to step inside. The stove was lit already, the filled kettle on its plate and tea spooned into two only-slightly chipped Dresdner cups he had acquired a year earlier as part-payment for a small job. She warmed herself, waiting while he cleared spaces around the shop that, hopefully, would be occupied by other, better customers during the coming hours.

When she had a cup in her hands he made a show of examining the Hettich. Its face was intact except for a small, neat hole below the one that accommodated the winding key. The rear panel was entirely unmarked also, hinting at nothing of what had happened in the small, crowded space between. The bullet – Soviet 7.62 mm ordnance - had gone in cleanly but then been deflected, wrecking everything it encountered and not quite escaping the resulting tangle. Knowing all of this already, he opened the back and pretended to assess carefully what he saw.

'I'm afraid it can't be fixed, Frau Siebert.' He spoke formally, as a priest would when inviting a congregation to recite the Lord's Prayer.

She looked at the clock sadly. 'But it's such a small hole.'

'There's a great deal of damage inside. It would need rebuilding, and I can't get the parts.'

He kept no log of her visits, but was certain that their exchanges hadn't varied by so much as a word in the months she had been coming to him with hope in her heart and a damn big, useless clock in her arms.

'My husband Erich bought it for me, our tenth anniversary.'

Unlike his wife, Erich Siebert didn't care about the clock. Fischer couldn't say whether it had been occupying his thoughts on the particular morning in January 1943 that his unit was wiped out by an unluckily well-aimed BM-13, but all mortal matters (horological or otherwise) had fled his attention thereafter. Frau Siebert didn't seem to be fully aware of her loss, any more than she was of her countless previous visits to *Fischer's Time-piece Repairs*, Curtius-Strasse 23.

'Well, at least you have it still, even if it can't tell you the correct time. It's a pretty piece, a good ornament for your mantelpiece.'

As always, the words seemed to comfort her a little, and she said nothing more as he re-wrapped the clock with a ridiculous show of reverence and then poured more tea into her cup. Being of a cynical bent, he had at first suspected the routine to be a sham, her means of obtaining a couple of hot drinks each morning and the human company that Erich could no longer provide; but there was a quality to her detachment, a degree of imperviousness, that couldn't be pretended by any mimic. It was quite obvious that Frau Siebert's clock had stopped in every sense, and wasn't likely to be repaired.

When her cup was drained for the second time she picked up the Hettich, nodded her thanks and allowed him to hold open the door for her. It was raining now and the brown paper wouldn't do its job for long, but neither clock nor owner were capable of being much affected for the worse. He stood in the porch, watching her shuffle off towards Kadettenweg, letting the drops refresh the side of his head where hair couldn't grow, hoping (as he always did) that he would see her the following day.

The rain was going to keep people indoors until they needed not to be, so he decide to sweep the shop floor and rearrange his sparse furniture in such a way as to provide a more satisfying retail environment (he had a few repaired but unclaimed clocks, sitting on a plank between two chairs in front of the window, that were touting earnestly for new owners). This task consumed less than half an hour, and, having no items currently in need of repair in the tiny backroom that served as a critical ward, he resigned himself to another day of speculation upon whether his brilliant investment opportunity was turning out to be such.

A good friend, Adolph 'Earl' Kuhn, had once considered the matter and concluded that Otto Fischer knew as much about business as he (Kuhn) did about Opera; that someone who had grown up in steady, paid employment was poorly equipped to launch himself upon the seas of speculation, particularly in the doldrum'd pool of post-war German Commerce. To this, Fischer had insisted (as his dead wife had once insisted to him) that a smashed nation was a land of opportunity: that all wars, however devastating, brought vigorous new growth eventually. Kuhn could hardly deny the point (having been solely responsible for resurrecting - in fact, creating - the recorded jazz market in poor, unsuspecting Bremen), but opportunities required the means to grasp at them, and in his opinion Otto Fischer's tarpaulin-lined mittens were not up to the challenge.

Fischer had a great affection for Kuhn, who had nurtured his friend's monies as he would his own during the former's dark years of imprisonment. He had equally great faith in Kuhn's business acumen, and knew that a future with *West Side Records* would have been the prudent choice; but the offer to resume their partnership following his release had not been hard to refuse. A man had to let go, even of safe, profitable things, if something new were to be given room to breathe and grow.

He glanced around the fourteen-month-old empire that had sprung from this revelation. It was small, shabby and sounded wonderful, the non-synchronisation of a dozen clocks dusting his ears with the patter of tiny cogs, all of whose movements (being, as they were, moving) owed their resurrection to him. The work was painstaking and intricate but satisfied the soul, and was due to pass into actual, financial profit no later than 1990, if the present volume of trade could be sustained. Naturally, he'd be dust and bones by then; but he comforted himself that the pharaohs hadn't let death get in the way of a sound, long-term plan.

By nine o'clock he had seen no further custom, and decided to re-fill the kettle for when Jonas Kleiber arrived. Kleiber was a recent acquaintance, a rake-thin young man employed three doors away at the offices of the *Südwest-Berliner Zeitung*, a hopeful but struggling journal. He was what pulp fiction referred to as an 'ace' (more accurately, an 'only') reporter, whose roving brief allowed him many minutes of the working day to himself and who often used them to avail himself of Fischer's hospitality. In another age he might also have been called a philosopher, a quality that hardly assisted him in his chosen career. He was interested in trends, perceptions and much-disrupted realities, while mere events he saw only as the rough weave from which a proper view of life might be fashioned. This attitude did not endear him to his editor, who employed him only because the profession, like most others in Germany, had suffered a catastrophic pruning of its ranks, courtesy of one rather large, relatively recent *event*.

Before the kettle could whistle the door opened and the object stepped in. Though the morning was reasonably warm he wore a woollen scarf wrapped around his neck, its ends tucked rakishly into a thick twill jacket – his *standing-around-for-hours-doing-bugger-all* outfit, as he had introduced it during the depths of the previous winter.

'Ay up, Otto!'

A reluctant boy-soldier during the war's final weeks, Kleiber had been captured by the British outside Wesel and served almost a year thereafter on a farm in the south Pennines, during which interlude he had acquired a working knowledge of the local dialect, two mangled fingers (victims of some compulsory dry-stone wall rebuilding) and a taste for those parts of sheep that more civilized nations feed to dogs.

'Ay up, Jonas. What's the news?'

'Nothing that's fit to print. Or otherwise. Here, I brought chocolate.'

Kleiber only ever came bearing gifts if he intended to make a day of his visit, and Fischer assumed that he was avoiding his editor once more.

'Did you get another final warning?'

Kleiber smiled brightly. 'I'm as much a reporter as Heydrich was a show-girl, apparently. It's probably true - and anyway, he's not in the best mood. Trudi didn't come home again the night before last.'

The *Zeitung*'s owner-editor, Herr Grabner, had married very late, and unwisely. His wife was at least two decades his junior and far prettier than a sensible, ugly man should have had expectations of. Worse, she was prone to sentimental feelings for American soldiers. As their home stood less than half a kilometre from Camp Andrews (the largest concentration of US forces east of Frankfurt), Herr Grabner had ample opportunity to find his circumstances trying.

'You'll have to give him a scoop, then. There must be something going on somewhere.'

'What, Korea? Who gives a fat fart?'

'Stalin's death? Anything new?'

'Yeah. He's still dead.'

'Come on, Jonas, try.'

Kleiber scratched his head. 'We can't do any more about England's new Queen, it's getting stale. Last week's Italian General Election's going to be old news after next week's. As for Hungary's new government-in-waiting, I refer you to my statement on Korea.'

'That's it? The world's gone quiet?'

'Strangely, it has. The most we can say about either Germany is that summer's coming - and, if you're an East Berliner, that you shouldn't become poorly.'

'Why not?'

'The construction workers on the new Friedrichshain hospital site went on strike yesterday. They're fed up with Ulbricht's work quotas. And not eating.'

Fischer, who rarely listened to the radio, hadn't heard the news. Strikes were not common events in the DDR, and usually permitted only in order that the Party could acquiesce upon some insignificant point and validate its role as the workers' friend (what one of its leading members - and Fischer's closest friend - would characterize as *kissing the Prols' arses with a half-pucker*).

'Is it serious?'

'Is it ever? I'm sneaking across the line later, to talk to a few bricklayers. Hopefully, they're throwing up barricades, otherwise we're going to have to run with the Lichterfelde flower show.'

They drank tea and ate American 'chocolate' (which, even to German mouths starved of luxury, could most charitably be described as *ersatz*). Just before ten o'clock, Fischer's business came dangerously close to turnover when an elderly gentleman stopped in front of the shop window and carefully perused the timepieces displayed there. The disappointment of his going roused the proprietor to a rare burst of intent.

'I'm going to paint this place. Something light and welcoming.'

Dumbfounded, Kleiber peered around at the flaked, shrapnel-pitted walls, their distressed memory of better times the very essence of Berlin *a la mode*. 'Why?'

'Because the war's over. The future's light-beige. Or antique cream.'

'Are you sure? We've become very comfortable with turd-brown and rubble-grey. It would be a pity to ditch the national aesthetic.'

'Be optimistic, Jonas. Believe in the *Wirschaftswunder*!'

Kleiber laughed. 'You *are* a cock, Otto. When the Ivans give back the East, France stops taking our coal and the Americans and British let us defecate without filling in the paperwork beforehand, I'll believe. Until then we're just clever, busy monkeys.'

So far, Fischer's morning had offered little promise of any sort of future uplands; but rain, economic stasis and the Kleiber diagnosis couldn't dampen his uncharacteristically positive mood. He glanced around his premises, seeing them transformed by light, paint and time into something slightly staid and enduring. It needn't be just clocks – he might branch out into gramophones (with whose bowels he was much more familiar). Then, he could draw upon his experience in the recorded music market and carry a tasteful selection of classical titles, perhaps become Decca's official agent in south-west Berlin. If a man with no un-severed roots had an advantage, it was that starting again was never traumatic.

He must have let his thoughts stretch into a reverie. Kleiber coughed, stood up and assembled his scarf for duty.

'Well, I'd better get on and speak to the striking masses.'

'Be careful. Don't get yourself noticed.'

'I won't. No Contax, no Press Card, no Cuban cigars. I'll just turn up on site, ask what's got them going and then get. If I don't get stopped at the line we can put it in this evening's edition.'

When the Third Estate had departed, Fischer made an early lunch of bread and cheese and resisted a third cup of tea. The crumbs were barely scraped from the table before the premises experienced a mini-boom, welcoming six customers in the space of the next two hours. One of them was the earlier promenading gentleman, who, to the proprietor's delight, offered a fair price for the 1937 Hermle that sat dead centre in the window display. More astonishingly, he withdrew a wallet from his jacket and offered the same in Deutsche Marks rather than attempt to barter some wretched family relic for it.

Fischer took his other customers' broken clocks, wrote out tickets, planned to purchase a strongbox (rather than continue to tuck money into his trouser pocket as had been his habit to date) and generally felt more like a man of business than he could recall. It made the afternoon pass on wings, and when he locked his front door at six pm he had a rare sensation of having not squandered the day.

He kept a small but pleasant home in three rooms directly above the shop. They were furnished extravagantly, with second-hand, Swedish-style furniture that drunken Soviet marksmen had somehow missed back in '45. Roman blinds rather than curtains hung in the windows, and the result had an airier feel than the traditional Berlin home (despite the polished mahogany floor he had inherited). It was by some distance the most respectable billet he had ever occupied, and on bad days he felt his wife's absence more acutely for it.

As with most widowers, his evenings dragged cruelly. Usually, he read a great deal and listened to his tiny collection of Wolf and Schubert *lieder* (on an instrument he had bought cheaply and repaired), then went to bed as early as didn't seem ridiculous. When loneliness pressed too heavily he sometimes visited a local café-bar and disgraced himself with two bottles of *Spezial* (never one, or three) while he read through the local papers, letting the pervasive warmth, nicotine and company restore a part-sense of being in a wider world than his trousers and shoes.

This evening, it wasn't loneliness that dragged him outdoors. He had money in his pocket, an unaccustomed sense of satisfaction and an urge to walk a little. He washed himself over the bathroom sink, carefully hid most of his takings under a loose floorboard, put on his boots and jacket and plotted a roundabout course to the bar. The earlier rain had cleared and there was a cool breeze, giving this particular outer edge of the city a freshness that even the Soviet checkpoints couldn't impede on its way in from the countryside. Many of his fellow Lichterfelders were outdoors and taking their time, moving with a little less purpose than their habitual foraging expeditions demanded. He joined them, almost at ease with things.

Almost, because old, familiar ghosts were promenading too, and his cruelly efficient memory raised them as he walked past the Botanical Gardens:

Here and here, Frauen Fuhrmann and Ziegler, sisters, were discovered dead and ravished, post mortem; down there, on Wildenowstrasse, Frau Mauer was displayed in a similar state, though the murderer hadn't bothered to be as tender in his addresses to her as he had to his first two victims; a little further on, in a café on Sophiastrasse (now closed down), a younger lady – little more than a girl - had committed self-murder by consuming bleach, because her fear of what Soviet soldiers did to German women had been greater than her love of life; in the same premises, a method-murderer was tried extra-judicially for his crimes, the sentence carried out immediately thereafter by KriminalKommissar Gerd Branssler's fists. All of them were as clear in his mind now as then, their files pristine, incorruptible, the content stored, catalogued and added to the considerable sum of what he knew of the world's bleeding corners. His only consolation was that none of them visited him in dreams any more. He couldn't have come to live in Lichterfelde, otherwise.

At the bar door he parted company with his ghosts. The establishment had no name as yet, beyond 'that new place on Schloss-Strasse', but was slowly attracting a reasonably respectable clientele (one that didn't believe that functioning kidneys and strong drink should be an either-or choice). Tonight the place was as busy as Tuesday ever was, the seating commandeered already, so he took a place at the bar with a group of men who knew each other well enough to share the day's news without ever feeling the need for introductions. To his surprise, they were talking about the strike in

East Berlin – which, he soon discovered, had bred a litter of similar. It was the general view that something big was happening (*big* being a far more satisfying canvas for uninformed speculation than *small*, or *insignificant*), and Fischer found it hard to be disinterested. The rumour was that an initial walk-out by about three hundred men was now being supported by thousands of their comrades in the construction industry, fired by the injustice of having new, larger work quotas imposed without further compensation. SED councillors and officials were said to have been arguing in the streets with the disaffected mob, trying to persuade them to stand down with the quite accurate (but largely ineffective) claim that the quotas had already been reversed. As one of the men at the bar observed, a head of steam couldn't be dispersed by mere truth.

One of his older, excitable mates predicted a Berlin-style revolution, the workers marching on the *Neues Stadthaus* to despatch a few SED councillors from the upper-storey windows. His dour comrade disagreed; it was always the way of these things to have a brief, rowdy display followed by arrests and show trials, with the ringleaders sent off to mine radium for a few years. Fischer didn't offer an opinion (he much preferred to listen to bar-room wisdom than spout it), but he couldn't see a pleasant ending to the business. The DDR had suffered a wretched year - a near-famine during the previous winter, a horribly-underperforming industrial sector and a half-panicked purge of such dangerous elements as youth, pensioners', Jewish and women's groups (which had accelerated the already arterial-strength flow of its citizens westwards to find a better life in the other Germany). Under the circumstances it was hardly surprising that the SED and their lumpen masses were not on the best of terms. A multi-party democracy had a safety valve, allowing the electorate to kick out one set of useless timer-servers and elect another; but when the ballot card offered only one 'choice' the masses had to take what they were given or find another way to express their ire.

It was a matter about which he could do nothing, of course, yet it preyed more than it should, and his second bottle of *Spezial* took an hour to drain. He had hoped to see Kleiber walk in (more to reassure himself that the boy was safe than to get the latest news), but by nine o'clock he hadn't appeared and a comfortable mattress was beginning to call, siren-like, down the length of Schloss-Strasse. He gave everyone a nod, walked out into the beginnings of dusk and plotted the shortest route home, letting the south-westerly wind drain his lungs of a habit's worth of other men's cigarette smoke. The beer had numbed his head pleasantly and the ghosts allowed him some free time - almost as long as it took him to reach Curtius-Strasse.

At the corner of Prausestrasse and Drakestrasse a small crowd was occupying the pavement and gutter, forming a circle, looking down at something. He didn't want to know, but avoiding them would involve crossing the street and making a point too obvious to deny to himself, so his feet kept him on a collision course. He willed the gawpers to stay where they were, to keep their secret to themselves;

but a policeman, reaching the spot from the same direction as himself, pulled at shoulders and opened the circle, offering the view.

A middle-aged lady, lying face down in a pool of blood whose centre lay somewhere beneath her throat, still clutched in one hand a tattered section of ordinary brown wrapping paper. At a glance, one couldn't say whether it had in fact contained anything of value, but Fischer, had he been inclined or able to speak, might have offered an informed guess. His problem, other than the dizziness and strong sense of nausea that almost overwhelmed him, was how one determined the concept of *value*.

2

Sleep acted as a cosh, dulling his sense of purpose. He awoke by degrees, performed necessary evacuations and ablutions without being able to recall them later and opened the shop door fully an hour after his usual time. It took an effort of will to expose himself to the possibility of human contact.

It arrived within minutes, disguised as an intrepid reporter. Kleiber entered cautiously, the expression on his face telling Fischer everything.

'The murdered lady? Was it …?

'Yes.'

'Fuck. Who'd do that?'

'Anyone in desperate need of a broken mantel-clock.'

'Did she have money?'

'I never saw any. I think she existed on my tea and air. I suppose this counts as news?'

Kleiber pulled a face. 'It would, normally. But Herr Grabner's wetting his pants about the troubles.'

'What, the strikes?

'He's hoping for more, naturally, bad news being the very best news. I'm supposed to find out where it's happening the most today and stick with it like … what sticks?'

'Limpets? Leeches?'

'Yeah, those.'

'So it looks serious?'

'I don't know. I got word that something else was happening on Stalin Allee, so I went for a look. By sunset yesterday it hadn't blown up into anything spectacular. The workers elected a couple of representatives to go and speak to the FDGB and Ministry about their grievances. That was about it, though; they tried to get a march going but loudspeaker vans told them to break it up, and after that I came back west.'

'Wasn't that premature?'

Kleiber had made only a start on rebutting this implied slur upon his courage when the shop door opened once more and Pastor Lemke stumbled in. Fischer's mood, low already, sagged further. The Pastor was a frequent visitor, his enduring mission to argue the case of a clock that sat some thirty metres above a local pavement, silent since an altercation with British bombers that had seen much of its steeple and church below go absent without leave. It was Lemke's belief that the clock – *his* clock - was a symbol of Germany itself; that its repair and restoration would be a profoundly moving symbol of the national resurrection. Fischer had declined to indulge the metaphor on numerous occasions, explaining that his skills extended to domestic clocks and the simpler wristwatches; that the maintenance and repair of industrial-scale movements was a specialist field, now largely fallow. Lemke had taken these rebuffs as the necessary stations of his personal cross (though of course he would never have put it that way) and persisted, gently and infuriatingly, at the approximate rate of two pesters per week.

Fischer had no idea if he was capable of doing the business or not, but his ex-paratrooper's acrophobia wouldn't allow him to try. The steeple was clearly fragile still, its repairs to date confined to those that would prevent it collapsing outright on to the passing citizenry. He had no intention of testing whether it was in fettle to support a clock repairman.

The Pastor seemed agitated this morning, far from that serene state of calm with which he usually pressed Fischer to Do the Right Thing. Having tripped over the doorstep he steadied himself against a table and pulled his jacket down from his midriff, the limbs twitching slightly for want of further pastime. Fischer wasn't in the mood to read moods, but a building pressure of something that needed urgently to be let out wasn't difficult to sense. He lifted the kettle.

'Tea, Pastor?'

Hastily, Lemke held up a hand. 'Thank you, Herr Fischer, no. I have no time. Have you heard?'

'Heard what?'

'The strikes in the east?'

'We were just speaking about them. The construction workers want more money for less work. It doesn't seem to be amounting to much.'

As he spoke, Fischer changed his mind about the expression on Lemke's face. He was agitated, yes, but as a child might be as he took off his coat to join a birthday party. The Pastor was about to explode with something approaching joy.

'Don't you listen to the radio? It started yesterday with barely three hundred workers, but by the afternoon there were twenty thousand at least with them.'

'Really?'

'Apparently, one of the strikers stole a loudspeaker van and drove around, urging workers to join their comrades. This morning it was reported that forty thousand had gathered by dawn. *Forty* thousand!'

'This was American radio?'

'But it's happening! Yesterday they demanded that Ulbricht himself speak to them, but he didn't dare. It's the end! He has to go!'

Most of Lemke's colleagues east of the line had been harassed, locked out of their churches, and, if needing further discouragement, imprisoned; youth organizations associated with Churches had been closed down or absorbed into the *Freie Deutsche Jugend*, and God Himself had been asked politely to pack his bags and fuck off somewhere else. Even a man of staunch Christian principles could get spiteful in the face of all that.

Kleiber climbed off the table that his bony rear end had hardly begun to warm. In contrast to Lemke, he didn't seem the least happy about the news. 'I suppose I'd better go back and be the fearless face of the Free Press. Where's it happening?'

'Everywhere in Mitte! Unter den Linden, Potsdamer Platz – wherever the largest crowds can gather.'

'Shit.'

Fischer raised his eyebrows. 'Surely it's best to be where the action is?'

Kleiber nodded at Lemke. 'He's just mentioned a couple of ideal places for armour to deploy. That sort of action doesn't need my company.'

'If history's being made, shouldn't the *Südwest-Berliner Zeitung* be there?'

'Oh, shut up.'

With that pleasantry, Kleiber stepped out on to Curtius-Strasse. Before the door could return to its jamb three men had entered in his place. This was the most humanity the premises' current owner had ever entertained simultaneously, and for a moment he had a brief, glorious vision of more inventory shifting. It took only a second glance, however, to (dis)satisfy himself that the new arrivals would be even less likely to purchase a time-piece than Pastor Lemke. Two were civilians in suits, the third a *SchuPo* officer; all were wearing the sort of face that wasn't going to take any nonsense from whoever got in their way.

'Herr Otto Fischer?'

Lemke shook his head and pointed a bony forefinger at the correct party. Three heads swivelled to the shockingly mutilated fellow in the collarless shirt, sleeveless sweater and shamefully shabby trousers.

'Would you come with us, please?'

Like most citizens of the new *Bundesrepublik*'s awkward city-enclave, Fischer hadn't yet worked out whether *please* carried the same implied threat as it had under the previous regime. The air between them didn't seem to be charged with menace or a subtle hint of future violence, but that might mean only that he couldn't read unfamiliar, American-taught signals.

'May I ask where?'

The policeman glanced briefly at his suited colleagues. One of them gave him the nod.

'A friend wants to speak with you.'

'Can't he come himself?'

'He's at Rudolph-Wilde Platz, the *Rathaus*. He won't leave the building, and he says he's not talking unless you're in the room.'

3

Rolf Hoeschler's uniform lay on the bed, splayed as if touting for a new owner but lacking the tailor's window to advertise the fact. He had been staring at it for some time now, trying to order things in his head. Downstairs, his boy Engi was moving around, doubtless organizing his breakfast or clearing the mess from the same, or packing his school bag in that efficient way that Rolf still couldn't help but admire after all this time. His own education had been a long, stubbornly-resisted process - of being forcibly shoved out of the household each morning and then monitored like an incoming air-raid until he was safely in the clutches of his teacher. Engi had never needed herding; he wanted to know things like other children craved cake.

Children. The boy was almost seventeen now, deemed to be a man by any recruitment officer. How had that happened? A father – even an imitation one, with no papers to prove anything – needed to turn his back for no more than what to be seemed a moment and the clock turned monstrously. Only last week he had asked for a razor, for God's sake.

Hoeschler had no good reason for the pride he felt. Six years earlier, the boy – the child, then – had been an orphaned street rat, a pickpocket, an unrecorded-death-in-waiting, a part of the flotsam of a war that had stolen ten million childhoods. With great luck, the strenuous but half-competent efforts of a new guardian who hadn't the first idea of what it was that parents did and the warm, ungrudging help of friends, the waif had filled out, lost his fear of everything that moved and had then then jumped, two feet-first, back into the world's daylight. If he was more interested in practical things than academic achievement, that was fine – a boy could do very well with a technical qualification in a nation that sorely lacked engineers and mechanics.

But now he might not have that chance. Hoeschler had searched desperately for a painless way to tell him, knowing that there was no time, no gentle way to get from here to there. Their old life was over, its official demise due in less than an hour; what could be said to ease the shock of that?

The thought of time woke him from his trance, and he dressed quickly. When he was done the uniform lay there still on the bed. This was a working day, a day in which *VolksPolizei* would be busier than at any time in living memory, and for once he wouldn't be with them - in fact, if he got any of the next few hours' complicated dance-steps wrong he would be adding to their workload considerably. Imagining his colleagues' faces as he was dragged into Keibelstrasse added considerably to the morning's unpleasantness.

'It's seven-thirty, Rolf.'

His distractions had muffled the creak of stairs. Engi was in the doorway, a mug of *Venag* held straight out, the once-habitual tremor long-gone from his limbs.

'You're going to be late.'

There could have been no finer prompt, and Hoeschler took it quickly, before his courage failed him.

'I'm not going in today.'

'But it's a work day.' Almost before the words were out, the expression on Engi's face was shading from curiosity to anxiety.

'Do you remember the game we used to play? The one with the bag?'

Slowly, the boy nodded. The 'game' had simple rules and a maximum playing time of three minutes - three minutes to gather things necessary for a life on the run, their sum not to exceed the space provided by a single shoulder bag. They had practised it often but not for some years now; it belonged to a different, darker time, or so they had both allowed themselves to believe.

The coffee cup was on the floor in a moment, and this time Engi negotiated the stairs like a wall heading for the ground. They both knew which bag and where it was – a faded Wehrmacht rucksack, hung for so long behind the pantry door that it had become as much a part of the fittings as the brass hook that held it. Half-filled already with a map, compass, matches, thick socks, gloves and ten dry *consum* rations (Red Army issue, 1950 vintage), it awaited only water, a torch, the Tokarev that Hoeschler kept taped beneath his bedside table and whatever perishable foodstuffs their kitchen could provide on the unwanted day the game finally became something else.

As he removed the gun from its hiding place and two magazines from the drawer, Hoeschler felt the irony keenly. They were enacting a drill, the last controlled manoeuvre of a day in which plans, stratagems and expectations were likely to explode as soon as they were tested. He should be savouring the moment, he told himself, because that was exactly how long it would last.

He hadn't quite finished tying his bootlaces before Engi was back in the bedroom, fully dressed himself and carrying the bag over his shoulder. The schoolboy's clothes had gone; he had put on his hand-me-downs from Hoeschler and looked like any one of the thousands of teenagers, apprenticed to an industrial concern, who slouched their reluctant way to work each day across East Berlin. Luftwaffe-grey paint on a foggy morning couldn't have provided better camouflage.

'Where are we going, Rolf?'

If he told the boy nothing it wouldn't matter - he would still follow, silently, trusting absolutely that circumstances warranted it, that alternatives had been considered and dismissed. But the question was too important to ignore, because *where*, wherever it was, wouldn't allow any further possibility of *here*. The bag game was to be played only when something bad was bracing itself to entirely kick down the door of Normal.

'Many places. To your Aunt Anneliese's first.'

'Is she coming with us?'

It was an intelligent question, as Hoeschler had expected. The woman was as close to the boy as anyone other than a mother could be, and if shit was falling (which the bag said it was, and soon) he would want his few indispensable people accounted for.

'She is, yes.'

'What about the twins?'

'They'll have to watch for themselves today.'

'But we'll warn them?'

'We'll try.'

Engi had just two friends, his 'cousins', both now grown and out of the family nest. One of them lived in Pankow, the other in Friedrichshain; both had jobs, romantic attachments and lives that were about to be soiled by association. They were guilty of nothing but their blood, which might be no mitigation whatsoever.

'I don't think Aunt Anneliese will go without them, not if …'

If. It hung heavily for such a small word, and Hoeschler realised that the boy had worked everything through already. They were about to run, and whatever chased them would have long legs and a longer reach. There was only one place they could have any chance of safety, and that was another world entirely. It was likely that he'd have to convince her, to speak to the situation's brutal realities. Of all that could or would happen in the coming hours, he feared this task the most.

He held out the Tokarev and magazines. 'Put these in the bag, below everything else.'

When Engi had done it he looked up, expectantly. He seemed calm, calmer by far than his adopted father felt. Perhaps the street rat had simply laid dormant these past years, enjoying the unfamiliar security and sustenance, storing up against the day when real life recommenced. Hoeschler's guilt lessened a little, soothed too easily by what he wanted to see.

'Right.' He stood and glanced around his bedroom for the last time. 'Are you ready?'

'Yes Rolf.'

'Stage one, then - five streets, to Gartenweg.'

4

Fischer hadn't previously set foot in *Rathaus Schöneberg*. Before the war he may have walked past it during one of his infrequent trips to Berlin (though he doubted it), and after the Soviets had fought their way through it in 1945 its attractions had become a moot point for anyone who wasn't an urban archaeologist. When the Americans came they had it rebuilt in the original style, and even donated a 'Freedom Bell' (though what freedom this represented to a half-city surrounded by hostile armed forces wasn't obvious). It arrived with great ceremony, apparently, but Fischer hadn't thought to attend the installation. For some months following his extended stay at Sachsenhausen holiday camp, an expedition to the end of a cul-de-sac would have left him breathless and out of sorts.

He examined the Rathaus' monumental central tower as the DKW *Meisterklasse* approached across Rudolph-Wilde Platz, his professional interest piqued by the massive clock it housed. Unlike Pastor Lemke's precarious treasure, this time-piece looked as if a direct hit from an 85mm tank gun wouldn't disturb it (though obviously one would, and had). In fact, the whole building attempted a statement of inviolable authority, a sandstone-cliffed edifice that now housed West Berlin's Senate. This being modern Germany the statement was only partly honest, given that the senators inside couldn't pass wind without it being approved and ratified by the

Allies. Still, if an institution wanted to pretend more power than it actually possessed, this was a fine place in which push the bluff.

To Fischer's surprise, the two suits and *SchuPo* officer took him in through the front entrance, as if he had been somebody. The interior was impressive - much too tasteful to be one of Speer's designs, but with a long and intimidating approach to a magnificent staircase, the sort of psychological ordeal the Führer had loved to inflict upon visiting diplomats. He passed the trek trying to decide if the architecture was neo-classical or neo-baroque, while a couple of onlookers peered down idly from one of the upper galleries, probably thinking that modern democracy's embrace of the common man could be taken too far.

At the last moment the four men swerved around the staircase and aimed for a door in shadows under the lower colonnade. One of the suits opened it, stepped aside and waved Fischer through into a small meeting room, of a size to accommodate a modest sub-committee or a discrete beating. Thick curtains were drawn across the single long window, creating a gloom that a lonely table lamp couldn't dispel. Two men, barely more than dark shapes, stood against a wall. In front of them, caught at the boundary of the feeble illumination, a man in working clothes sat with his thick arms folded, giving as fine an impression of permanence as the building that surrounded him.

Fischer hadn't allowed himself to speculate beforehand, and the shock was greater for it.

'Hello, Freddie.'

Friedrich Melancthon Holleman, a large gentleman with features that hinted equally at a very successful or disastrous career in the boxing ring, looked up from the table and smiled broadly. 'Otto! Tell them who I am, would you?'

'Tell …? That's complicated.'

'See? Didn't I say that?'

One of the shadows detached himself from the wall and stepped forward, holding out a card for Fischer's perusal.

'Dietrich.'

The card said *Robert Dietrich, Commercial Representative, South German Industrial Development Company*. Fischer looked up.

'You're one of General Gehlen's people?'

The other man's face twitched, but he hid the surprise well. 'Why do you say that?'

'I've had dealings with the Org. A long time ago.' Fischer waved the card at the seated man. 'He's Beckendorp, Kurt - *Inspecteur der VolksPolizei* at the last time of asking, though he may have moved up a little since then. He's also Friedrich Holleman, formerly an *OrPo rottmeister* and lieutenant-pilot, Luftwaffe.'

'Call me Holleman, please. It's what I was born with.' The big man stood and steadied himself against the table.

One of the suits who had accompanied Fischer stepped forward.

'You wish to defect?'

'I *have* defected. You can send me back if you want. I'd prefer that you didn't.'

The room's official presence took a few moments to consider the offer. Dietrich, having recovered and walleted his card, coughed.

'What do we get? A defector brings something useful with him, and we already know everything about *VolksPolizei* that we'll ever want to know. Since the Fifth Directorate's work was handed to the Ministry of State Security we've lost interest in you. No offence.'

Holleman beamed at him. 'None taken. They offered me a transfer to MfS, and I told them where they could place it for safe keeping.'

Fischer didn't care for the direction the conversation was taking. 'Tell them who else you are, Freddie.'

Dietrich snorted. 'He's told us he's two men. If he's a third we're sending him back.'

Holleman shrugged. 'You can confirm who I am with General Gehlen. I doubt that he's forgotten either of my names. Speak to Wessel, if he's not available. I think Herr Fischer meant *what* else I am.'

Mention of Dietrich's two most senior bosses had put a thoughtful expression on several faces. Holleman moved quickly to occupy the pause.

'I'm a whore, a professional liar - a reptile, if that's not libelling the species.'

The class, Fischer murmured to himself, pedantically.

For a moment Dietrich looked bewildered, but he was a sharp one. 'You're … a politician? SED?'

'There's no other sort, where I come from.'

'How senior?'

'I have the ear of Fritz Ebert, you might say.'

'Not his balls? We'd give you an excellent price.'

Fischer was beginning to warm to Dietrich. He didn't seem to think much of his catch, but nor was he cursed with the arrogance of so many of his kind. The best they could hope for was that he was someone who thought things through.

The talking suit coughed. 'How is it that you're so close to him?'

Holleman looked pleased, as if he'd been hoping for the question. 'That was Kurt Beckendorp's doing, not mine.'

'But you're …'

Fischer interrupted, to head off more of Holleman's unproductive teasing. 'Beckendorp was the identity I found for Freddie when he needed to hide from the Reich. It seemed right at the time. The man and his family had died during the British terror raid on Hamburg, so there wasn't likely to be any physical evidence remaining. He'd been Luftwaffe like us, so I managed to access copies of the ID papers. But it turned out that he had prehistory.'

This time Dietrich got the point immediately. 'A *kozi*?'

'As red as they come. He was alleged to have killed several policemen during the Hamburg Uprising, in '27.'

The suit's eyebrows went up. 'That would make him royalty.'

Holleman smiled modestly. 'It did, once I'd managed to persuade the Ivans I wasn't the *wrong* sort of communist. They tend to assume it, usually.'

'So what's your rank in the party?'

'Officially, I'm only a city councillor, representing Weissensee. But I'm told that there's a junior minister's seat waiting for me in the DVdI, if I don't fuck it all up.'

Dietrich smiled faintly. 'Defecting would qualify as fucking it all up, I assume?'

For the first time, Holleman lost his own smile. 'I can tell you what's going on in the heads of the Politburo and Planning Committee right now, and it isn't all the same thing. I also know which of your organizations is giving gainful employment to our people.'

'Names?'

Holleman shook his head. 'I wasn't that close. In any case, I'm not going to send men to the wall.'

'The organizations, then.'

'Yours, for one.'

Dietrich's mask went back into place, more firmly than before. 'What do you want?'

'Not much. Safety for my family, a chance to make a modest way. Somewhere to put our heads until I can provide for them.'

'Not Berlin?'

'How could we be safe here? Somewhere far west – Ireland, if you can arrange it. The Rhineland, if you can't.'

Dietrich, the suits and the uniform annexed the opposite end of the table and for the next few minutes talked things over in low voices. In that pause, Fischer examined his friend more closely. Holleman 'work clothes' were more probably his gardening wear, a well-used ensemble equally suited for passing invisibly through checkpoints or being executed above a shallow trench. He had put on weight in the two years since they'd last met, a respectably hearty spread that probably gave his half-amputated leg a deal of grief when required to move any distance on its steel-and-wood prop. Fischer had noticed the wince when he stood.

'Are you alright, Freddie?'

Holleman pulled a face. 'I don't know. This is the strangest thing I've done since the last one. Do you think they'll send me back?'

Fischer glanced at the huddle of whispering officialdom. 'They daren't. Everyone who comes across the line has to be checked. In any case, your name's on one of Gehlen's files already. I just hope you're right about what you can give them.'

'Otto, your eyes would bleed if you caught sight of what I know, believe me.'

Freddie Holleman had risen far with very little native feel for the political arts. It had been the cause of considerable satisfaction to Fischer for some years now, to see a man so obviously destined for life's harder latitudes somehow claw his way into a temperate zone, unsoiled by most of the usual crimes that smoothed the passage. But now he was turning around, pointing himself right back at the Hard, throwing away everything that was quiet and comfortable. There had to be a better reason for it than stupidity.

The conclave at the other side of the table started to break up. Fischer whispered the other of his two most urgent questions.

'What about the family?'

Keeping his eyes firmly upon his approaching fates, Holleman spoke out of the side of his mouth. 'It's taken care of. I hope.'

Dietrich pulled a piece of paper from his pocket, flattened it on the table's highly polished surface and began to scribble notes. 'You're going to Pullach, to be questioned.'

Holleman nodded. 'I know. Just not today.'

The other man looked up. 'Why not?'

'You're going to want me here.'

'In Berlin? Why?'

'To be your crystal ball.'

5

As Dietrich and the other suits left the room Fischer had his next question ready, but Holleman was answering it before it saw free air.

'They sent us out on to the streets yesterday, to argue with the workers.'

'As police?'

'No, as SED councillors and union officials. The Party gave us lists of responses to arguments, the permutations worked out like a fucking catechism. To any possible complaint, protest or plain gripe about working conditions, we could offer perfectly reasonable counters.'

'And?'

'It bounced off.'

'The strikers didn't listen?'

'They didn't try. I was sent to the Block 40 site, to harangue them until they dispersed. When I'd finished I got the sense that they hadn't heard a word. In fact, it was the other way around. By the time they'd laid out their grievances any faith I might have had in what I was saying had gone in the breeze.'

'So, you're disheartened. It's hardly a reason to give up everything.'

Holleman rubbed his eyes, which looked as if they hadn't closed for a month. 'It's not that. You know things haven't been going well, over there?'

'I read the newspapers. They seem to relish your pain.'

'Well, there's enough of it. The economic plan that Ulbricht's tied us to? It's unravelled like wool in a kitten factory. Coal, Steel, Copper, Agriculture, Construction – there isn't a single sector that's meeting its targets. Obviously, that's why the work quotas are going up. The thing is, when the economy crashes there's usually a scapegoat lined up. We can – we do - blame private businesses, off-the-book traders, hoarding farmers and any other enemy of socialism that comes to mind. This time, it's *our* people who are the enemy. The construction workers I spoke to yesterday, they told me they're building homes for the masses while they sleep in pig-huts. They haven't seen their families for months, and they get paid so little that even if they had the free time – which they don't, because of the quotas - they couldn't go for a beer, or to the cinema, or even sit for an hour in a café with a cup of swill warming their hands, talking shit about football and easing pressure a little. Everything they earn goes home, and it isn't enough, and these are the people who are building the Utopia that Uncle Walter keeps saying is right around the next corner.'

'But they dispersed, you said.'

'Yeah. And then some cheeky bastard rounded them back up again last evening. And …'

'What?'

'It isn't just Berlin. Overnight, we were getting reports from Leipzig, Mansfeld, Görlitz, Magdeburg, Jena – almost everywhere there's heavy industry and more than two workers to get together and say fuck it, we're out. It was barely dawn when I left Keibelstrasse, but we'd already got the call from the *Neues Stadthaus*, telling us to mobilize everyone and everything. I doubt there's a single policeman in the city or the central DDR who's going to be enjoying time off today.'

Fischer finally saw something of what this was about, at least for Freddie Holleman. 'There's nothing Ulbricht can afford to offer, not to calm something this big.'

'No, which leaves the *schlagstock* – or at least, I hope that's *all* it leaves.' Holleman shook his head. 'I don't mind acting the arse in uniform, it's part of being police. But I wasn't SA back then and I won't be now. Fuck the pension.'

'When did you decide?'

'Probably when I heard about the pig-huts. No *muschi* with a Party card can argue down that sort of thing. I told Kristin last night, that it had come.'

'What had?'

'The day I've been warning about for years, the one on which she'd have to throw away her life yet again for the idiot she married.'

'The idiot who's given her a better life than most German wives could expect?'

'She deserves better than another rent-arrears flit.'

'You said that the family was taken care of. How?'

'You remember Rolf? Rolf Hoeschler?'

'How could I not? We nearly died together in '41, and then again in '48.'

'He feels the same about this as I do. I told him that if I ran I'd make sure that any terms I could get from Gehlen's people would include him and his boy. He's going to bring out Kristin.'

'What about your sons?'

'I spoke to them last night. They …' Holleman's eyes filled. 'For twenty-three years they've gone the same way, like two grains of sands on a tide. When I told Franz he said fine, Dad, I'll see you over there tomorrow. But Ulrich isn't coming. He has a girl and it's serious – Kristin thinks she may be pregnant, though he hasn't dared admit it to her. He told me not to worry about him being a Beckendorp, he'll be able to fix up new papers, no problem.'

'It's never no problem.'

'I told him that, but he's like me – plenty of balls and not enough between the ears. He said he's been wanting to find new work anyway. He has a degree in Chemical Engineering and he's tired of operating a lathe.'

'I suppose …'

'What?'

Fischer thought about it a little more before he spoke. It wasn't kind to raise hopes about something like this.

'*VolksPolizei* and MfS are going to be overworked for the next few days and weeks, that's for sure. If he can arrange these papers quickly – and if they're good enough - he might be lost in the bureaucratic fog for a while at least. Perhaps for long enough to be persuaded that he should come west.'

'He'll be stubborn.'

'Then his uncle Otto will go across the line and have a word, tell him about the opportunities the Federal Republic has for young, well-educated families.'

'Does it?'

'The economy's growing fairly strongly over here. It must have.'

Holleman shook his head. 'I hope you're good at moving large rocks.'

'If there's a child coming he'll have to think about more than himself, won't he?'

'Yeah, I hope.'

Outside the door, several voices were arguing a point. Fischer turned his back to the door and whispered. 'You mentioned *the things you know*. What did you mean?'

'It's …'

'What?'

'I don't know if I should say, not until I have to.'

'Good, Freddie, that's good. I was going to tell you not to give them everything at once. They'll offer you as little as necessary in return, it's their way.'

'I expected that. I was just going to hint at it – enough to get them interested.'

'In what?'

'In helping to prevent a bloodbath.'

6

In a small, shabby office, in an only slightly less shabby building on E Street NW, Washington DC, Sergei Aleksandrovich Zarubin, formerly a middle-ranking officer of *Ministerstvo Gosudarstvennoy Bezopasnosti SSSR*, examined a document under the gaze of two Americans. They were wearing grey suits that were almost identical to his own, from which he had deduced that Brooks Brothers were the spies' outfitters of choice.

He was proud of his suit. It was the first he had ever owned that was made for him particularly, and not to a template labelled 'average'. He had purchased it almost three years earlier, in the first, glorious flush of wanton consumerism that had *consumed* him (he loved the English language!), when it seemed that he might find steady, secure employment with the Central Intelligence Agency. Unfortunately, his over-clever mouth had assassinated that hope, leaving him with one good change of clothes and a very occasional, poorly rewarded role as *special advisor* on Soviet affairs.

It had surprised him (and not pleasantly) that the United States was no less a nation of ideologues than his own. As a defector, he was expected to have seen the light, to have experienced a full, damascene conversion from the darkness of socialistic principles to the radiance of freedom, democracy and a rather unpleasant dessert that involved mothers spoiling apples. This, unfortunately, had become apparent only after he had made several droll observations regarding the similarities between Russian and American intelligence agencies - their habit of proceeding confidently on the twin pillars of wishful thinking and stabs in the dark, and their common inclination to tell their masters exactly what they wanted to hear. Americans liked to think that they had a well-defined sense of humour; clearly, it wasn't one that extended to self-deprecation. The recipients of his wit had been two stony-faced handlers (young men whose very few years on the job had given them a lifetime's ration of easy superiority and condescension), who hadn't smiled once while draining him of information on MGB matters. Once squeezed dry, they had pointed him at the exit in possession of the smallest stipend the Agency could authorize with a straight face.

Thus cast out, he had since taught two semesters of Russian Literature as visiting lecturer at a provincial (in every sense) university; translated a new edition of *The Brothers Karamazov* for a small New York publishing house; tried his hand (and failed heroically) at writing articles on ordinary life in the USSR that might interest a general American readership; and, most shamefully, spent almost an entire summer squiring the middle-aged heiress of one of Philadelphia's most venerable German families, his qualifications being a pretty face, his perfect command of her ancestral language, that damned sense of humour (far more effective upon willing ladies than grey suits) and his ready Russian cock. At least he had eaten well during those months, though even that simple pleasure had been tempered by his constant hopes for the arrival of the lady's menopause.

But now he was briefly valuable once more. Given no warning, he had been summoned the previous day from his apartment in Brooklyn (a garret, to be charitable), provided with a train ticket (second-class) and met at Union Station by one of the two men who now stood over him. He had hoped for a decent breakfast at least, but his morning's rations to date had amounted to no more than hot coffee and something sticky that Americans blame upon Denmark, pushed in front of him with the document they demanded he parse.

Parse, because it had been translated already, and badly. The CIA's Directorate of Intelligence had too few Russian speakers - and, in fact, only one native defector, a poor bastard from Minsk named Yuri Sheremenko, whose disillusionment with his new home had fermented (literally) into a habit that kept him almost comatose for twelve hours of every day. His younger American wife, not being familiar with the heroic nature of Russian inebriation, had long since departed with their mongrel kids, adding to Yuri's disaffection considerably. Zarubin would have pitied the man more, had his self-affliction not required that a substitute be found when necessary, thereby raising cash that helped to meet an outrageous Brooklyn rent.

Clearly, it wasn't Yuri who had translated this mess. Zarubin glanced up at his audience. 'May I see the original, please?'

'Why?'

The trick, he had found, was not to insult the department and still get one's way. 'The state of the document, the franks upon it, the circulation list – they'll all help me to more fully understand what's happening. Official Soviet documents can sometimes be rendered intentionally abstruse – it's paranoia, you see?'

Reluctantly, one of them nodded and departed, while his colleague's frown deepened slightly to restore the equilibrium of the room's discomforting aura. Zarubin smiled pleasantly and reapplied himself to the job. The meat of the business wasn't much. Clearly, the CIA had at least one man in Moscow, but from the evidence he wasn't someone senior. Since 5 March that year they had sought no intelligence that didn't relate to Stalin's death and what came next, yet they remained as uninformed as Roman citizens had following Caesar's assassination. As then, an unlikely triumvirate had stepped into a vacuum - three men who shared only the unpleasant experience of having earned Josef's displeasure at one time or another, but who now pretended a unity that even Yuri at the bottom of a bottle wouldn't have believed for a moment. To add to the confusion, each of them seemed to be behaving wholly out of previous character. The monster Beria was arguing that all the gulags filled with men and women he'd somehow not executed should be emptied and closed; Malenkov the arch command-economist had discovered his inner capitalist and was trying to re-align the Soviet economy to produce gewgaws for the masses; and Krushchev the consummate purger and buttock-kisser was slandering Stalin to anyone who'd listen. It was hardly surprising that the Americans wanted enlightenment.

This latest piece of intelligence was nothing helpful. It was a brief summary of appointments to the new Praesidium of the Central Committee (the body replacing the former Politburo), made during the previous year's 19th Congress, with a transcript of Stalin's valedictory (he hadn't known it at the time, naturally) speech thereto and a short appendix naming the men appointed to implement Congress' decisions. As the latter had yet to be published even in the Soviet Union, one might draw any conclusion from the bare statement.

Obviously, the Americans wanted some deep insights from him regarding the bunch of unknowns now appointed to the Praesidium – Shkiryatov, Zverev, Ignatov, Pgov, Yudin and the rest - insights which he would offer gladly, because they would all be fiction. He had as much understanding of these men as anyone outside the Kremlin - which was to say, none whatsoever. For all he knew, Stalin had drawn their names from the Moscow telephone directory the night before their promotions were announced. It was no secret that the old ogre had become much more playful towards the end.

Nevertheless, the list appended to the piece offered some clues. The fact that Malenkov's name headed it – underlining his then-appointment as the Party's First Secretary - suggested that he had outmanoeuvred his rivals even before the old man was gone. That was hardly surprising; he had been the Soviet Union's rocket-science supremo since the end of the war, and the successful development of the technology had daubed his reputation with gold dust. If the Soviet Union was a normal nation, governed by the laws of political physics, Malenkov would be the man to bet upon.

But it was always wiser to think of the Kremlin as one would a particularly wilful Renaissance city-state. The document referred to events occurring more than six months earlier, which made it out of date, if not obsolete. The day after Stalin's death a new ten-man Praesidium had been announced, with Malenkov and Beria the first two names given. Krushchev's had been tenth – which, ostensibly, marked him out as the fellow tasked with closing the door behind the rest and organizing the tea and biscuits. Yet just eight days later, Malenkov had resigned as First Secretary and the new boy's name had moved to the top of the re-issued Secretariat list. Who had been bribed, assassinated, exiled or blackmailed during the intervening week was anyone's guess, but clearly, Krushchev had built a power base in the corridors where plots were hatched, incubated and tickled fondly beneath their fat chins.

And Beria? He knew where more bodies were buried than any other man, because he'd done most of the burying. It would be like him to let Malenkov and Krushchev fight it out and then allow himself to be raised as the compromise solution. It was probably why he had embarked upon a campaign to convince everyone – the surviving *everyone* - that he might be human after all.

The sum of it was a flipped coin, though Zarubin couldn't tell his American friends that, not if he wanted further paid work. He decided it would be wisest to give a tentative nod to Krushchev, if only because he knew already that they possessed the least, and the least reliable, intelligence upon the man. *Watch this one*, he would tell them with a serious expression on his face, and if he was proved wrong what did it matter? God alone would know from which direction the shank was coming, into whose back it would plunge and whose bloodied hands would lift the crown thereafter.

The spinning pencil had just stopped in Krushchev's direction when the other American returned with the original document and dropped it onto the table. Zarubin glanced at it briefly. It was, as he'd suspected, a TASS release, something the CIA's operative could have picked up on a Moscow street corner and therefore as useful as whatever the *New York Times* said regarding the same subject. Despite this, he nodded knowingly and opened his mouth to offer the informed opinion he'd plucked out of the air moments earlier.

It stayed open as he recalled suddenly that his old boss and fellow defector Maxim Shpak had served in the Ukraine for a year immediately after the war. It was highly likely that he knew more about Krushchev than most men in the Western Hemisphere, the republic having been the latter's personal fiefdom at that time. At the least, he might recall a few anecdotes that could be fashioned into something resembling insights. With luck and a favourable breeze, a second Brooks Brothers' suit might come from it.

The pause had worked for him, made them think that he was pondering the material on the table. He closed his mouth suddenly and gave them what he hoped be a deeply thoughtful frown.

'I'd like to consider this for a few days.'

The agent who'd remained in the room gave him a sour look - but then, his face seemed incapable of anything more. The other one nodded slowly. He seemed marginally gratified by the implication that the business might be worth further thought.

'Sure. But we want a written report.'

'Of course. I'll mail it from the New York office. Would next Tuesday be acceptable?'

'Yeah, fine. The payment's the same, though.'

A father of six plain daughters was no more careful with money than the CIA. Zarubin nodded but pushed anyway.

'I need to do some research. Might I claim reasonable travel expenses? With the proper receipts, obviously.'

He had long known that he was being followed, if not every day. He was a commie *and* a turncoat, and therefore could be trusted with nothing. But receipts provided a paper trail, and his answer to their next question would, if not reassure, convince them that he would be a dolt to admit to such, if his intentions were bad.

'Who will you be meeting during this time?'

'Just one man, Maxim Shpak, whom you debriefed with me.'

'Why?'

'He may know – or be able to posit - something more about what's happening in the Praesidium right now.'

'He's uncooperative.'

At his interrogation, Shpak had refused to give them anything more than details of his then-current responsibilities (unlike Zarubin, who had readily offered a rich and intricate canvas of Moscow politics and infighting, no more than ninety percent of which had been fantasy), and being allowed to remain in the US represented the entirety of his reward for betraying his own country. Cast adrift, he had wandered aimlessly for more than a year before being sucked into one of the very many strange, minor eddies that coursed through the vast American Sea.

'What Mennonite isn't? He'll speak to me.'

7

Since he had known her, Rolf Hoeschler had resisted the invitation to call Frau Beckendorp by her given name. Her husband was his boss, and the Beckendorps being almost a second family to Engi, a further sense of obligation had made him uncomfortable with familiarity. Eventually – less than a year earlier - he had succumbed, and now she was changing the rules once more.

'Don't call me Anneliese.'

He was confused for a moment only. She had never liked the pretence of being someone else, and now that her husband had crossed the line it could be dispensed with. He told himself to practise *Kristin*, industriously.

She had packed a small bag, as instructed. But there was also a briefcase, her husband's, placed next to it in the hall of Gartenweg 16 when he and Engi arrived. She notice his glance, the slight frown, and counter-attacked immediately.

'It's photographs, mainly. And the boys' certificates.'

'Birth?'

'All of them. They won almost everything they ever went in for.'

Though not a biological father himself, Hoeschler knew he couldn't argue the matter without blood – his blood – being spilled, so he didn't try.

'None of the photographs show them in a uniform they shouldn't be?'

'We burned those a long time ago.'

He nodded and picked up both bag and case, but she stood there still, coatless, and he sensed that the first difficult moment had arrived.

'What's wrong, Anne … Kristin?'

'Ulrich, he won't come. We can't leave him behind.'

'He's a man now. He makes his own decisions.'

'I'm his mother.'

'And a burden to him, if you stay.'

Her eyes lit furiously, and he rushed on before the ignition occurred.

'They'll try to associate him with his father's crime, but it's difficult. He doesn't live with you anymore, so he can say convincingly that he knew nothing about it. He's tainted, yes, and any career he might have made here is dead before it begins; but that's about all there is to it. If you stay, you become the poisoned link. They'll assume – they'll *know* – that you knew about it, and you'll be treated badly. At the very least, they'll use you as bait to drag back your husband. Ulrich loves you, so he'll try to intervene and be sucked into it. Which means that your other boy will probably get involved, too. Everyone's worse off if you don't leave.'

The bare, obvious truth only made her angrier, but she snatched at her coat and pulled it on. He smiled, trying to seem more at ease than he felt. The briefcase was a mistake. It would look right only if he carried it, but he wasn't dressed for office work. Neither seventeen-year-old boys nor women had any need for such things, so it would draw attention, make them unusual. For a moment he considered altering the plan, to take them closer to where there would be trouble today in the hope that they would be lost in the wake of something bigger; but police would be there in great numbers, and at least some of them would know his face and wonder why, on this of all days, he wasn't in uniform. In any case, changing the route wouldn't address the problem of what happened when they reached a checkpoint and had to explain the item.

He told Engi to carry the briefcase under his arm, where it would be partially hidden by the bag he had slung from his shoulder. Hoeschler picked up Kristin's bag – that at least was the right item, something that would do for a weekend but not a new life. They were going to cross a guarded line into the west, a line at which their assumed intentions would be scrutinized closely. The state had lost a lot of its citizens in the past year, and was getting sensitive about the problem.

They stepped out on to the front path. She locked the front door, testing the handle to make sure. It was pointless yet predictable, and when she turned, the corners of her eyes were moist.

'Seven years, we were here. I thought …'

'I know.'

Twice now she had fled a home with her husband – *because* of her husband. Germans had becoming familiar with the refugee's life - kicked out of the old East, hounded from the Sudetenland, self-exiled from point to point in what had been Germany but was now something subtly else - but Kristin Holleman had begun the journey long before the rest; had been a vanguard for the fashion in reaping what others had sown. Hoeschler wondered if it made her the best of wives or the most willing of martyrs.

They walked quickly down Gartenweg and Feldstrasse to the bus-halt on Klandorferstrasse. There was a small queue waiting, mainly ladies but also a few male workers, on their way to day-shifts. Hoeschler's stretched nerves made him watchful; he examined their faces, looking for hints of awareness of what the day was going to be, and saw only the slightly bored, wanting-to-be-somewhere-else attitude of people expecting only what marked their usual lives. Perhaps they didn't listen to the radio; or perhaps they did but didn't believe what they were told. Berliners had got used to doubting what Authority said, even when it was someone else's Authority.

The first bus that came was a stopping service into Mitte. They boarded it and took seats towards the rear, where fewer passengers would pass by and have the opportunity to be curious. Engi, as always interested by everything and anything, took a window seat, leaned his head against the glass and inspected the world as it went by. Kristin Holleman's gaze was with her mind, somewhere far else but directed carefully ahead. Hoeschler glanced at them both, as anxious (as a cat-herder might be) that the plan was working so far as he would have been if it wasn't.

And what a plan - a moment snatched, a hurried evacuation, the lottery-roll of passing through checkpoints with self-signed inter-zonal passes and then a descent upon a sanctuary that might be there or not, with either a bed or a park bench upon which to contemplate a future bereft of friends or prospects. And all of it for the sake of principle, whose exercise might not make the world better in any way and possibly considerably worse than it presently was. The only comfort he could take was that it had been Kurt Beckendorp's (or rather, the resurrected Freddie Holleman's) plan, and not his own.

When the bus reached Danzigerstrasse in Prenzlauer Berg he stood up, and his hapless companions followed. So far he had seen no crowds, no gathering groups of aggrieved workers, but his policeman's eye unerringly twitched out the deployments at street corners, the small plain-clothed squads ready to intervene if trouble found the elbow room to take the chance. He noticed also the behaviour of civilians that passed them by. Unlike their fellow Berliners in the outer city it seemed that they had already seen or heard something, and moved as they had in the bombing times, with heads down and a firm need to be elsewhere soon.

A few metres from their halt, Hoeschler found a western-bound BVG service and bundled Kristin and Engi onto it. It was a ring-route that skirted inner Mitte and went as far as the Sophien II, which was ideal for them. The cemetery's northern, Bernauerstrasse boundary formed part of the demarcation line, so once there they would have little time to fret about things before they were across it and safe.

From the moment the bus departed, Hoeschler's hopes were dashed. At the Prenzlauer Allee junction a police roadblock was diverting all westbound traffic to the south, towards the eye of the coming storm. Almost immediately, however, the flow re-routed again, taking a succession of staggered shuffles through minor roads. Minutes dragged as they crawled forward, sometimes moving in the general direction of the demarcation line, at others meandering as aimlessly as if the purpose of a bus service was to keep a group of Berliners in mobile detention for the day.

He forced himself to seen calm, even though his nerves were lighting like flares. He tried to convince himself that traitors weren't such until they reached the line – that they were still guilty of nothing, could be suspected of nothing; but a quieter, persistent voice reminded him that a senior *VolksPolizei* officer had already crossed it that morning, and at least one of the trip-wires with which all fearful, paranoid societies surrounded themselves must have been triggered by his passing. The Beckendorp family, that Lazarus-like resurrection ordained by Otto Fischer exactly a decade earlier, was now a matter of State concern.

When they turned into Anklamerstrasse for the second time he almost grabbed Kristin's bag and led his charges off the bus, but a few moments later their driver tired of the game and decided to depart the board. While the forlorn convoy of lost vehicles continued straight ahead he turned right into Strelitzerstrasse, and, less than two minutes later, parked a few metres from Bernauerstrasse and the demarcation line.

'We don't go any further west today!'

Every Berliner who used public transport had heard the phrase countless times since the city's bus company had divided into separate east and west institutions, but it raised a few smiles this morning. Gamely, the passengers disembarked, resigned to having their commute extended. Hoeschler kept Kristin and Engi seated until everyone else was out on the street then paused, half-standing, as a *VolksPolizei* street patrol arrived and began to examine pockets and bags. This wasn't usual. At most, one might normally expect to have to produce papers and then be waved on, but the tensions created by events happening elsewhere were breaking the surface, making ordinary things extraordinary. Today, the border had become a line between peace and something else, making a difficult passage much more so.

Hoeschler considered the odds. He decided – he hoped - that the briefcase might not be a problem, if whoever examined it could be persuaded that the lady was going west to see a sister, someone who might be interested in old family photographs. Her bag was an overnight thing, nothing suspicious, and the boy she was with lent credibility to the story. But the Tokarev in the shoulder bag couldn't be explained away, because of course the papers that Hoeschler carried – papers he had long kept ready for a day such as this – were those of a man who wasn't police. Civilians didn't carry standard issue Soviet side-arms unless they were planning a private war, and that was precisely what the authorities feared.

He took the shoulder bag from Engi and whispered. 'Go with your aunt. Smile at whoever gets in your face and do what they say. I'll meet you both on the other side.'

Without a word Kristin and Engi got off the bus just ahead of Hoeschler, who turned as he stepped down into the street and moved behind the bus. The three-man patrol was too busy with the twenty or so passengers to notice him, and the moment he detached himself from the rest he became anonymous, just another worker on his way from somewhere to somewhere else. Head down, he turned left into Rheinsburgerstrasse and then left again into Brunnenstrasse, which brought him back up to the demarcation line a couple of hundred metres east of where the bus had stopped. In the meantime, he had dropped the Tokarev and its ammunition into a pavement coal chute, a donation likely to bring considerable anxiety to the innocent Berliner who dug it out on the next cold night.

Someone had deployed wire along Bernauerstrasse, solidifying the invisible line and more or less advertising the fact that trouble was expected. On the other side of the new barrier several members of western Berlin's uniformed *Bundesgrenzschutz* were marking out their territory and getting themselves noticed. Unusually, they weren't armed, which Hoeschler assumed to be the decision of an intelligent superior who wanted to keep the pot off the boil. He turned west before any of them noticed him and walked directly back to the bus and patrol.

The passengers, including Kristin Holleman and Engi, had dispersed. Relieved, he presented his papers to an *anwärter* and waited. The man was either myopic, semi-literate or over-officious, because it took him fully two minutes to read what a kindergartener could have absorbed in thirty seconds. When he looked up his practised glare almost begged to be slapped from his face, and had Hoeschler been in uniform he might have volunteered for the job.

'The purpose of your journey?'

'I work at the Rheinmetall-Borsig foundry, in Tegel.' He smiled and shrugged. 'It's a long way, but the money …'

Workers from eastern Berlin passing to the west were interrogated far less rigorously than those coming the other way, because the present state of the East German economy made a steady, western-sourced wage almost a token of patriotic endeavour. The glare stayed where it was but the papers were returned without further pause for effect. Twenty seconds later, Hoeschler was over the line. His diaphragm, which had been practising its spasm reflex since dawn, stood down.

He glanced around, unconcerned that he couldn't see his fellow travellers. Probably, they had put themselves far enough from the line that no one would notice them waiting. He decided to search logically, starting with the block's length of Strelitzerstrasse that ran north from Bernauerstrasse and branching from there into the parallel streets.

Half an hour later the spasms were back, double-timing to punish his premature assumption that a bad day might have any smooth edges.

8

Dietrich had returned with a notebook, coffee, pastries and the offer of a nearby bathroom. Fischer's feeling about him gained padding. He was going to do this efficiently, smoothly and probably without threats, which suggested that Gehlen's recruitment policies had improved considerably in the six years since Fischer had put himself - very briefly - on the same payroll.

Holleman seized the chance to empty his bladder, and while they were waiting they helped themselves to the coffee. It was real, a better blend than Fischer could ever recall experiencing (but then, he'd had plenty of time to forget what coffee should taste like). As he savoured it he noticed that Dietrich was examining the view carefully.

'When were you injured?'

'Forty-two, the Eastern Front.'

'I missed it.'

'The East?'

'Everything. My father was a diplomat. At the Lisbon Embassy.'

'Doing his bit for the Kriegsmarine?'

Dietrich smiled. 'Dispatches, oranges and torpedoes. And sometimes letters from home.'

'You weren't old enough to serve?'

'By the time you met with your bad luck I was, but getting out of Portugal was difficult. To be honest, I didn't try too hard.'

'Wise man. There were far worse places to be. I saw quite a few of them.'

'What service were you?'

'Fallschirmjäger, 1 Regiment.'

Dietrich's eyebrows rose slightly. 'The Cream.'

'It soured, considerably.'

'And now you repair clocks.'

'If you have a broken gramophone I could mend that, too.'

Dietrich poured more coffee into their cups. 'How do you know Beckendorp – I mean, Holleman?'

Briefly, Fischer gave him their mutual history, omitting sensitive matters that might count in the balance of what value the Organization would put upon Holleman's defection (as he did so, the object in question returned from the lavatory and remained uncharacteristically silent while excerpts from his biography were rehearsed). It didn't amount to much, and as Fischer spoke two things struck him: that their relationship had comprised a series of glancing, frantic encounters prompted by personal crises, and that wiser men would have been far less pleased to see each other than he and Freddie usually were.

Holleman had managed to get half a pastry into his mouth when Dietrich dispensed with the informalities.

'Give me something.'

'Wha …?' The defector struggled to control the lump in his throat and swallowed heavily.

'You said that *they* aren't saying the same things. In the Politburo. Give me an example, with names.'

For almost a minute, Holleman stared at the table, brushing crumbs from his chest and stomach. His half-elated mood had faded, the earlier relief of having crossed the line now crowding against the consequences of it. He coughed again, and looked up.

'Did you know that Franz Dahlem was kicked off the Central Committee last month?'

Dietrich frowned. 'I didn't. I assume that *we* do, that it wasn't a secret. What was the cause?'

'*Political errors*. That could just be bad breath, of course.'

'Ulbricht and he aren't the best of comrades.'

'To put it politely, no. Dahlem was the unofficial opposition.'

'To what?'

'To the Moscow emigrants. This, also, isn't a secret. Since before there was a DDR, two groups within the SED have been at each other's soft parts - those who spent the war in Moscow, pressing their lips to Stalin's arse, and the ones who didn't. Stalin never trusted the ones who didn't.'

'Stalin's dead.'

'You heard?. Well, his bereaved Germans worry about where the Soviet Union's going next, and, like any good *kozis*, they've decided in the meantime to empty their own latrines. Paul Merker was sacked last November for allegedly being a French poodle, though the real reason was that he criticised the Josef - Adolph Pact back in '39 and they've wanted to do for him ever since. Dahlem was a close friend of Merker's, so it's only natural that he's in their sights too. But really, it's about more than settling scores.'

Dietrich didn't seem convinced. 'There's nothing new about different sorts of communists fighting. They hate each other more than they hate the West. What else could it be?'

Holleman shrugged. 'You're not thinking about the … what isn't he thinking about, Otto?'

'The woods? The bigger picture?'

Holleman pointed a finger at his friend and continued. 'Ulbricht's getting rid of the opposition for more than the pleasure of it. For as long as Stalin was alive the two Politburos were as far apart as twins in a womb, except that while the Soviets did everything that Josef told them to out of fear, the Germans did it because they knew that he knew best. Now, they're getting a taste of how things might be different. I suppose you know that Ulbricht reversed the new work quotas under pressure from the Ivans?'

Dietrich nodded.

'That was Semyonov's doing, and he more or less runs the Soviet Control Commission in Germany. What hurts more, he made it clear that the economic problems the quotas were intended to address won't be relieved by Moscow this time. Their economic plan's as fucked as ours, so we're on our own and Ulbricht's beginning to feel like a squirrel on a thin branch. Until the succession's sorted he has no pull in the Kremlin, and if it goes the wrong way he never again will. In the meantime ...'

Holleman shifted his artificial leg to search out a more comfortable position that wasn't there.

'... a lot of people in the SED – not the Moscow emigrants, obviously – think we've been moving the wrong way for years. The nationalizations have been a disaster, they say, and this concentration on heavy industry at the cost of everything else is just repeating the Soviet mistake. They want us to produce more stuff that people will buy in the shops, like Malenkov's arguing for the USSR – to build an American-style economy without capitalism, so to speak. Demand, they say, will allow production to take care of itself. At the moment, we're building the cart then searching for a horse to pull it.'

Dietrich's attention was beginning to wander, but he made the effort. 'Dahlem's one of these?'

'I don't know. Possibly. He's enough of a politician to use it if he gets the chance. Like Merker, he's down but not yet *out*, and for the first time Ulbricht's vulnerable. Semyonov has made it more or less clear that he thinks the present leadership of the SED's a bunch of cocks. There are a lot of reasons for that, but what's really got his back up is the cult of Ulbricht.'

'I didn't realise there was one.'

'There isn't yet, not quite. But, being a true Stalinist, the man wants some of the trappings. His latest stab is arranging golden fucking chariots and petal-scattering wood nymphs for his official sixtieth birthday celebrations at the end of this month. In the middle of a self-inflicted depression, this isn't sitting well.'

'I'm sure our analysists will find this fascinating, but …'

'Let me finish, please. I was giving you the background to the real business.'

'Which is?'

'Now, today. The strikes. They're going to be big.'

'We guessed that.'

'I mean *massive*. About the only large, heavy-industrial concern that's not likely to come out is the cushy, overpaid lot at Stalinstadt. Ulbricht's already made himself look weak by reversing the work quotas, and yesterday the Party itself turned on him. Brandt, Jendretzky and Herrnstadt more or less told him to issue a statement acknowledging the justice of the workers' grievances. If he doesn't get a grip on what happens today – on the streets *and* within the Party - he might as well start planning his memoirs. I'm saying, he isn't going to be soft.'

'I wouldn't imagine so.'

'It's why I'm here, and why you need to do something.'

'Me?'

'You, plural, the *wessies*. And, if possible, the Allies too.'

'What *something*?'

'Nothing.'

'Eh?'

Fischer was as puzzled by this exchange as Dietrich looked to be, but then he recalled his previous evening's thoughts about democracy and how it relieved its itches.

'Freddie, you're saying they shouldn't interfere?'

Holleman shrugged. 'They *can't* interfere, not practically. But the first thing Ulbricht's going to do today is to blame foreign agitators for what's happening, and if he finds evidence for it he'll have every excuse to be harsh. Look what he did to the Jewish leaders – sorry, the *cosmopolitan elements* - earlier this year. Give him the chance and he'll scrape every other imagined fifth-column off the plate too.'

Dietrich's puzzlement seemed to deepen slightly. 'Forgive me, but surely it's very much in our interest that Ulbricht be *harsh*? What better way to loosen the SED's grip than to encourage a festering wound?'

'If you don't care about blood on the streets, fine. But what if *VolksPolizei* and State Security can't handle what's coming? MfS have brought several hundred of their provincial personnel into the city, but it isn't going to be enough to cover every street corner. And they daren't strip DGP personnel from the border, not on a day when thousands of citizens might try to make a dash to the west.'

'What about *Kasernierte* police?'

'KVP won't – can't - move without Soviet authorization, so if they do it means it's already too late and everything's out of German hands. Yesterday morning, my boss, Waldemar Schmidt, asked Semyonov for permission for *VolksPolizei* to disperse the Stalin Allee strikers and arrest their ringleaders. He was refused, but if it looks like we're going to lose control of the streets Semyonov will have to intervene.'

Dietrich shrugged. 'It would contribute to the eventual collapse of the DDR. We've already absorbed more than a hundred thousand of her citizens this year; the process would only accelerate if striking workers are suppressed brutally.'

'It would also destroy any chance that the opposition within the SED might get rid of Ulbricht. Fear would cement his arse into the General Secretary's chair until his corpse got ripe.'

'Again, would that be a bad thing? Do you recall what happened to Heydrich? The British only arranged his assassination after he started to rule the Czechs intelligently. The Allies don't want flexible, economically-literate men running the DDR; they want the idiots to continue as before.'

'Christ!' Holleman slapped the table. 'When have things ever gone the way you clever bastards expected them to? If you make folk desperate they do desperate, stupid things, whatever common sense tells them. We're already raising a wire fence between east and west to keep our people in - a fucking fence, it's unbelievable! What will the Politburo do if they see a collapse coming? Will they say *fair enough, the better system won*? Is Moscow going to let the DDR fail and welcome a re-united, western-allied Germany? The Soviets have the Bomb now, and they're far more scared of the system failing than they are of another war. Look ...'

The hand that had thumped the table opened, pleading. '... if you stand back and do nothing, you lose nothing. If you do *something* and the shit starts flying, what will you do next? How far are the

Allies willing to go? How many Germans would be make an acceptable casualty list?'

Dietrich said nothing for a few moments. One of the other suits coughed quietly to get his attention and then tapped his wristwatch. He nodded, irritated.

'What is it that you think I can do? Or General Gehlen, for that matter? We're an intelligence-gathering organization, that's all. It's the politicians who make decisions on where and what we do. And even if we could influence our own leaders, what would the Americans, or British, or French care for that? They'll sit back all right, enjoying the spectacle of the DDR and Soviet Union sliding into the shit, perhaps putting out a foot occasionally to help nudge the business along. It's entirely in their interest, as they see it.'

Holleman rubbed his face. 'I know, and it's mad. In the past year, both Stalin and Churchill – and I never thought I'd mention those names in the same breath – made speeches calling for a demilitarized, neutral, united Germany. In other words, both sides have argued for pushing the so-called Iron Curtain a couple of hundred kilometres eastwards, at no political cost to the West. Why wouldn't you want that?'

Gehlen's man shrugged. 'Because even if Stalin was being sincere for once, he's dead now and it doesn't matter. In any case, some people believe that the collapse of the Communist model is an inevitability. For them, anything that relieves the economic and social pressures upon it, even in the short-term and to save innocent lives, is counter-productive. My own boss thinks that way. The Americans too - they don't want peaceful co-existence with the Ivans; they want them neutered, preferably in the literal sense. They look at the two Germanies – the expanding, increasingly prosperous west, soon to be part of their military alliance, and then the half-crippled east, a growing burden upon their principal enemy – and anything that alters that picture looks like appeasement. If the worn-out, dying men are calling for a reasonable, sane accommodation, it's because only those without money in a game can see its risks clearly.'

He looked at Holleman with something like sympathy. 'Believe me, I don't disagree with you. Like any German who didn't spend the war in Moscow I'd much prefer that we were allowed to make our own mistakes. But we have what we have, and whatever happens today we'll have it tomorrow, too.'

Fischer put his hand on Holleman's arm, to quell whatever response this immoveable truth goaded. 'What about the more obvious provocations?'

'Such as?'

'Berlin politicians, people in this building, opening their mouths without considering the consequences. And American radio in Berlin – they've been devoting a lot of time to the strikes. Can't something be said to the effect that all comments have to be cleared first through the Allied Control Commission?'

'But the Americans themselves run RIAS. What could we do?'

'You have no-one in Kufsteinerstrasse?'

'No. We don't set foot in there, unless it's to provide intelligence when they're putting together a broadcast, which happens rarely.'

Fischer nodded. He hadn't expected better. 'Who, exactly, is responsible for output?'

'The Americans, obviously - their Information Control Division. Don't look for any favours from them.'

'Why not?'

'You've heard the content - it isn't subtle. Each Sunday they broadcast excerpts from their Declaration of Freedom, for Christ's sake. If the strikes are going to be as bad as Herr Holleman says, the Control Division will probably regard it as manna from Heaven. Their intended audience is in the east, not west, so if they can spray gasoline onto the flames they probably will.'

Holleman slumped, as if a stopper had been pulled and his anima allowed to bleed out. 'I might have well have stayed over there.'

Dietrich finished scribbling in his notebook, put away his pen and looked up. 'No, you'll be valuable enough. We know what's going on in the Politburo and Central Committee only after it's happened, not before or during. Any light you can throw upon who hates whom will be gratefully received. You might even be offered a pension.'

'I don't want money, just a chance at a job. Any job.'

'I'm sure the *LandesPolizei* would welcome your expertise. And you …' he turned to Fischer; 'In a couple of years there'll be a *Wehrmacht* again – though of course, they'll call it something else. You could be an instructor, if you want steadier work than timepieces.'

'I volunteered once. Twice would be wilful.'

'Your choice.' Dietrich glanced at his watch. 'I've arranged for incident reports to be wired here directly from Pullach today, so as soon as we know what's happening you can give us your views. I'll mention what you've said, but I doubt they'll do anything beyond putting a note on your new file.'

Holleman nodded. 'If you can get information on how the demonstrations are being handled, I can offer an opinion about if and when the Soviets are likely to get involved. Once they do, there won't be anything more I can add usefully.'

'Understood. Is there anything else you need?'

'My family. My wife and a colleague will be coming across the line this morning, if they haven't already. They know to find a policeman and mention that people at Schöneberg's *Rathaus* should be informed.'

'Of course. I'll ask the telephone room to let me know immediately. Now, I have to speak to Pullach. You won't be placed under guard, but please don't think of leaving the building.'

Holleman's face fell a little further. 'Believe me, I daren't.'

9

'For years, their way of life fascinated me. It may be why I chose to study in Germany before the war. Of course, it was the Volga community that drew my attention originally, but now they're gone, to Siberia or Heaven. It's ironic that I had to come to America to find what remains.'

Maxim Shpak had grown a beard. Zarubin had expected it, of course, yet he could hardly keep his eyes from the object. It was luxuriant near the chin, a red celebration of primitive anabaptistry; but as it grew distant from its home follicles it straggled more than a retreating army, giving an impression of what Americans called cotton candy, falling off its stick.

'There are plenty of Russian Mennonites in the United States, Maxim Petrovich. Why didn't you go to live with them?'

Shpak pulled a face, sending the ends of the beard in several directions. 'That would have meant Kansas, or Nebraska. I owe God only so much suffering.'

'You've fitted in well here?'

'They've been very welcoming. Of course, I had to drop what I imagined was German and learn *Plautdietsch*, but now I feel at home. Did you know that my community is one of the oldest in America?'

'I didn't. It seems a pleasant place, this valley.'

They sat in a pew in the Meeting House, an otherwise empty building whose lack of ornamentation made a cow-barn seem as frivolously ornate as an Orthodox Cathedral. Shpak's very plain hat sat on his lap, and his trousers had ridden up to reveal a generous half-length of bony shins. Memories of the uniform of a Colonel of MGB (it had fit the frame with no greater success) seemed like the flitting wisps of rumours long gone.

'It's very fertile, yes. My farm – my father-in-law's farm – is over towards Reedsville. I hope you don't think me rude that I didn't …?'

'Invite me over? Of course not. What truck would a good Mennonite have with a sinner like me?'

'Are you, still?'

'You mean the heiress? No, thankfully. In other ways, as much as ever. How is your wife?'

'Also fertile.' Shpak's face coloured slightly. 'She's ... younger. This is a very conservative community, almost as much as the Amish. The age difference isn't considered ugly.'

'You have children! My congratulations.'

'One and another on the way. Sergei Aleksandrovich, I feel that this visit isn't about your need for familiar company in a strange land. May I ask what you want?'

This was shockingly direct, even by the old Shpak's standards. Zarubin had to assume that the not-even-slightly-mechanized farming life made great demands upon a man's time.

'Yes, of course. Nikita Krushchev.'

'Ah. CIA work, presumably?'

'I wouldn't ask, otherwise. There's nothing about Soviet politics that makes me long for the old days.'

'I knew him, actually.'

'I was hoping so.'

'It was for a few months only, from late '46. I was still NKVD in those days, and some of our units were sent to Ukraine to flush out Insurgent Army elements while he was Premier and head of the Party there. We must have met ten or twelve times at most, and then he got on Stalin's bad side by begging for food for his people. All that came of it was a few soup kitchens and Kaganovitch, sent down to steal his job. Until that moment I thought Krushchev a little simple-minded, but he reacted to the setback very shrewdly.'

'How?'

'He went to bed, sick, for several months. By the time he was well again, Kaganovitch had become equally sick of Ukraine and got himself recalled to Moscow. I'd transferred to MGB in the meantime, the partisans were all dead or sent to the gulags and

Krushchev, re-instated as Party Secretary in Ukraine, got on with his collectivization of farms. We never met again.'

'When he left Ukraine in '49 he went to Moscow and immediately became head of the Party there. Do you know how it happened?'

Shpak shrugged. 'I know rumours. Stalin was getting paranoid - excuse me, even *more* paranoid. The Leningrad gang had been smashed, but that imaginary group of plotters made him see conspiracies everywhere. Krushchev had been out of the Centre for too long to be suspected, and it worked for him. Politburo meetings had stopped almost, and any of its business that needed to be done happened at Stalin's house during the all-night dinners. What happened there I can't say, obviously. I suspect that, as with all failing absolute monarchies, the courtiers vied for the King's affections in order to advance their respective causes.'

'What is Krushchev's *cause*, particularly?'

'I never knew. He hid his ideals quite well, if he had any. His great skill is that he's diffident – he doesn't push himself forward too obviously. He isn't egotistical in the manner of Malenkov, or Beria, or Kaganovitch – or, if he is, he takes care to keep it under a lid. No doubt this was what made him attractive to Stalin.'

'So he was forgiven for caring about whether Ukrainians starved or not?'

'Apparently, though his advance wasn't obvious until recently. He wasn't one of the men raised by the 19th Congress last year.'

'No.' Zarubin considered what he'd been told. The only surprising or curious thing about Krushchev's elevation was that it hadn't stopped with Stalin's death. There was no other apparent power base upon which he could rely, other than the Moscow Party he led. That was significant, but not enough to allow him to displace Malenkov as First Secretary *and* keep Beria sulking in his tent. Yet here he was, one of the three men who would almost certainly succeed Stalin – if not quite as dictator, at least *primus inter pares* by a healthy distance, the only hands that mattered upon the wheel of State. It was enough to make a cynic (which Zarubin most definitely was) wonder if there were bodies down a well somewhere.

Shpak was considering his knees. 'It's a confusing situation, certainly.'

'It is. Malenkov and Beria have far more experience of real power, but was it *really* real? No one farted without the Boss's permission, not after 1937. Who knows if any of the Old Guard have the ability to think independently anymore? Perhaps Krushchev has the advantage of not having been long domesticated by collective terror.'

'Perhaps.' Shpak stood up. 'I have to go now, Sergei Aleksandrovich. I have cows to milk.'

'Isn't that a dawn chore?'

The older man's face reddened. 'It is, but this conversation makes me uncomfortable, and there really isn't more that I can say. There'll be a bus outside soon to take you back to the station at Belleville' He offered his hand. 'If I ever come to New York, I promise that I'll let you know beforehand.'

'Thank you. And if I ever have reason to revisit this particular part of the seventeenth-century, may I announce myself?'

'Of course. I'll introduce you to the family, but we'll speak of suitable things, not Moscow.'

10

Having for the first time that morning a few minutes in which to think of more than the moment, Fischer decided that Freddie Holleman looked older, and by more than the eighteen months since they had last met (at the twins' twenty-first birthday celebration, during which, surreally, a badly mutilated, ex-Luftwaffe stooge of the capitalist system had shook hands with several high ranking members of East Berlin's SED and inquired, politely, after their health). It wasn't so much the wrinkles – he had always maintained a healthy crop of frown lines - as the slight stoop, as if the weight of a particular world was finally getting the upper hand and Atlas was looking to his pension plan.

Their eyes met, and Fischer realised the appraisal was proceeding both ways. They had found a coffee-room on the third-floor of the *Rathaus*, and occupied a table away from the clutch of City employees who were breaking up their morning with gossip, cakes and a beverage quite unlike (and much inferior to) the private stock that Dietrich had accessed earlier.

'You look older, Otto.'

'Thank you, Freddie. I *am* older.'

'How's the clock business?'

'I want to say *ticking over*, but that would be a very British joke.'

'Eh?'

'Never mind. You aren't wearing the uniform, so I can't tell – did you get your promotion?'

Almost two years earlier, the man generally understood to be Kurt Beckendorp had been closing upon the rank of Chief Inspector of *VolksPolizei*, a mere two steps below the summit occupied by Waldemar Schmidt himself. At the time – or rather, during those few hours at the birthday party at which Beckendorp's SED colleagues had gone out of their way to pat his shoulder and offer knowing looks – Fischer had sensed that his friend was dreading rather than relishing the prospect.

'No, thank Christ. I think Zaisser put in a word against me. I've never been as close to MfS as I was to the Fifth Directorate. If it had been up to Jamin I'd probably have had Schmidt's office by now.' He stared out of the window. 'And had to deal with this shit.'

'You sound almost fond of Jamin.'

Erich Jamin, Director of the once-dreaded and now-defunct Fifth, was not a man embarrassed by a surfeit of admirers. His short but notable early career in Dirlewanger's SS brigade might have had something to do with that, or his latter habit of arranging *night and fog* disappearances of enemies of the State. He certainly wasn't someone who felt the need to attract the affection of colleagues.

'He was alright, as monsters go. After we had that brawl in '48 he began to act more as if his Directorate was part of the police – which it was, of course – and I always kept him informed about what we were doing. Since State Security took over the business it's as if they and *VolksPolizei* occupy separate bunkers.'

'Zaisser doesn't cooperate?'

'Zaisser would be very happy to have *VolksPolizei* confined to traffic-directing duties. He's entirely devoted to expanding his own forces. They have about ten thousand active duty men now, none of whom bother to liaise with us. Can you believe it? Ten thousand - that's more than 'Stapo had in '39.'

'You have no regrets, then?'

'About crossing the line? No. I'll tell you if I miss the house and perquisites when I've had time to think about it. Watch out …'

Dietrich lowered himself into an unoccupied seat. He had a sheaf of papers in his hand and the flustered air of a man ordered to take command of a missing regiment.

'You might have what you wanted.'

Holleman tried to recall what it was that he wanted. 'That would be …?'

'I've spoken to an acquaintance at RIAS. However his bosses might decide eventually to play it, the Station Director's given strict instructions that the news is to be reported today without embellishments - no salt, just the wounds. Chancellor Adenaur's already pleaded for calm, and yesterday evening the Minister for

All-German Affairs went on RIAS to suggest that the strikers shouldn't lose their heads and do something stupid.'

'That's … good.'

'There's some bad, also. Last evening, RIAS recorded an interview with the prick Scharnowski, who urged his members – and anyone else who'd listen – to assemble and demonstrate in support of the eastern strikers. They didn't broadcast it immediately but referred the decision to the Americans, saying that if they hadn't been told what to do by 5 o'clock this morning they'd put it out. They heard nothing, so out it went. That – I mean, the silence - may be what frightened the Director into banning any further provocations. Anyway, in West Berlin, *Bundesgrenzschutz* personnel are being deployed at the line with orders to try to stop any of our trades-unionists crossing the line to do the solidarity shit with their eastern brethren. What's going to happen elsewhere along the internal border, I can't say.'

Holleman shook his head. 'Still, it sounds as if someone's thinking.'

'For the moment, yes. I assume that whether they continue to do so will depend upon what happens next.'

'That's what gives me the gripes. So far, the strikers have been doing it by the rules – electing strike committees, sending delegations to speak with the Party, listing their demands and not kicking anyone. If it stays that way, Ulbricht can do the dance again – pretending to care, offering small concessions that he was going to offer anyway and then have the workers go home, happy that they imagine they have a say. But ...'

'If they're joined by non-union troublemakers or *wessies*, it becomes a mob.'

'And Ulbricht has his excuse. Western Fascistic elements will have infiltrated a legitimate industrial negotiation to spread dissent and undermine the State.'

Dietrich leaned forward and lowered his voice. 'If that happens, what will State Security and *VolksPolizei* do?'

Holleman pulled a face. 'I don't know. That sounds dumb, doesn't it, from a senior *VoPo* officer? But everything changed eight days ago, when the Ivans made Ulbricht back-track on most of the programme he's been pushing for the past year. Since then, no-one in the Party's been able to find their arse with both hands. Before 9 June, I'd have told you confidently that we'd be ordered to go in feet-first if it looked like we were losing control of the streets. Now, who knows? If the Politburo's paralysed by indecision, who's going to take the initiative? If no-one does, and the crowd thinks it's got the Party on the ropes, Ulbricht only has the one option ...'

'He calls Semyonov.'

'And Semyonov calls Moscow. Whoever's on the other end of the line won't want to appear weak or indecisive, not when a three-way arm-wrestling competition's underway in the Kremlin. There'll be just one objective, to restore order. The cost won't matter, not today at least.'

Dietrich's finger's drummed on the table. 'We can't guarantee that absolutely no-one crosses the line to join the strikers today.'

'Of course not, you're not used to keeping people in. We've had a lot of practice, and we're still crap at it. If someone wants to cause trouble, they will.'

Fischer had been silent, listening to a lot of what wasn't his business, but something struck a jarring note.

'Aren't you hearing *anything* from the Americans and British?

Dietrich sat back in his chair and glanced around. 'Not yet. At least, if Gehlen's being told something he isn't sharing it with his employees.'

'If the Allies deployed troops from their Berlin garrisons at the line, it might shore up the police effort. At the least, it would show the Soviets that they were trying to calm things.'

'I can't say for sure, but I doubt that the Allies have *any* idea what to do. They couldn't have seen things coming if we didn't, and by the time they've decided what their policy should be, events will be over the horizon.'

To Fischer, it sounded credible. From what he'd been reading in the newspapers since the previous 5 March, western governments had been almost as paralysed by Stalin's death as had the Soviet Union.

In the lingering glare of that political explosion, Walter Ulbricht's DDR had become a mere shadow play, something that not even the German sections of foreign ministries would have been considering too carefully.

Dietrich turned back to Holleman. 'We need to wait and see what happens, obviously. But *what* we see, and when we see it, may not be enough to be helpful. Herr Holleman, I think it's time you made yourself useful to us.'

'How do I do that?'

'If things start to go very badly today, Ulbricht's going to try to cut the telephone lines between east and west. It hasn't happened yet, but let's not be complacent. You must have subordinates you can trust, at least until they know what you've done. Can you contact someone? Someone who might know if plans are being laid for *badly*?'

11

Panic didn't come easily to Rolf Hoeschler. As a former paratrooper he was familiar with degrees of anxiety – about his harness, the flight-path and how prepared the enemy beneath them might be for an operation planned by mad bastards back at Headquarters; but not outright panic. Members of the Fallschirmjäger regiments had been carefully chosen, their fatalistic tendencies nurtured, and, following parlously dangerous operations conducted with characteristic élan, rewarded with colossal quantities of medals, local girls and alcohol. Had more of his comrades survived these operations, no doubt there would have been less booze and *muschi* to go around; still, it had been remarkable how swiftly the liberal application of both had medicated shattered nerve-endings. Even the medal ribbons came in handy, when toilet paper couldn't be had.

Panic would have been pointless, unthinkable. A man, flung from an aircraft into darkness, likely to be lit up like a duck on a fairground firing-range, was far beyond the point at which loss of bowel control or a tearful appeal to a dead mother might ease the tension. Hoeschler recalled such moments as remarkably calming, a brief passage during which all mortal concerns had been laid to rest, or at least placed in escrow pending a resolution one way or the other. The closest he had ever come to actual nervous collapse during his time in uniform had been the fault of a jammed Mauser, the garnishing turd upon a day in which he had been pinned down for the best part of twelve hours by men who had objected strenuously to handing over their airstrip to the Third Reich. Fortunately, the shared pain of it had taken off the corners, leaving him no more than acutely perturbed about the heat, the crossfire, the dirt he was obliged to eat, the raging thirst it brought on and the very real possibility that General Meindl – the monumental foreskin who had ordered them to be dropped on Maleme – would cut his losses and pull back.

That stretched moment of anguish counted now as military history, yet once more Hoeschler's Mauser had jammed. He had been trusted with a mission and failed in it, spectacularly, more so than if he had merely walked up to the first *VolksPolizei* patrol that he, Kristin and Engi encountered and confessed everything. At least then he would know where the woman and boy were, and who was dealing with the business. Perhaps, with great luck, he might have been able to weave some sort of extenuation, a blatant play to faint possibilities that would delay their interrogation long enough for the day's coming confusions to offer some further, undeserved chance of escape. At the moment he was blind, utterly without a means of proceeding. If he had a map of Berlin spread out before him, he could confidently have waved a hand and said 'they're here, somewhere. Probably.'

Standing on the north side of Bernauerstrasse once more, he tried to clear his head. He recalled – he believed that he recalled – that the patrol that had examined the bus passengers' identity papers comprised three men. When his own papers were surrendered minutes later there had been three still, and looking across the road now even his disordered mind could confirm the same number. If Kristin and Engi had been arrested, there would be fewer remaining, at least until the prisoners had been delivered into custody.

But then he wondered if there had been a police van parked nearby, just out of his peripheral vision, in which a couple more *VolksPolizei* hopefuls had awaited detainees. No, he had been careful to check in all directions - he reassured himself that even in his nervous and distracted state it was the sort of thing that would have registered strongly, immediately. It was, after all, what he had feared the most.

So Kristin and Engi must have crossed into West Berlin, but where were they? It wasn't conceivable that his boy would have allowed her to just wander off, even if she'd been addled enough to attempt it. Nor would she have approached a *SchuPo* patrol to announce her arrival in the west, for the excellent reason that he hadn't yet told her where or to whom her husband had surrendered himself. Most of all, Engi wouldn't have allowed her to simply abandon Hoeschler, not unless …

Ulrich. He thought that he had convinced her, but what mother would allow logic to calm her fears for a son? Had they escaped more easily than he had hoped, and then turned straight back? It only seemed impossible until he recalled the stubborn set to her face. Engi would have argued strenuously, but she was his aunt in all but blood, and an intimidating one at that. Hoeschler himself wouldn't have enjoyed the conversation, so what chance would a seventeen-year-old have, one who worshipped both her and the son she imagined she could save?

He recalled Ulrich's address, one of the four-storey blocks that had risen around Vinetastrasse's u-bahn station in Pankow. He and Engi had taken bread, salt and honey there the previous year, to help warm the pleasant one-bedroomed apartment on the first floor. From that same occasion he also recalled Liesa, the pretty, timid girl who had taken Ulrich's heart and locked it in her safe-box. Over the space of two hours he had managed to coax about a dozen words from her, and only then because, in the presence of the fearsome father-in-law-to-be, every other guest had seemed relatively unthreatening.

Would Kristin use the u-bahn? If it hadn't yet been closed to prevent striking workers getting into central Berlin it was the logical choice, the quickest way to get to her son's home. The trouble was, he might not be there. He worked for a metal fabrication concern in Heinersdorf, a small business just about hanging onto its independence in the face of the remorseless nationalization of eastern Germany's industries. His working day should have started already, but this was not a day like others. He might have decided to stay at home, to keep away from the trouble; he might be marching at the head of a strikers' column, one of many converging on the *Neues Stadthaus* to demand better working conditions and higher wages; he might have thought fuck all of this, me and Liesa are going to have a quiet picnic in the Bürgerpark until it's all over. That was the problem with mad, spur-of-the-moment decisions – they needed at least a sliver of predictable circumstance if they weren't to fall to pieces.

The same problem made following Kristin and Engi equally difficult. He couldn't know where they were at that moment; couldn't predict where they would be an hour from now. All he could say with reasonable certainty was that at some point soon, Kristin would knock upon Ulrich's apartment door, and …

If he was at home, she would speak to him. If he wasn't, she would leave a message. If the former, then either she would persuade him to come West with them or fail – in which case she would surely return with Engi and try to find her husband; if the latter, a locked door could be opened with a boot. The message would offer some clue as to what and where next.

He would draw attention if he tried to re-cross the line through the same patrol, and his face commit itself to several memories. He turned and walked eastwards along the north side of Bernauerstrasse until he found another gap in the temporary wire barrier at the junction with Ruppinerstrasse. Opposite their eastern counterparts, a three-man *Bundesgrenzshutz* patrol stood almost at parade-stiffness, giving a slightly self-conscious impression of being a nation's bulwark against the communist hordes that might try to jump the line that day. Hoeschler presented his identification, pretended to yawn and asked how their day was going so far. The one who had taken his papers shrugged.

'Quiet as church, so far. On your way home?'

'Yeah. The night-shift turned into half a morning too. Was I offered a choice?'

'Well, get to bed soon. It's going to get mad on your side, later.'

'That's my plan A, mate.'

A friendly pat on the shoulder sent him into the road and through the wire. At the other side, he was processed without comment or more than a momentary glance, by men who looked as if they had far more on their minds than a worker heading home at a curious time of day. He walked south along Ruppinerstrasse until he reached a bus halt and boarded the Prenzlauer-Berg service that arrived within a minute.

He was beginning to think that he had a chance – perhaps even odds – on reaching Ulrich's apartment before Kristin managed to avoid him once more, when the bus came to a halt so suddenly that its passengers lurched forward in violent synchronization. They were almost at the junction with Granseerstrasse, Arkon-Platz to their left, and in a moment Hoeschler realised that a matter of time had become something else. Spilling out of the children's park and entirely filling the street in front of them, a vast procession of men moved slowly but inexorably, punctuating whatever they were chanting with raised fists. It was an army by any measure, marching to a war that no-one could have foreseen even forty-eight hours earlier, but which now seemed as inevitable as any the Führer had planned.

12

VP-KriminalKommissar Albrecht Müller was staring at a convenient wall when the telephone on his desk spoiled his morning. This was a considerable achievement, given that the day was already promising to rank with one, ten years earlier, upon which he had first witnessed a client being executed. Having then been a defence lawyer in the People's Court, a mere guillotining shouldn't have crept up on him unawares; but it had, and horribly, just like the news that had swept through Keibelstrasse earlier like a dose of camp-fever, piling unpleasantly onto their existing expectations of the coming hours.

He was looking at the wall because he could avoid other men's eyes that way. He was tired of seeing in them what he was feeling, weary of sensing the collective absence of understanding. He worked with some good men and a lot of bad ones also – it wasn't the fear of what they might have to do today that was casting the pall, but rather the sense that a master plan had gone missing.

They were waiting. Patrols were out on the streets and reports were coming in, confirming the scale of dozens of unauthorized industrial actions that were converging, congealing into something that threatened the political fabric of their young state. It was a moment of decision, and no-one was making one.

Their ultimate boss, Waldemar Schmidt, was doubtless conferring with other senior decapitated poultry, clucking that something needed to be done. Yet no orders were filtered down to the non-coms, the ones who would be coordinating the response on the streets. Without adequate direction they would be as useful as perforated condoms, and as likely to cause something unfortunate.

And then the bloody 'phone rang. Müller didn't quite leave his chair, but his already-fraught nerves submitted another request for leave. He picked up the receiver, said yes when asked by the exchange operator if he would accept a call from an unidentified party and then nearly parted company with the contents of his colon when the voice of a non-person betrayed Albrecht Müller as someone who was an acquaintance of non-people.

'Müller, it's Beckendorp. Can you speak?'

For a few moments, Müller wasn't sure that he knew the answer, his larynx being as paralysed as much of the rest of him. He cleared his throat twice, swallowed, glanced around to see if he was being watched and then tried something simple.

'Ah …'

'Listen, you've probably heard rumours about me this morning. Ignore them, it's all crap. I need to know how you've been told to deal with antisocial elements today. I mean, your operational orders.'

'We haven't.'

'What?'

'We haven't been told anything.'

'Don't be a comedian. Has the use of arms been authorized yet?'

'No, really, we haven't been told anything. They sent out street patrols at dawn, as many men as we had below the rank of *unter-kommissar*, but without any orders other than to protect the *Stadthaus* and ministries, to make their presence known and to check papers more carefully than usual. That's it, so far. We're waiting to hear more. Are you saying that you didn't defect …?'

'What about MfS?'

'They brought in several hundred extra men from other states yesterday …'

'I know. What are they doing with them?'

'They're out on the streets, but I don't think they have clear orders either. In any case, they have no radios, so how they're being coordinated I couldn't say.'

'What time is it?'

Müller checked the wall-clock. 'Almost ten o'clock.'

'Jesus. No-one's making decisions.'

'We guessed that, Comrade …' Müller paused. The acting Chief Inspector for East Berlin had called them in at eight am that morning to give them the news that their boss had crossed over to the enemy, having left a note for his own superior explaining precisely that. The facts being discharged, he then referred to Beckendorp as a traitor, a western stooge, a betrayer of the People and an unspeakable cunt, and demanded that any officer who subsequently heard from the aforesaid should report it immediately. It was all the sort of thing that couldn't be walked back as an error of judgement or a professional misstep, and under the circumstances *comrade* seemed a little out of date. Müller owed Beckendorp a great deal, but loyalty couldn't survive the ultimate act of disloyalty. He swallowed again.

'Why did you do it?'

There was a long pause at the West Berlin end of the line. The other party was breathing hard, but Müller doubted that his question was the cause of it. What a mere *KriminalKommissar* might think of his boss's betrayal probably counted for as much as the canteen cockroaches' opinion of that day's menu. He had no idea why, but it seemed that Kurt Beckendorp's mind was still on what was happening in East Berlin that day, though he was now, irrevocably and from choice, a *wessie*.

'A lot of reasons. You'd better report this conversation the moment you put down the 'phone.'

'I will.'

'Listen, I might call again later, if the lines are still open. I'll announce myself, so you'll know. It's alright, no-one will put it on you, as long as you warn them that it's coming. Who's your new boss?'

'They've moved Petersen up to acting Inspector.'

'Good, he's not a prick. Tell him about this call, and that there may be more. He'll want to listen in, that's fine. Tell him ...'

'What?'

'That I want to see Soviet troops deployed today about as much as he does.'

'Do you think it will come to that?'

'I can't see how it won't, if Ulbricht isn't telling State Security or DVdI how to deal with it.'

'*Why* isn't he?' Beckendorp might be a traitor, but Müller had a trusting faith in the man's understanding of the SED's bowels.

'Perhaps he's as confused as everyone else about what's going on. Uncle Joe isn't around to give orders anymore.'

'Who's going to make the decisions, then?'

'The Soviet Control Commission, obviously. Which means Semyonov.'

'You've met him. What's he like?'

'He's fond of Germans, though not so much that he won't do whatever needs to be done. What are you working on right now?'

The question was so absurdly out of place that Müller didn't answer for a moment. In fact, he needed the time to push away the day's events and recall what it was exactly that he did for a living.

'The Spittelmarkt murders, mostly.'

'Good. If Petersen tries to move you off the case, point to your record. You're the best murder man I have. Had, I mean.'

'Me? Really?' The praise of a traitor was still praise, and to Müller it was as unexpected as a pay rise.

'You're dogged, and you don't get bored. That's what catches killers, if anything does.'

'Thank you. Please don't give me a reference.'

'I won't. Goodbye.'

A sense of solitude struck Müller as he replaced the receiver. If he had become the department's best murder man it was because he'd had Beckendorp behind him and Kalbfleisch (his long-time colleague, an accomplished grafter and blame-dodger, recently ascended to happy, pigeon-infested retirement) by his side. With both props removed, and a new, unwanted reputation to uphold (even if no-one but himself knew of it), he feared that the homicidal element of Berlin's underworld had been dealt an unbeatable hand.

And now he had to confess to his new boss that he was in touch with a – with *the* – traitor, stooge, betrayer and unspeakable … what the Chief Inspector said. What that might do to a career wasn't to be considered without a man's nerves first being calmed by strong liquor, and local bars wouldn't be open for hours yet. He stood, tried to breathe regularly and pointed himself at the corridor where Beckendorp used to live. Petersen was a reasonable, thinking man, someone who had worked his way on the strength of his skills as a policemen, not as a politician. It wouldn't be foolish, Müller told himself, to hope that he might not be looking for a sacrificial object on his first day in a new job.

13

Zarubin had found the Olivetti in a pawn shop near Kaiser Park, haggled for it and paid only a little more than twice what it was worth. The shop's proprietor, perhaps haunted by the merciless quality of his victory, had thrown in new ribbons and the best part of a ream of watermarked paper. The latter was very fine, of a sort that would make a subliminal statement about the verity of whatever was typed upon it.

The would-be author was staring at the machine, willing inspiration and English grammar to come to him before he melted to a puddle of émigré grease under the small wooden stool upon which he had been squirming restlessly for almost an hour now. His apartment, workplace and refuge (a top-floor box in a brownstone building on Neptune Avenue) lacked that fabled token of American technological prowess, air-conditioning; and although his two windows faced directly toward it, the Atlantic rarely shared its bountiful breezes with streets north of Ocean View Avenue.

Cold he didn't mind, but the heat … Since coming to America, he had tried and failed to get on with her summers. They were worse, and more humid, than anything he recalled experiencing during his brief posting to Baku, just before the war. Perhaps he had been tougher then, or readier to bear discomfort if it meant being out of Moscow, but these days, the effort of sucking vigorously to acquire next to no oxygen wore him down horribly.

He didn't suffer alone, unfortunately. Mrs Weinstein, the old lady who lived immediately below him, complained volubly of the heat to anyone who would listen, and to her cat when no-one cared to. Her voice carried impressively, so Zarubin was able to share valuable insights not only into climatic conditions but a dead husband (Fred), the Italians down the street and the price of bagels also. What the cat thought of it all he couldn't say, but as he passed it on the stairs sometimes they shared a glance of hopeless longing to be somewhere else.

That *longing* was beginning to worry him. A sense of non-belonging was only natural, given that his defection and transplantation to America had been a matter of necessity, not choice. Perhaps he should have spent the last three years trying harder to adapt to the very different lifestyle and mores of his adopted county, rather than allowing every reverse, irritation and surreal conversation to add to the store of his discontent. He didn't mind so much that his intolerance of Americans and Americana was becoming less socio-political and more the sort that priests felt for Satan; but what it might mean for his peace of mind disturbed him greatly. He feared that he was becoming homesick.

He had chosen to live in Brighton Beach because it didn't, to his knowledge, house any other Russians. Not even one. He had most definitely not wanted to spend his declining years on a park bench, listening to forlorn reminiscences about sunsets over Lake Limen, or borscht the way a mother used to make it, or the goat that had been a first love. New beginnings had to be just that (he'd told himself), and a new American shouldn't bind himself unnecessarily to old ways. Yet an instinctive reluctance to fall too willingly into that new identity had left him between two places, not quite in touch with either.

He sometimes wondered if he should have settled in Nyack, where old tsarists still groped their rosaries and said tearful prayers for the souls of Romanovs. Being of assorted noble stock, their daughters would be considerably more personable than those of the descendants of serfs, and almost certainly reserved for Old Country matches rather than marked down and sold off to local men with names like Randy, or Harvey, or Hiram. He might have fit it, somewhere like Nyack. Of course, his membership of MGB would have needed to remain a matter unspoken, but his blond hair and blue eyes would be great assets among such company, hinting at the right sort of bloodline for breeding purposes. With effort and luck, a dowry might have provided at least a short-term solution to the financial issues with which he currently shared garret-space.

But the smell of incense make him sick, and the prospect of a life tied to folk who believed Nicholas II to be a fucking saint even more so. What-might-have-beens were a fool's occupation, and Sergei Aleksandrovich wasn't one of those. He was in *the* land of opportunity (or so the sales-brochure insisted), so if he wasn't climbing the ladder it must be because he hadn't yet spotted its lowest rung. His first mistake had been to assume that the CIA lavished money upon its agents and contractors, when in fact his present part-employment was at best a means of meeting the rent. He had assumed also that his identity, *per se*, would be a marketable commodity, which it turned out not to be (at least, not to anyone who wasn't an over-sexed Pennsylvanian German heiress or putative White Russian father). The so-called 'Cold War' was too young still for Americans to realise that they needed a far greater understanding of the Soviet mind, so universities, strategic planners and other interested parties had yet to rush to tap his experience (available to any and all at reasonable recompense).

Which left commerce. America was a land of aspiration, manifested by the accumulation of desired objects. As a child of communism, Zarubin was not a natural entrepreneur, and as a stranger to America he would have had trouble understanding the market even if the system was comprehensible to him. No doubt there were men, new to this land, who brought with them ideas, seeds from which mighty empires could and did grow; but someone raised to believe that money corrupted absolutely was unfairly handicapped at the starting-line.

There was, of course, an infantry-level to commercial activity, but he no more wanted to be an insurance salesman than he did the husband of a pious Russian wife. He had already seen the dark side to the American Hallucination – the lives of those, who, told that they could be anything if they tried, had tried and failed anyway. He had watched the grey, hope-fled procession of men who held down three jobs and still failed to make elusive ends meet, trooping their way to the nearest bar, their rent-monies ready to squander on liquid balm. He had wondered at the forty-year complexions of women in their late-20s, ground down further by un-unionized factory work than they would have been by a wind coming east off the steppe, and lusted for none of them. When he considered any of the many possibilities at the bottom of Capitalism's greasy pole, he was obliged to acknowledge the wisdom of Maxim Shpak's choice.

Stop thinking, and start Thinking. The paper in the typewriter remained unsullied by ink, and he had promised to deliver a report to the CIA's Beaver Street office by the following day. He hadn't even thought of a title yet that was bureaucratically bland enough not to make them suspect he was teasing once more. *Malenkov, Beria, Krushchev - What in God's Name's Going On?* wouldn't do, though it was perhaps the most accurate reflection of what they were thinking. *Reflections on Political Dynamics in the Post-Stalin Kremlin* sounded like a proposal for a PhD or a marching song by Gusev, and equally digestible. His personal preference (for its honesty) was *Just Give Me the Money and Read it Carefully*, but that would serve only as a concise notice of resignation.

Soviet Leadership after Stalin. He typed it with two fingers, satisfied that whatever was stamped on a box of nails couldn't be more nondescript. The next part was easier – a summary of the state of the Praesidium immediately preceding and following the old bastard's death. He knew enough English synonyms for panic, cluelessness and naked positioning to make this a substantial section, and for once he could be entirely accurate without compromising the security of the USSR (which, to his surprise, remained a concern to him). His most difficult task was then to draw conclusions from the present morass that made sense enough to stand convincingly, if and when they were proved to be wrong – difficult, because there had been no process-based transfer of power within the Soviet hierarchy since 1917. One might as easily predict an outcome by crushing a hundred-rouble note, flinging it into the pack of contenders and guessing whose hand would lift the thing triumphantly from the maul.

He wasn't complaining – it was this chaos that had provided him with his latest employment, modest though it was. Predictable things needed no special insights or experienced eye to interpret, and therefore generated no cash. Even a low-grade operative at E Street NW, asked to offer (for example) an opinion on the result of the next British election, had access to mountains of intelligence that would allow a stab at a reasonably shrewd prediction. He would have no need to consult a British defector, or crystal ball, or chicken giblets, or even *The London Times'* political columns. But when it came to the Kremlin, the Americans had as much idea as would a medieval Russian peasant asked his opinion on the White Horde succession question. Zarubin was their only realistic interpreter at this point, and he owed it to them to be convincing.

In his opinion (the genuine article, not the one he'd necessarily present), Malenkov remained the likeliest winner. He'd surrendered the General Secretaryship of the Party to Krushchev, but he remained Premier and Chair of the Praesidium (probably, the rest of them hadn't wanted anyone to spring too quickly out of the trap and thus had insisted on the splitting of offices). More importantly, he wasn't detested as Beria was - except by Zhukov, of course, who owed him at least one heart attack. He was intelligent, reasonably personable, could hold his drink (a greater political skill than most Kremlin observers realised), and – to Zarubin's knowledge – had no history with which he could be beaten too severely. His only potential weakness was that he had a habit of pinning himself to causes too prominently, and if they failed he might follow.

Beria's only advantage was that he was an insider, and a friend of Malenkov's. Given his history of elbow-deep bloodiness, his own mother and Christ would have signed the death warrant, if asked. Recent efforts to re-fashion him as someone with a soul only emphasised what had preceded that fantasy, and if he was to survive the present manoeuvrings it would only be by dint of making himself invaluable to whoever looked to be the likely winner. Hopes of his being the compromise candidate fell on the matter of him not knowing what the word meant.

Which left Krushchev. Shpak had offered little enough, which more or less summed up what was known. Somehow, the man had hovered just below the highest strata of Soviet power for almost ten years, crossed Stalin and survived it, worked hard and made very little impression on anyone. He was not known as a thinker (not necessarily a disadvantage), had no known enemies, no strong ideological convictions and no ties to any particular strand of thought on *what next*. If a man wanted to put himself late into a race, there were far worse places from which to attempt it.

Were there other possibilities? It didn't seem likely, though nothing could be ruled out entirely. Neither Molotov nor Bulganin wanted the job, Kaganovich couldn't do it and Zhdanov – once Stalin's likeliest successor – had somewhat hampered his chances by drinking himself to death. No one else was known to be in the betting, so what remained were the permutations.

It was fairly obvious (barring a surprise round of mass executions) that no-one would be able to rule as Stalin had, not for years to come. One might assume then that alliances would be made, old debts settled and new excuses for purges devised, and at the end of it one man might or might not have pulled away from the pack sufficiently to fear no rival; but to arrive at even this anodyne conclusion might be to see the future thought the past's lens. It was equally possible that the conditions which allowed Stalin to become their Red Tsar were gone forever. Revolutionary fervours had cooled, the Whites weren't coming back and the Soviet Union had lost enough men during the Great Patriotic War to dim the most sanguinary appetites for more of the same. A generation of survivors was as likely to seek to govern by committee, for a while at least. Consensus had one great advantage - it hid bad decisions in a crowd.

But a consensus upon what? The Americans were already into their stride, painting Communism as the existential threat to civilization that Nazism had been. *They* hadn't lost enough men in war to be sick of it yet – look at Korea, the back-end of the arse's arse, an excuse if ever there was one to make trouble for its own sake. How would the tired men in the Kremlin react to a taste for more confrontation?

They were already discovering that the maintenance of a vast war machine in peacetime was more expensive than the Soviet Union could afford. The near-disastrous results of the latest five-year plan had sharpened minds, made some of the wiser heads consider whether goading the Americans into re-arming massively had been a bad mistake. Malenkov had already mumbled a few tentative public noises about halting the atomic race; the economic implications aside, he seemed to think that the possibility of ending all sentient life everywhere might not be an entirely good thing. Neither Beria nor Krushchev had yet spoken on the matter, though each must have been aware of the potential danger of tying themselves to a rational strategy – that if Eisenhower didn't reciprocate, the architect of a policy of rapprochement would be painted as a weakling and disappeared quickly.

The future direction of policy cannot be determined with any accuracy until the shape and nature of the post-Stalin Politburo is established (perfect – both considered and obfuscating). *However, it is almost certain that the new Leadership will face conflicting imperatives: that it will be measured by its success in addressing currently unfavourable domestic economic conditions while maintaining a strong posture in the face of growing concerns regarding the absorption of the Federal Republic of Germany into the anti-Soviet alliance. Failure to address either or both issues satisfactorily will almost certainly result in further political developments which cannot presently be anticipated.*

Zarubin sat back on the sticky stool. His stream of consciousness had run to almost three pages by now, and it said just about everything that might be said. None of it amounted to anything substantial, but for what he was being paid it was more than a bargain. He wondered for a moment whether it might be wiser to split it into two instalments, thereby covering a further month's rent. It was a sad fact, however, that a man with a poor hand could only bluff so much before he was found out (unless, of course, he was dealing with idiots, which the CIA mostly weren't). It was better, on the whole, to give value for money and be thought of well for it than incline one's only customer to look elsewhere for future work.

This nakedly capitalist revelation pleased him, and raised his mood for the better part of the five minutes it took him to write a carefully non-committal, concluding paragraph. But then the heat either overcame or woke Mrs Weinstein, who launched into her poor fucking cat about their landlord, Mr Kowalczyk, and his reluctance to squander money on plumbing improvements. Several moments later the rhythm section commenced (old Miss Gerber, whose party wall with Mrs Weinstein was thinner even than the floor between storeys, deploying a shoe on the wall in a vain effort to stifle her neighbour's monologue), and Zarubin gave up any hope of doing more. He put on his outdoor shoes, jacket and hat and went for his daily walk, a form of exercise he had previously not considered as such but from which he now derived considerable mental benefit. Outside of the commuting rush, Brighton Beach was pleasantly quiet, its streets straight and logically laid out, and he had found that he could wander much further in the head than his feet took him in the hour or so he usually devoted to his regime.

It was a fine afternoon, much fresher outside than in the confines of the steam-bath that passed for his lodgings. He walked down 6th Street, thinking about his report and how it might be improved, and had almost reached the waterfront when a possibility struck him so forcibly that he stopped suddenly. He could re-write the report, drastically, and make it work for him in a way that he hadn't remotely contemplated until this moment. Cautiously, he flipped the notion, turned it around, examined it from different directions and found two possible worsts. The first of these was relatively minor – the CIA might regard him as an idiot and dispense with his future services (which weren't exactly guaranteed to be required in any case). The second was more problematic, involving his quiet but definitely irreversible execution in some wooded place. He had no way of assessing how likely this *worst* was, which if anything made it an even worse worst.

Still, he thought more about the idea as he followed the boardwalk as far as Coney Island. If anything he over-argued the dangers, and it came to him suddenly that this had very little to do with prudence. He was out of place here, short of money, opportunities and prospects, a self-uprooted wanderer with no real idea of his eventual destination. All of that was cause for concern for a man approaching his thirty-fifth birthday (it would fall, ironically, on the 4th July); but none of it moved him nearly as much as the other thing, the problem that made this new, dangerous possibility so attractive to him.

He was definitely, and quite possibly clinically, wearied by every single aspect of his life in the western hemisphere.

14

Josef (he didn't know why they had chosen that particular name, unless it was nostalgia for the good old bad days, recently passed) tried to think quickly. Obviously, he couldn't reveal himself and what he was, but this policeman was going to take his time. Perhaps it was his sense of helplessness making him over-compensate; but a robust set of identity papers weren't going to be nearly enough to satisfy him (that was fair enough; their previous owner had died in an interrogation cell two weeks earlier, his heart too weak for the business at hand).

'Where are you going?'

It was a difficult question to answer innocently. At eleven am, a young, apparently healthy man should have been at his workplace. Had he been on shifts it was too late to be starting an early day, too early to be on his way to the late one. And if he was on nights, why wasn't he presently in bed? On any other day, he might have convinced the fellow that he was taking leave to tend a sick wife or mother; but not now, not moments after the last of several hundred angry strikers had marched past, fists clenched and eyes hard upon the small, nervous *VolksPolizei* patrol that had stood by and attempted nothing. He was, in a way, their small recompense for that.

He cleared his throat and looked the *unterwachmeister* straight in the eye. 'This is all shit. I'm going home before anyone thinks I'm with those idiots.'

'You don't agree with what they're doing?'

'Why should I? I work in pharmaceuticals. We're paid well enough.'

As the policeman considered this Josef kept his eyes anxiously on the man he was following, who had almost crossed the park and would soon disappear out of its eastern gate. They had been on the same bus, had got off with the rest of the passengers and watched the marching strikers for a few moments before queuing obediently to have their papers checked once more. It was just foul luck that Josef was being detained, while his target, just two places ahead of him, had been allowed to proceed almost immediately.

'Where do you work?

'At Temmier.' As soon as he said it his arse clenched. Apart from Bayer, Temmier was the only pharmaceutical company that he knew was sited in or near Berlin. Only it wasn't, anymore. As the words left his mouth he recalled that the Ivans had stripped out the plant back in '45, after which the company relocated to the west, somewhere in or near Hamburg. What remained was a hole in the ground, probably.

The *unterwachtmeister*, his lips pursed, considered this stupid lie for a few moments and then handed back the papers. 'You'd better go straight home, son. It's going to get bad soon.'

Trying not to seem hurried he pocketed his papers and walked as quickly through the park as he dared. His target was now out of sight, but he had been moving directly into the western stretch of Fürstenburgerstrasse. There were no roads branching from it until it terminated at Schwedterstrasse, so unless his destination was somewhere along that stretch (a possibility Josef didn't allow himself to consider), there was a good chance he could be caught before he reached the latter street, and that was very necessary. It was at Schwedterstrasse that two possibilities – east or south – became three, because the demarcation line swung directly north a few metres from its northern end. If he didn't catch sight of his man soon, the pursuit was over.

The striking mob had been moving south, not east, so Fürstenbergerstrasse was relatively quiet. A few delivery trucks were parked on its northern side, but the passing traffic was thin. There were enough pedestrians on both sides of the street to partially obscure the view, however, and it took him a few moments to spot what he was reasonably certain was his man (unfortunately, the fellow was fairly average in every sense, even to his grey clothes). He followed the inner pavement, keeping several other Berliners between himself and Comrade Nondescript.

Having a moment now in which to think, he began to wonder what was happening. He had begun his stalk at Gartenweg earlier that morning, and for a while it had been straightforward; but then the man, the woman and boy had split up, crossed, and then re-crossed the demarcation line. This had either been a ploy to lose any potential surveillance or the mark of a plan falling to pieces. He hoped it was the former. Once people began to improvise – or worse, to blunder around half-panicked – it became impossible to anticipate their next steps. If the fellow ahead of him was merely trying to be slippery, that was fine. He couldn't recall ever having been thrown by a deliberate deflection.

At the end of Fürstenburgerstrasse, his target turned northward without glancing back. Josef accelerated, not pausing as he came into view on Schwedterstrasse but crossing immediately to the eastern side. The manoeuvre required that he look both ways before stepping into the road, neatly disguising his interest in the other man if he happened to turn at the wrong moment (he didn't). Not bothering now to remain concealed he walked briskly, holding back only so much as would allow him to remain behind his target should he, too, cross the road.

It all went to hell as they reached the junction with Kremmenerstrasse. He should have noticed the bus approaching, seen the halt and realised that he was too far away to do anything about it. In ten seconds, his prey had jumped into the open door and left him with only the route number searing a hole in his head. Twisting the knife, the bus was followed almost immediately by a *VolksPolizei* van, which, had he been able to use his genuine papers, could have been commandeered immediately, its driver and crew abandoned peremptorily on the pavement while he chased Berlin's public transport unnoticed. Today, however, discretion wasn't optional. His task was one to which no taint of evidence could be attached.

He stood for almost five minutes, trying to decide what to do. There was a single answer, obviously, but it was one that he would have sipped battery acid to avoid. It required that he admit failure to men who didn't accept less than competence; who had a habit of not offering second chances to cocks who let unsuspecting folk off a hook they hadn't even felt as it went in. Thoughts of what they might say and do kept him looking at the police telephone across Schwedterstrasse much longer than was sensible, but eventually he re-crossed the road, dialled the exchange and gave the name that would put him through, unmonitored, to Department II.

'Yes?'

The voice carried a note of expectancy, which made a bad experience worse. He cleared his throat.

'The group separated. I followed one of them but lost him, less than ten minutes ago, on our side.'

The pause on the line lasted for moments only, but seemed to stretch horribly.

'It's not disastrous. We now have a confirmed location - the *Rathaus*, Schöneberg.'

His relief lasted as long as it took for the address to register in his preoccupied mind. He was tempted to groan, but kept his voice steady.

'I assume you want me to extract him from there, before …?'

'It would be difficult to portray it as an accident, otherwise. I'll leave it to you how it's handled. Move quickly – he won't remain in Berlin for long.'

Josef replaced the receiver and considered his options. Almost certainly, the job would have had to be carried out in West Berlin in any case, but he hadn't expected this complication. Typically, a man either ran with family or arranged to rendezvous as soon as possible thereafter – it was human nature, to seek that early reassurance after a dangerous passage. He had expected to catch the objective before he found an initial sanctuary, but this one had been clever. Under the circumstances Josef was left with only two opportunities, and realistically, the first of these – to call off this chase, go straight to the *Rathaus* and extract the objective physically – would be suicide by any other name. If he wanted to survive the day he needed to re-secure one of the levers that would prise the man out.

He corrected himself – not *one* of the levers. The woman was the only sure means by which he could do the job. He didn't know the fellow he was presently following, or the boy; didn't know what either of them meant to the objective, if anything. Only *she* would get him to a place where he could do his job and make her a widow.

But where was she? He had three addresses – hers, and those of her two sons. It didn't take more than a few moments to decide what came next. She wasn't going home, he was certain of that. If she chose to go east, to the son who lived in Friedrichshain, it would take her a while - more importantly, it would allow him the time and space to correct a wrong guess before she could retrace her steps and cross to the west once more. The other one lived in Pankow, and if she was on her way there he had to follow, because she would be only a few hundred metres from West Berlin – hell, she could jump on a bus on Wollankstrasse and be over the line in just five minutes. It wasn't as though he had a choice.

15

By 11.30am it seemed that both Freddie Holleman and Dietrich were growing new nerve-endings. The former was checking his watch every two minutes, while Gehlen's agent gave the curtains the same attention. It was enough to make Fischer feel unwanted, the little boy whom no-one had wanted at the party.

From the canteen they had returned to a different room, a corner office on the second floor that looked out over Rudolph-Wilde-Platz. Whoever lived here on other days was something substantial in the City Government, a man who could requisition the sort of desk that senior officers used to plan offensives upon (or shove bomb-filled briefcases beneath). The carpet it sat upon looked new, or at least untrodden, and the spines of books that filled the wall-to-wall cases had yet to be distressed by browsing. Clearly, the occupant wasn't required to do his own walking, or reading.

Fischer played with a novelty pen-holder (a faux-cigarette case, opened and propped at 45 degrees) and thought about his poor abandoned clocks. Apart from his role in keeping his friend from exploding or saying something indiscrete, he couldn't see why his continuing presence was deemed necessary. The two other men knew far more about the business at hand, and where it might lead.

It came to him suddenly that Dietrich's colleagues had been absent for more than an hour now. The policeman was long departed, probably to organize his men in a vain attempt to prevent most of West Berlin from crossing the line, either to join in the trouble or enjoy the spectacle from the stands. Some sort of history was writing itself across the city, and the three men in this quiet, still room were as insulated from it as if they stood upon another continent. For one of them at least, that was a problem.

'Where *is* she?' Holleman was bothering his watch once more. The habitual squint of his right eye had begun to move slightly, which to Fischer was clear evidence of a mood. Soon, he would twitch, stand, sit down again, try to find some position in which the stump of his leg didn't remind him of the missing bit and none of it would help. Freddie Holleman didn't do patience very well, not upon matters of Kristin.

'Does she know to come straight here?'

'Rolf does. He wouldn't make any detours.'

'Your people may have closed down public transport already. Crossing the city will be an ordeal with crowds moving around, all the checkpoints manned and access roads blocked. It's too early to worry, Freddie.'

Whatever Holleman thought of this sage observation was interrupted by the return of one of the suits. He was in a hurry, his anxiety adding to the room's present, ample store. He whispered something to Dietrich, and both men glanced at the defector, giving a faintly pantomime quality to whatever drama they weren't caring to share. It put an edge on the last of Fischer's own patience.

'What's happening?'

Briefly, Dietrich parted the curtains once more and examined the view. Not being intimately familiar with Rudolph-Wilde Platz, Fischer couldn't recall any singular feature that might keep someone's attention to this degree. It was a broad, utilitarian space, too-recently ruined for the repairs to have fully taken yet. The best that could be said for it was that it gave the re-built *Rathaus* enough cleared space to be seen properly from three directions.

Gehlen's man turned from the window. His mouth was working slightly, as if the brain were taking a run at what it wanted – or didn't want – to say.

'We've had word from one of our own across the line. About Comrade Beckendorp.'

Holleman sat up. Dietrich had as good as blown a Gehlen man's cover. It must have cost him a great deal to admit it.

'What have you heard?'

'That your name's been scraped from the Pension Fund. A decision's been made, about making an example.'

'Oh, fuck.'

'It's worse. MfS have someone here, or at Pullach. They must have, because they already know that you're in this building.'

Holleman closed his eyes. 'That's alright. It was going to happen eventually. At least this place is secure …'

'No, it isn't. We've lost control of Rudolphe-Wilde Platz.'

Fischer reached the window before Holleman, but both men realised at about the same moment how efficiently sound-proofed this expensively-appointed office was. Two storeys below, the entire expanse of the irregular square was filled, chokingly, with Berliners.

Holleman gaped. 'What the hell are they doing?'

Dietrich shrugged. 'They probably tried and failed to join the strikers across the line. If they can't demonstrate there, they'll do it somewhere. This is where West Berlin's Government lives – what better place to be angry about something?'

'Something? What have those well-fed bastards to complain about?'

'Anything, then. But this building isn't secure and can't be made so. We need to get you somewhere else.'

Holleman shook his head. 'I'm not going without my wife.'

'I'll leave word that she's to be looked after, if and when she arrives. Once it's safe, we can bring her to you from here. If she doesn't make it across the line it doesn't matter where you are.'

'I won't leave Berlin.'

'We can't guarantee …'

'Wait.' Fischer knew that Holleman would have to be drugged, tied and carried out by four large men if they wanted to put further distance between him and Kristin. He turned to Dietrich.

'How did you find me?'

'What?'

'This morning. I'm not in any business directory. How did you find me?'

Helplessly, Dietrich waved a hand. 'Herr Holleman told us where you live.'

'Then unless he carved my name onto his desk before he left this morning, we can assume that no-one over there is going to make the connection. And even if they did, they couldn't find me, not immediately.'

'We can't secure your premises, not without being noticed.'

'A safe-house doesn't need to be secured. It just needs to be off the map, yes?'

'It won't be so for very long. MfS are good at finding people in Berlin, East or West.'

'It doesn't matter. As soon as Kristin Holleman's safe you can put them both wherever you want. In the meantime, who would think to look in Lichterfelde?'

'You're the registered tenant of your premises?'

'No. My landlord doesn't care to pay too much to the State, so for cash, no receipt I get a good discount. Nor am I on the voters' list, as no-one's yet moved me to make my mark on their behalf. I haven't even got around to updating my papers to give a current address.' He lifted them from a pocket. 'I still live a cellar in Friedenau, apparently.'

Dietrich nodded. 'I'll arrange transportation. Obviously, we won't be leaving through the front door.'

'And not in a *ShuPo* van, I hope?'

'I'll find something unremarkable.'

Unremarkable turned out to be anything but. When Dietrich, Fischer, Holleman and the suit descended to the *Rathaus*'s underground delivery bay they were confronted by a Borgward Hansa 2400, the size of a small ocean liner and resplendent in its distinctive, deep red finish. Fischer noticed that the suit's face had coloured to something similar.

'Please don't scratch it. I've only made three payments so far.'

Dietrich took the keys from him. 'All the doors are hinged at the rear. I thought it would be easier for Herr Holleman to get in and out of more quickly.'

With Holleman prone in the rear seat, covered by a blanket, they had a difficult journey. On a normal day, the drive from Schöneberg to

Lichterfelde might have taken twenty minutes; today, the Hansa was forced through Steglitz's more exotic byways by successive droves of marchers, their composite grudge deployed as an animate barrier to traffic. It took the better part of an hour to navigate the last of the demonstrations (a small railway engineers' demonstration, moving north along Hindenburgdamm) and a further five minutes to park the car behind Curtius-Strasse, and all the while Fischer sat half-crouched in the front passenger seat, trying to keep the memorable right-side of his face from catching the attention of passers-by, while Holleman griped almost without drawing breath from beneath his cover.

The rear entrance to *Fischer's Time-piece Repairs* lay at the end of a narrow access passage, with a high fence to either side that concealed their arrival from windows in the adjacent properties. The Hansa remained in the alley, entirely blocking it, with a Police Business label tucked under the windscreen wiper to deter reprisals upon its expensive panels.

The premises' rear door was used for little more than rubbish ejection. Its mortice lock was stiff, so when Fischer inserted the key he twisted hard to compensate. Nothing moved, not even a hint of give. Puzzled, he relaxed, breathed deeply and tried again, bracing himself against the door for purchase. For all that it helped he might have been tilting at a block from the Atlantic Wall.

'What is it?' Dietrich, who had been on rear-guard detail up the passage-way, stepped past Holleman.

'Nothing. It's just …'

A bad possibility occurred. Fischer grasped the doorknob, twisted and pushed, and the door swung open. In the space of a moment he tried and failed to recall having unlocked the door earlier that day or the one before, and then Dietrich was through it before him, a Beretta drawn from its armpit holster and raised to face height.

In the cramped corridor between shop area and rear kitchenette a man turned suddenly. He was surprised but then moved quickly, reversing, trying to put space between himself and the muzzle. Hurriedly, Fischer reached out a hand and grabbed Dietrich's wrist.

'Don't. He's not that sort of assassin.'

16

It took a while to bring Jonas Kleiber down from the state of euphoria an aviophobe experiences when touching tarmac once more. He jabbered about nothing, couldn't sit down, and, after much patting of shoulders, eventually subsided to a state of nervous semi-collapse with a mug of over-milked, heavily-sweetened tea in his trembling hands.

Fischer's other two guests regarded the young man curiously. Holleman was the more reserved, though he relaxed slightly once he'd noticed Kleiber's mutilated hand, as if acknowledging the dues that had been paid to the brotherhood of foul luck. Dietrich offered a cigarette and then lost interest until Fischer asked Kleiber about his day so far.

'You've been over the line?'

Kleiber took another sip of his tea. 'Yeah. And I'm going back soon. I would have stayed over there, but my boss told me to report my initial impressions, and the public telephone exchanges have been shut down.'

'By MfS?'

'No. Just after dawn the Soviets put men on all the railway stations, telegraph and post offices. They kept them open until about an hour ago.'

'What's happening?'

'It's growing. Until noon, I'd have said that it was purely an industrial action. Men were marching like soldiers, all of them union strikers, all with their own people. But now citizens have joined them – even women with their kids – and it's getting strange. As I left, 'Down with the Quotas' had become 'Down with Ulbricht', and discipline's going to fuck. At Stalin Allee the crowd became a mob, got harangued by one fellow for a few minutes and then headed off to Hohenschönhausen to free the prisoners. Some of them threatened to break up any police station they found on the way.'

'Christ.' Holleman shook his head. 'What are the police doing?'

'Nowt.'

'What?'

'Sorry, I mean nothing. Well, next to nothing, at least. I heard that a small station in Friedrichshain's been smashed up already and the police just stood by, watching as their file-cupboard was emptied and a bonfire started outside.'

'You've seen no official reaction at all?'

'No-one seems to know what to do. Some of the police are armed, and I spotted a couple of squads with automatic rifles, but none of them have left the shoulder or holster – or they hadn't, the last I saw.'

'They still don't have orders, then.'

Kleiber looked at Holleman curiously. 'Are you … someone official?'

'Until this morning I was …'

Dietrich coughed. 'Perhaps we won't say too much.'

Fischer, who had been checking the view from the shop window, turned. 'You can trust him. For a journalist, he's quite averse to reporting things'

'That's commendable. But if he's going back across the line I don't want him to know anything that might be beaten out.'

Kleiber's face paled but he held out a hand to Holleman. 'Jonas. Please to meet you.'

'Freddie.'

Released, the hand swivelled towards Dietrich, who smiled tightly and shook his head. 'Better if we don't become friends.'

'Ah. Right.' Kleiber glanced anxiously around the shop. 'Sorry, Otto, I used your key. Herr Grabner was shouting down the 'phone at his wife when I got back, so I thought I'd hide until he's calmed a bit. But you weren't home.'

About six months earlier, Fischer had trusted a duplicate key to Kleiber, considering him to be the local acquaintance least likely by far to covet stock. Until this moment there hadn't seemed cause to regret the decision; but then, the thought of what bloodstains did to an unfinished wooden floor hadn't occurred to him.

Holleman was chewing his lip, regarding the clocks around him without seeing them. He picked up a pair of forceps, passed them from hand to hand and replaced them on the counter, and Fischer was certain that he wouldn't recall the instrument a minute later.

'What's wrong, Freddie?'

Holleman ignored the question and turned to Kleiber. 'Have you had any problems crossing the line?'

'None. When I went east this morning at Adalbertstrasse my papers were checked briefly. When I returned along Lindenstrasse there was no-one at all. Before today I don't think I've *ever* not been stopped on Lindenstrasse coming west.'

'They're giving up.'

'What do you mean?'

'At dawn we were told to send out small patrols and spread them thinly, to try to cover all but the smallest access roads. We knew it wasn't possible to do the job properly, not without being able to call on the paramilitaries; but if places like Lindenstrasse have been uncovered it's because there's been a redeployment, or …'

'What?'

'Or they're being withdrawn. Fuck.'

It took Fischer a moment to get to the only possible meaning. 'The Ivans are about to go in.'

'At the least, Schmidt and Zaisser have been told to get their men out of the way in case the Red Army wants to put in armour. And if they're thinking about it, they probably mean to do it.'

'What do they have in Berlin?'

Holleman shrugged. 'Enough. A motor-rifle brigade at Karlshorst. Seven mechanized divisions within fifty kilometres of the city, mostly at Wünsdorf, Schönebeck and Eberswalde. And more than enough elsewhere to handle trouble in the rest of the DDR, if it comes to that.'

'Would Moscow need to sanction a response?'

'Technically, yes. But if Semyonov hasn't spoken to the Kremlin about it already he isn't doing his job. We have to assume that they can – and they will - move at a moment's notice. But …'

'But?'

'The commander of Soviet forces in Germany – that's Grechko – has been in the job for about a month, and he's a question mark still. Will he be cautious because he hasn't found the Officers' Mess yet, or go the other way to prove he's not going to let Germans tread on his new boots?'

Dietrich shrugged. 'Semyonov's the Political Secretary. Grechko will do what he's told.'

'Yes, but once an operation's under way Semyonov won't try to interfere with tactics. It isn't like the war anymore. Commissars don't stand behind generals with pistols cocked.'

Kleiber had been listening to this while he drank his tea. His mood seemed to be lifting considerably. 'Well, if there's going to be shooting, Herr Grabner can't send me back in, can he?'

Despite the subject matter, Holleman and Dietrich laughed. Fischer tried not to smile as he patted the young man's shoulder. 'I'm afraid he can, Jonas. In fact, he'll probably make you take the *Zeitung*'s official camera with you this time. Nothing sells newspapers more than blood on the streets.'

'Shit. I'll quit, then.'

'Don't you need to give notice?'

Appalled, Kleiber stared down into the tea-leaves, trying to spot a future in which he didn't become a heroic statistic of war journalism. When he'd taken the job it had been a genuine choice - Herr Grabner had offered it the same day that a porter's position opened at a slaughterhouse near Grossbeeren (secured by a an ex-comrade of his father, the man who had brought home his personal effects). At the time, Kleiber's mother had been alive still, so the opportunity to earn both a wage and a little 'spoiled' meat each week was a powerful incentive, offset only by his utter conviction that the first time he saw a cow killed he'd burst into tears. So journalism had won, but only barely, and now he could see that he'd been deceived. He'd had no illusions that a job with the *Südwest-Berliner Zeitung* might open the door to international assignments, fashion weeks or even the company of hard-drinking literary types in dark, iconic bars; but the pale promise of reporting local allotment competitions and interviewing district councillors hadn't been made more tempting by any hint that he might one day stretch his potential under an advancing Soviet tank. On the whole, executing livestock now seemed the lesser evil. He sighed and stood up.

'I'd better go, then.'

Fischer unlocked the front door and almost had to push him out on to Curtius-Strasse. When he returned, Dietrich was scribbling something on a piece of paper.

'I have to leave too. I'll be speaking to Pullach about the situation, probably to General Wessel himself. Should I give him any message?'

He was looking at Holleman, but Fischer spoke first. 'Remind him that he and Gehlen wanted Kurt Beckendorp very much, back in '47. He might think that a defector isn't nearly so valuable as a turncoat in the enemy camp, but Herr Holleman knows a lot more now than he did then, and about many more people. He might well become your resident expert on the Politburo.'

Dietrich nodded. 'Wessel isn't someone to bear a grudge. I assume you gave him some reason to, back then?'

'Perhaps. It wasn't much, but I think we embarrassed the Organization.'

'A lot of people did, I wouldn't lose sleep about it. Like other modern Germans, we've learned to treat past enemies as present friends.' He turned to Holleman. 'I'll begin to arrange accommodation for your family, somewhere in the DBR. It will be unremarkable but safe. You won't be joining them for some time, naturally.'

'I know. Thank you.'

When Dietrich was gone Holleman sat down heavily on a stool (purchased for the old and infirm customers who comprised the majority of the business's through-trade) and examined Fischer's retail empire. This requiring no more than a few seconds, the mildly distracted expression on his gnarled face soon faded back to anxiety.

'How many entrances, Otto?'

'Front and back, obviously. A fire-ladder to the bedroom window.'

'Not defensible, then.'

'Not with this.' From a drawer, Fischer pulled a PRM 1892. 'I bought it last year to deter clock-abductors. It cleaned up nicely, but I worry about the ammunition.'

'How much do you have?'

'Five rounds. I'd have to be desperate to use them.'

'Marvellous. Perhaps we should barricade the doors.'

'Against whom?'

'I don't know.'

'Do you have many enemies, Freddie? I mean, apart from the fellow who's been detailed to pop you?'

Holleman looked strangely at his old friend. 'I'm a senior policeman *and* a communist politician. What do you think? And if I wasn't despised enough already I added massively to the list this morning. Even people who hate each other hate me more.'

The question had been teasing, but it struck Fischer suddenly how final a step Holleman had taken. He had been one of the minor pillars of the regime, a stalwart SED man with comfortable, State-sanctioned perquisites, who, on the day the people turned against their leadership, had washed his hands of both and fled west. At that moment he was probably feeling like Vlasov, though without the comfort of a friendly army at his back.

'Sorry.'

'It's alright. I had no choice, really.'

'Really? If *VolksPolizei* are being restrained, you wouldn't have had to …'

'It's not just that.'

'What else?'

Holleman glanced around the small shop once more. 'Today can't end in a way that would have kept me where I was.'

'How's that possible?'

'I might tell you later, if something less rusty than what's in your pistol hasn't passed through my head by then.'

17

Lieutenant-Colonel Andrei Voloshyn rubbed his eyes and stifled the yawn that had been brewing for five minutes. It wouldn't have looked good, not in front of men who had enjoyed precisely as little sleep as himself. As the Regiment's commander for less than six months, he wanted to prove himself to them as more than just a pair of red tags.

He turned his glance from the direction of Potsdam, back down the road towards Wollin. This short, wooded stretch was currently filled with Red Army vehicles, principally BTR-152s and a mongrel selection of trucks, with four T34s out front on making-a-point duty. Aside from the most recent bi-annual military exercise, this level of firepower hadn't departed Schönebeck since he had taken up his present appointment.

He'd walked up and down the column twice now, letting the men in the trucks see his face and seeing in theirs something of what they thought of the day's delights so far. Up at 3am and fed hastily, they had been in full combat dress for the past six hours and sitting here, bored, for three of them. And they were the lucky ones. Knowing that a certain order – *if* it came – would require that the column move instantly and rapidly, he was not allowing anyone to leave their vehicles, so the men in the APCs were probably steaming gently by now, comforted only by the protection that their metal coffins afforded from the occasional passing deer. A lot of them were young, conscripted after the war ended; they hadn't known its privations, didn't have the experience of what real shit was. Right now, they would be thinking that *this* was hardship.

His command – 248th Motor Rifle Regiment, 10th Guards Tank Division – comprised three mechanized and one tank battalion, a total of 2711 men. Two battalions, the 2nd and 4th, remained at barracks, which gave him roughly twelve hundred men for today's business. From his briefing, he knew that other formations, totalling approximately a division's strength, were providing similar impediments to traffic on roads around Berlin at that moment, waiting for the word to move in.

They hadn't practise for this one. The 248th had long been designated the unit that, if things came to it, would cut and hold the Walkenried-Ellrich road for the first twelve hours of hostilities and then, consolidating with the Front, advance into the Federal Republic. A manoeuvre eastwards hadn't been contemplated; it had always been assumed that a few battalions from Wünsdorf would secure West Berlin while the bulk of Soviet forces in Germany confronted the Allied armies. Today's operation was unexpected - and, like all unexpected things, capable of being buggered badly if attentions wandered.

He turned to the radio car once more, and got another shake of the head from Lieutenant Pankov. The man was doing what a good adjutant should, which was to display all the nerves that a commanding officer could not. Voloshyn himself had to maintain an appearance of imperturbable readiness, to reassure the men that someone, somewhere, knew what the hell was going on. He was certain that he was radiating precisely this quality, because he had practised it diligently and often in front of his bedroom mirror. It required a certain blankness of expression, and that he not twitch, nor move to do something and then forget quite what it was, nor swallow too visibly, nor lose his temper for any reason whatsoever. It occurred to him suddenly that he should have yawned – it would have been a small flourish to hint at the utter lack of anything *unexpected* that he and his men might … well, expect.

Pankov, on the other hand, was giving a fine impression of a startled hare. He had the responsibility of letting his commander know when the orders came through, of transmitting the same to other officers down the column and of keeping both Karlshorst and Wünsdorf informed of their movements throughout the coming day, all of which could test the strongest nerves, particularly if something went wrong.

And so much might do precisely that. Their preliminary orders had been bloody ambiguous, which was definitely not the Red Army way. For the first time in his career, Voloshyn was leading men into a potential combat situation having been warned to avoid combat *if feasible*. Before he could ask if that meant retreating from trouble, the stipulation had been modified slightly: only if his men were directly threatened were they to employ their firearms, and even then in a non-lethal fashion unless responding to fire directed at them. In his opinion this hinted more at a task for negotiators than a unit of an elite Red Army formation, but he was only a lieutenant-colonel, a creature whose initiative extended little further than to choose the best, least costly way to kill an enemy. That, apparently, might not be required today.

So why the tanks? A policing operation didn't need mobile artillery, yet the day's deployment schedule had specified it. If small-arms fire wasn't permitted he couldn't see how 85mm cannon could do the job unless the situation was expected to worsen quickly, and catastrophically. Tanks in urban areas weren't very useful, other than for de-urbanizing them.

'Nothing yet, Comrade *Podpolkovnik*.' Pankov hadn't needed to come across from the radio car to pass on news that wasn't news, but Voloshyn probably would have done the same, given that a watched kettle never boils. It would be like their masters to know instinctively when a man was furthest from his post and send through orders at that moment, so perhaps he was trying to urge them on. As picturesque as it was, they were all becoming heartily tired of this section of the Lehniner-Wald. No doubt many of the men of the 248th came from similarly verdant landscapes and on other days might have found a hint of home in it; but this was no more than a jumping-off point for much worse - or nothing at all.

'Give the men a piss-break. They go no further than the tree-line.'

It was against regulations during an operation, but so was turning off engines, and he'd ordered that an hour ago to save fuel (believing - perhaps naively - that the point of mechanization was to deliver men quickly into battle, not have them push their vehicles slowly into the same). It might earn him some hard words when the operation was reviewed, but only if the men performed badly, and he had no fears of that. His predecessor had pushed them hard, and Voloshyn hadn't cared to squander that good work. Things might go very wrong for all kinds of reasons today, but loose discipline wouldn't be one of them. His men would hand out flowers to civilians or shoot them in their throats, whatever was required.

His eyes on the horizon over which Berlin lay, he heard them climbing out of their vehicles behind him, their voices rising as if pre-offensive tensions and bladders were easing together. Startled birds shook treetops and rose up at either side of the road, and the movement nudged something within him. He finally recognized the scent that had teased his nostrils since they arrived here – it was wild thyme, of course, a staple of his mother's kitchen, long displaced from a professional soldier's memory. He had just started to feel pleased about this when a voice from the radio car went through Pankov like a tracer bullet. He sprinted back there, lifted the receiver, listened, spoke briefly and nodded to Voloshyn. The men closest to the head of the column were already rushing back to the road, tucking cocks or half-wiped arses hastily into trousers, but he blew his whistle anyway – a small nod to conformity to weigh against his recent indulgence. In moments, the road came alive with the ugly noise of more than a hundred engines revving furiously, and it was difficult to have the necessary confidential exchange with Pankov without shouting.

'Well? Do we go home or to war?'

His adjutant placed a finger in one ear and leaned towards Voloshyn. 'The concentration point is Adlershof. Three to four hours, via Potsdamer-Wald, Ludwigsfelde and Schönefelde. It's been posted already.'

The south-eastern Berlin suburb of Adlershof was home to the *Kasernierte Volkspolizei* Division – twelve thousand paramilitaries with absolute loyalty to Ulbricht's SED. If the 248th was to join them (with whatever units the Soviet garrison at Wünsdorf contributed), someone was planning for the worst of days, whatever orders said. From Adlershof the roads ran almost as straight as sight-lines into the heart of the city, an excellent means of putting force among throngs of civilians in the shortest time.

Voloshyn climbed back into his GAZ jeep and nodded to the driver, a largely mute Uzbeki private whose skills seemed to have been honed on anything but roads. Pankov took the seat behind and spread a map across his legs. If they took a wrong turn on the way to Berlin it would be his fault and his arse in the sling. After that, in a situation that promised to offer countless opportunities for fatal miscalculation, the sling would be reserved entirely for his commanding officer.

Only the previous day, Voloshyn had written to his sister in Novgorod to congratulate her on the news of her betrothal. He had tempted fate by claiming that he had nothing to offer in return (his posting being a notoriously quiet and uneventful one), and now he was leading the very worst sort of operation, against an allied, probably unarmed population in an urban environment – in fact, in Germany's premier urban sprawl. He might or might not be obliged to use force, might confront westerners joining the trouble from across the line that was hardly a line at all, might even - though God knew he hoped otherwise - come face to face with British or American units and need to make a quick decision about how close to a shooting war he could or should go.

He wished now that he hadn't rushed to put the letter in the camp post-bag. It would be a great pity for her to get his congratulations and word of his court-martial or death in the same delivery.

18

Hoeschler waited outside the apartment for more than half an hour before reason gave way to impulse. He had been lucky; the bus he had jumped on had turned right onto the ring road and taken him directly to Luxemburg-Platz, where he transferred to the u-bahn (its incoming services had been halted, but those out to the northern suburbs were running still). He was at the Vinetastrasse terminus in less than twenty-five minutes, and at Ulrich's front door in a further five. He told himself that Kristin Holleman could hardly have done it more quickly, not dragging along a reluctant teenager who would want to know why.

Thirty minutes later that conviction was slipping badly. She wouldn't be taking her time, not today; so, if she wasn't here it was because she had come and gone already or wasn't coming at all. If she had posted a message under the door he needed to see it, but an old lady who lived two doors down the corridor had come out twice while he'd been here, to peer suspiciously at the unfamiliar face. Not wanting to cause either attention or an aneurism he put aside thoughts of using his boot and went downstairs to the *portier*'s room. To have the apartment opened he'd need to use his warrant card, and he wondered why he felt reluctant about it - whether things went well or badly today he'd have no further use for the thing, other than as a memento of a past life. Perhaps it was a twisted sense of propriety, that made an inappropriately-waved authority offend his conscience while his ready betrayal of an entire nation hardly touched it.

The *portier* was a *portierfrau*, and younger than he'd expected - perhaps in her mid-40s, probably a war-widow with enough luck to fall into the most secure job that any modern German woman could expect. She gave his card a single glance before recovering a large bunch of keys from a hook behind her door.

'What's he done?'

He hadn't thought to imagine an offence, and it took a moment for the only correct response to occur.

'It's police business. He hasn't murdered anyone, though.'

'Good. We don't want that sort.'

She smiled as she said it, and he relaxed a little. The typical *portier* took his or her role very seriously, memorizing details of uncommon events every bit as assiduously as *blockhilfers* had under the old regime; but if she could joke about it she probably wouldn't be on the 'phone to her local station before he'd left the building. The last of his fears on that score disappeared on the first floor landing, when she half-turned and gave him a shameless up-and-down that almost loosened the belt on his trousers. Flattered, his mood lifted slightly but fell again almost immediately when she unlocked the door of Ulrich's apartment. There was no message behind it, and no-one inside.

He made a show of examining the apartment without actually opening a drawer or cupboard, taking his time in case Kristin, against all expectation, turned up. After five minutes he sensed that his credibility was beginning to fray, so he nodded at his new admirer and went back out into the corridor, waiting as she re-locked the door.

'When Herr Beckendorp returns please tell him that I called. It isn't anything serious, but he may be able to assist us with an enquiry. An acquaintance, we think.'

Having done his best to repair a reputation he'd knocked to the ground and kicked, Hoeschler smiled (putting a bit of warmth into it to keep the *portierfrau* amenable) and said goodbye. He wanted to be alone to think through a next step he could hardly conceive, short of fleeing west, holding up his hands to his former boss and confessing his utter failure to save the man's wife from a vengeful State. That wouldn't do, of course, not least because he'd be abandoning his own boy also. What he needed was inspiration, a hunch or an angel's voice, whispering in his ear, telling him where the hell they were.

Had she gone to Franz, her other son, hoping that a twin brother could influence his womb-mate? It hardly seemed likely. Beckendorp had told him that Franz was entirely willing to follow his family west – enthusiastic, even, to the point at which he may have embarked upon his own exodus already. Would his mother risk a journey right across Mitte and as far east as Friedrichshain on the slim chance that he was there still, ready to put off his own plans in the service of family? He didn't think so, yet he had no other …

Shit. He was thinking like a man, and this was women's business, plural. If Kristin hadn't been able to persuade her boy, who could, other than the one making his groin rule his head these days? It had to be Liesa, the mouse. Hoeschler had no idea where she lived, or where she might be found on a day in which Normal was taking a short holiday; but Kristin did, and she was probably on her way there now. It was a race that only she could win.

He was stood on the front step of the apartment building, his head dulled by its lack of options, when the old lady who lived two doors from Ulrich came out, glanced around furtively, and beckoned him with a finger – comically, because they couldn't have been standing more than a metre apart. He bent towards her and gave her an ear,

'It's Frau Amman.'

'Who?'

'Our building manager. You were speaking with her.'

'Ah, yes. What about her?'

Another glance around, and then they were close enough for Hoeschler to get the full benefit of her stale breath. 'She says things. About the strikers.'

A dutiful citizen, wielding the knife to best effect. Hoeschler recalled who he was, who he was supposed to be still, and didn't tell her what she deserved to hear.

'What does she say?'

'That they're right - that they have grievances, and the government should be ashamed of how it treats them. She said it yesterday, when she brought up my bread delivery. She should be dismissed.'

He frowned severely. 'Did you know that Minister Sellmann spoke to some of the strikers yesterday afternoon, and told them personally that they had a legitimate cause? It was on the news.'

'Oh.' The old lady deflated visibly. A denouncement had to be effective, otherwise it was regarded as anti-social behaviour, and there were penalties for that. Hoeschler almost wished he had time to drag it out, to teach the old bitch a proper lesson; but he was in a hurry and something had occurred to him. He tossed his head and she scuttled indoors like a frightened terrier.

Hartmann's. Why did he think of that? Obviously, because she had mentioned bread, but it had struck him with more force that a random recollection. It was here, in Pankow, and close by – the district's oldest and most famous bakery. Was that why he had thought of the name, or …

I hardly get to see Ulrich during the week. I have to be at work by four am, when they make the dough. But it isn't far, just along Wollankstrasse.

The apartment-warming party - he had been trying to disengage from a painfully awkward conversation, looking around to find the elder Beckendorp, but the mention of when she started work had struck him. It had made him think about how the lost generation of men had changed things - how, in the old days, the wives of bakery workers wouldn't have tolerated female staff for a moment, not working side by side with men who were stripped to the waist in front of their ovens.

Hartmann's was on Wollankstrasse. It had been there since the 1870s, a north Berlin landmark. She hadn't mentioned the name, but he knew of no other bakeries on the street. He held his breath. It was ten minutes away at most, and even if Kristin had been, gone and taken Liesa with her (a growing band of fugitives, all running from him, the DDR and common sense alike), his warrant card would extract a home address from the establishment. It was the most hope he'd allowed himself to feel for more than an hour, and he didn't spoil it by dawdling.

It took him less than five minutes at a half-run. The bakery was open, the wonderful smell of fresh bread announcing itself long before he reached the premises. A small queue of women stood outside, several of whom offered him a malevolent glare at him as he walked straight past and into the shop ahead of them.

He waved his card once more, at a young woman in a white apron who was taking money from a customer.

'May I speak to Liesa, please?'

It sounded over-familiar, but he had no idea of the girl's surname. He got a shrug.

'She's gone. About twenty minutes ago, with her mother. It's a family emergency, she said.'

'I need her address, then. It's urgent.'

It was an unusual request, so the young woman went to find her boss. A large, well-rounded and heavily-tattooed man in a damp vest returned in her place and gave Hoeschler a stare that seemed to question every fibre of his alleged integrity. In his present, anxious mood he almost wilted beneath it.

'Why do you want her?'

It was the wrong question, and Hoeschler took it gratefully. 'None of your business. Now get her address.'

The stare lingered for a few moments more, but it wasn't as though a choice had been offered. The man's last act of defiance was the pace at which he shuffled into the back to consult his employees' records, but he was in front of Hoeschler once more within three minutes.

'She lives on Görschstrasse, number 18, the top floor apartment.'

'No she doesn't.' The young woman had returned to her counter, and was shaking her head firmly. 'She moved in with her boyfriend, three days ago. But I don't know his address.'

The big man's eyebrows went up. 'That's right. She mentioned that she was thinking of it. It's done, then?'

Hoeschler didn't hear the rest of the conversation. The surge of hope that had carried him here on air dissipated instantly. At Ulrich's apartment, the *portierfrau* had opened the door wide and then stood in front of it, so the coat-hook that might have offered a clue had been on the reverse side, pressed against the wall. Still, he should have checked the cupboards. It would have saved him fifteen minutes and a lot of hope.

Out on Wollankstrasse once more, he applied himself to the mystery of whatever was going through Kristin Holleman's head. She had dragged young Liesa into the matter, so at least he knew now for certain that she was going directly for Ulrich. He wasn't at his – their – apartment, so unless he was wandering the streets aimlessly he was either at his workplace or marching. The trouble was, Hoeschler didn't have a name or address, and he was fairly sure that his inspiration had burned itself out with the hunch about Hartmann's. Ulrich operated a lathe, which meant he could be employed in any of the metal fabrication concerns scattered around East Berlin and its suburbs.

He'd said *it's a boring job. We all hate it.*

All implied numbers, more than a handful. He worked for one of the smaller, still-private companies that hadn't yet been clutched to the bosom of their command economy, but the definition of *small* slipped year by year as statutory reporting regulations were extended. Which meant, probably, that Ulrich was obliged by law to join the metal workers' union, and his company was responsible for organizing his membership. If he was on record, so were they.

He didn't know where the union records were kept, but that didn't matter. Keibelstrasse had directories listing contact numbers and addresses for official organizations. All he had to do was grip his balls, march into the nearest *VolksPolizei* sub-station and demand that someone call in and get the necessary details. Of course, he needn't volunteer that his career in the service had been voluntarily terminated some hours earlier. It was possible that an assiduous *wachtmeister* would make a mental note of the details of his warrant card and follow up, but that didn't concern him. If things went well this would be his last day in the DDR; if not, an illicit application for public domain information would be the least of the charges attached to the prosecution sheet.

This time, he didn't let optimism trip him. Ulrich had been working full-time for less than a year now, and his application for union membership might be sat on a desk still, or 'filed' to oblivion. Hoeschler knew how indolent *VolksPolizei* personnel could be when confronted by paperwork; he had no reason to suspect office staff in a factory or union headquarters of any greater urge to competence. It was at best an even chance – and his last, unless Kristin was overcome by a damascene fit of reason and allowed Engi to drag her west once more.

He recalled that there was a small *VoPo* station just north of Floragärten, where a *kriminalkommissar*'s warrant card would probably impress enough to quell awkward questions. He pointed his feet in that direction and his face at the ground, allowing his fear of failure to distract him enough for the shadow he had acquired at Vinetastrasse to remain just that.

Josef followed at a distance, pleased to have his work done for him. He decided that he quite liked this edgy fellow, the way their thoughts seemed to mirror each other. Obviously, he was – perhaps had been – a policeman, and so they shared something of a professional relationship, if a distant one. Having (like many orphans) a vestigial taint of sentimentality, he thought it a shame that the time was coming - and very soon - when this particular loose end to the main business would have to be dealt with.

19

Three days after dropping his research paper at the CIA's Lower Manhattan office, Zarubin received the expected summons. To his surprise, it was all the way to Washington once more, and he decided not to test their patience. Pausing only to wash himself and then climb into his precious grey suit, he was at Penn Station within ninety minutes to collect the reserved ticket. His train not having arrived, he put himself around a coffee and French toast at the standing buffet and admired the distinguished, sooty architecture while a continental mass of humanity swept by on its way to the day job.

The journey was as unmemorably efficient as always, and three hours later he was met at Union Station by a familiar agent, a young man who appeared to enjoy small talk as much as he might an improvised circumcision. The routine was broken only at the East St NW office, when they ascended straight to the fifth floor, a storey previously unsullied by Zarubin. He was ushered, but not followed, into a large, carpeted office.

A man in his 60's stood up as he entered. Until that moment, Zarubin had suspected the CIA to be an organization staffed exclusively by college sophomores, and he was pleased to feel merely his age for once. He grasped the extended hand (another novelty) and took the seat to which it then gestured.

'Excuse me.' The gentleman sat and turned his attention to a document which Zarubin recognized immediately. He had reached the penultimate page, the one where the conclusion commenced. It had been the most difficult section to rework, because it was there that an idea had been half suggested, a hint at which Zarubin had hoped the CIA would lunge without realising that they had been offered it. He wondered now whether he had been either too subtle or not sufficiently so. The gentleman who read it frowned in a way that suggested either a certain difficulty in seeing a point or disapproval at having had his time wasted by what Americans were fond of calling bullshit. Of course, it may have been merely a serious expression - that of someone giving due attention to a weighty matter. Which, of course, it was.

Eventually, the gentleman looked up. 'This is … unexpected.'

'Really?' Zarubin tried to look concerned. Of course it was unexpected. He had worked hard to make it so.

The older man removed his glasses and polished them with a handkerchief, keeping his gaze firmly on the Russian. 'It's the opinion of our Soviet Desk that Lavrentiy Beria is by some distance *least* likely to be the winner in the current contest.'

'Their reasoning being, I assume, that Beria has generated the greatest number of enemies within the political and military hierarchies of the USSR?'

'That, and the fact that he hasn't cultivated a significant power base outside of his now-defunct relationship with Secretary Stalin. He's a general without an army.'

Zarubin nodded, acknowledging the point. He didn't want to give the impression that he considered the CIA's Soviet Desk to be a bunch of morons, because they weren't, of course; but he was fairly sure they hadn't yet the confidence of their conclusions, being necessarily hamstrung by their lack of first-hand intelligence.

'On the face of it he would seem the third-placed runner, certainly. But there are circumstances, perhaps not immediately apparent to your men, which lead me to a different conclusion. I should say that I've discussed my opinion with my old boss, Maxim Shpak, and he concurs.'

The best of luck with checking that.

The CIA man glanced down at the report. 'You hint at it here without going into detail. May I ask what these circumstances are?'

The conversation remained polite, which Zarubin found immensely reassuring. He leaned forward.

As you're aware, Beria and Malenkov are close, if not exactly friends. They shared responsibility for the Soviet Union's acquisition of atomic weapons and missile technology, a task they discharged very successfully.'

The other man had sufficient grace or self-control not to wince. The Americans had expected their head-start with atomic fission technology to be of about a decade's length, not the mere four years it had taken the Enemy to acquire the Big Stick also.

'This has given both men a degree of standing that Stalin's death – and Beria's bloody record - can't entirely wipe away. Stature is a quality not to be underestimated with regard to the exercise of power *within* the Kremlin. It's true that his relinquishment of his role as Head of the MVD has taken away his 'army', as you put it. It's also true that the men who succeeded him aren't his appointees, so he can expect little support from them. But there's something else, something I had to discuss first with Shpak to give me a sense of how valid my hunch is. It's Malenkov.'

'What about Malenkov?'

'He doesn't want the job. Obviously, there'll be a more consensual style of decision-making for the foreseeable future, but he doesn't want to lead, direct or chair it. Far more importantly, he doesn't – he *really* doesn't - want Krushchev to do it either. He's quite prepared to support Beria, if that's what it requires.'

'You suggested that they weren't exactly friends.'

'They're not. For a long time, Malenkov feared Beria as much as everyone else did, but they seem to have reached a form of accommodation. As time passes and the novelty of a world without Stalin strengthens everyone's feeling of insecurity, Beria comes to be seen as the safe option, the one that pushes back the need to make short-term, possibly dangerous decisions about the future. It's clear that he isn't going to try to be a strongman - like Malenkov, he's getting too tired to make the effort. The years of fighting on eight fronts have taken their toll on all of the old guard, and Krushchev aside, there isn't as yet any obvious alternate contender among those with the energy to be enthusiastic. Beria can be expected to discharge his duties without trying either to raise himself further or force a successor upon the General Committee, and that makes him an ideal candidate in their eyes. I suspect that Malenkov will relinquish his own offices to him gradually, citing a desire for a peaceful retirement. And it's true, that's what he wants.

'You've been out of the USSR for three years now. How do you know all of this?'

A damn good question. 'I have a number of contacts still in what used to be MGB, men who aren't too doctrinal. Obviously, I don't want to risk their safety by giving names. I don't ever ask specific questions, but like most Russians they can't resist gossiping – and as you'd imagine, all the gossip that's worth repeating these days is about the succession. Additionally, I can make certain deductions based upon what isn't discussed or known.'

'What does that mean?'

'I visited Shpak for his opinion, but also one matter in particular. He is – he was – acquainted with Krushchev. We discussed the man's rise, its unremarkable nature until recently. We speculated upon what conditions had changed to allow it.'

'He's heading the Moscow Communist party. That has to count for a lot of it.'

'On the face of it, yes. But the Moscow Party looks more powerful than it is. For a while, its stature was enhanced by the corresponding fall of the Leningrad Gang; but more recently there seems to have been a corrective shift. It's doubtful that they alone could provide a sufficient power base.'

'Who, then?'

Zarubin shrugged. 'Absent any know patrons within the hierarchy, it has to be the Red Army. As you know, Zhukov has reason to detest Beria for his treatment after the war, and he doesn't think much more of Malenkov. It's also well known that he twice interceded for Krushchev during the war, when the man faced denouncements of his own. They're natural allies.'

'Yet Zhukov no longer commands the Red Army.'

'No, but he was recalled to Moscow from his Urals exile a month before Stalin's death, and the Old Man spent many hours with him during the time that he had left. It's seen generally as an *imprimatur*, and one of the reasons he was appointed Deputy Defence Minister recently. He's still loved by the Army of course, who have long had reasons of their own to detest Beria.'

The CIA man sat back in his chair and frowned at the desk. 'This doesn't really support your contention that the smart money should go on Beria.'

'On the face of it, no. But consider this – he's Deputy Premier of the USSR. Malenkov remains Premier and Chairman of the Praesidium, and while Krushchev is first-named on the list of the Secretariat, he hasn't actually been appointed First Secretary – not yet, at least. So, a short time remains during which Malenkov can move to block his progress. My guess is that within the next month, Beria will graciously accept the Premiership as Malenkov stands down, and both men will move to keep Krushchev where he is. Molotov won't do anything because he owes his return to the Foreign Ministry to Malenkov, and Zhukov won't squeak without being sure that Krushchev can react decisively against both Beria and Malenkov, which he can't.'

Zarubin paused to admire his work. He believed hardly a single word of what he'd just proposed, yet he knew that it sounded feasible. Whether it actually convinced, however, required something else, and that could only be supplied by his audience.

The CIA man was frowning still. 'Tell me about Krushchev.'

'As a man, he's quite attractive - approachable, has the common touch and doesn't bear grudges. But he's also impulsive and quick-tempered, and once something lodges in his head it's hard to shift. A typical Ukrainian, in other words.'

'His opinion of America?'

'Not known. But don't forget - if he succeeds against Malenkov and Beria, he'll have the unswerving backing of the Red Army, and Zhukov will be back. The flip side, of course, is that he won't do anything to test the Army's loyalty.'

'Such as?'

'Such as the thing that both Malenkov and Beria want as a priority.'

'Which is?'

'A decisive re-alignment of the Soviet economy away from its war-footing.'

The other man considered this for a while as he removed a pipe and tobacco pouch from his pockets and went through the ritual. As he did so a cuff rode up slightly, exposing a gold cufflink set with a single precious stone. If this was meant to give Zarubin a hint of where he stood in the hierarchy, it worked admirably.

When the room was full of rather sweet smoke, he placed the pipe in an ashtray and gave the Russian the full, frank stare.

'There are people in Washington who believe that it's in our interest for the Soviet Union's war economy to continue as it is.'

Zarubin nodded. 'Their reasoning being that the intrinsic weaknesses of the command-economy model will widen and rupture eventually, if the Cold War continues as before. It's certainly a possibility, given that the latest five-year plan is running into the buffers; but the logic underestimates the resilience of the Soviet population. They're quite capable of subsisting on bread and potatoes indefinitely if the nation's at war. And the Leadership has been insisting that it is, or as good as. Why? Because the convincing case is made by America every single day, and in public. As you may imagine, Joseph McCarthy is regarded as something of a godsend in the Kremlin.'

'So it would be difficult for present attitudes in Moscow to change.'

'Yes, but there are possibilities. Am I correct in thinking that all parties in Korea will accept the Indian armistice proposals?'

'Probably, yes.'

'Then the most immediate ground for friction between the US and USSR is about to end. There are other problems, obviously. For a long time, Stalin did nothing about NATO because he didn't see that it could be effective as long as the French refused to allow West German re-armament. But last year's European Defence Community Agreement changes that.'

'It hasn't been ratified.'

'That isn't the point. A re-armed West Germany is now accepted as an inevitability, even by De Gaulle. So, the Kremlin will consider ways to counter it, perhaps with a NATO of our own.'

'The USSR already has bi-lateral defence agreements with all of its satellites.'

'Yes, but there's no co-ordinating organization, no unified command. It's the next logical step, and will be seen as a justifiable response to the West's refusal to negotiate a neutral, disarmed, re-united Germany.'

'We refused because such an entity would very quickly become a Moscow puppet.'

Zarubin paused once more. He had to be careful now. Reds-under-the-Bed Syndrome had deeply infected the American psyche, and to ridicule the suggestion would end this conversation abruptly. He raised a hand, palm upward.

'I'm not arguing for it; merely stating the case. Whoever wins the leadership struggle in the longer term will do so by reason of his, or their, response to domestic and foreign pressures upon the Soviet system. Looking weak in the face of western aggression isn't something that any of them will risk, but the living standards of ordinary citizens need to be raised, urgently. It will be a balancing act, and the US may have an opportunity to hand the pole to one of the contenders.'

'A gesture?'

'Of course. I wasn't suggesting anything sincere. And it would need to be done discreetly, perhaps through the Swiss, because a candidate seen to have America on his side would be tying himself to a firing post. On the other hand, being able to wave a provisional concession from the enemy would, if timed correctly, do a great deal to enhance his standing in the Central Committee. The task is to identify the man who might be most amenable to such an approach, and to decide what you want from it. And while you're thinking of that, just remember this: it was Beria, less than two months ago, who asked publicly: *What is East Germany? What does it amount to? It's not even a real state, just one kept in existence by Soviet troops.*'

That was it, the lot. Zarubin had nothing left to prod with, other than his foot. The CIA man picked up his pipe again and tried to suck some life into it while examining the grain on the desk between them. It was impossible to judge accurately, but from the evidence of the questions he had asked, this particular American was neither an ideologue nor a fool, and that was almost the best that Zarubin could have hoped for. As he waited he breathed regularly, concentrating on keeping his face as disinterested in what came next as the desk that was getting all the attention.

Eventually, the pipe was replaced by a pen, and a paragraph's worth of scribbling further tested his nerves. Still, it was better than a brief scribble that an outright rejection would require.

The other man looked up, 'I need a comprehensive report, three or four pages, for the Director. How quickly can you do it?'

A promise of eternal youth couldn't have been more welcome to Zarubin's ears. 'Forty-eight hours. I'll bring it to the New York Office.'

No. Forty eight hours is fine, but you can write it on your way to doing something else for us.'

'What is it?'

'You were stationed in Berlin-Karlshorst, at the MGB station there?'

'Yes.'

'We need you in Germany. Ulbricht's Government and the Soviet Control Commission appear to be falling out spectacularly, and we don't have insiders to tell us what it means. Will you go?'

Zarubin revised his earlier assessment - eternal youth didn't come close matching this. It was as if he were being offered the opportunity to stamp his own application form on Judgement Day.

'Of course. Do I have time to go home and pack a bag?'

'No, we need you on the ground by tomorrow. You'll be attached formally to the Berlin office, which means you'll be a Federal employee. You're required to take the oath.'

The Russian nodded solemnly. This took some effort, as he was simultaneously quashing a desire to jump to his feet, dance and flick his fingers.

'Of course. I'd be honoured.'

20

Having been asked, Fischer gave Holleman the tour of his home above the shop. Polite noises were made, and the tasteful décor clearly intimidated a man for whom domesticity had fallen much like nets did upon wild game. But their perambulation took less than ten minutes, after which all the working timepieces on the premises were pressed into service once more.

'Where the hell *is* she?'

It was past one o'clock now, and Fischer's easy reassurances were beginning to echo. There were a dozen perfectly good reasons why Kristin Holleman might not yet have made it to West Berlin, and about as many bad ones. The fact that Rolf Hoeschler hadn't sounded an alarm might not mean anything, or that they had already been swept up by a vigilant *VolksPolizei* patrol with orders to watch out for a woman, a boy, a man and three furtive expressions. He couldn't say either way, and Freddie Holleman knew it.

He was still trying to think of something to say that was comforting without being transparently soothing when he noticed that he was being examined carefully once more.

'Otto, I said you looked older.'

'You did, Freddie. Thank you.'

'But it's more … tired. You look tired. Aren't you sleeping?'

'Well enough, for an ex-soldier. If I'm tired it's not for lack of sleep.'

'What, then? It's not life, is it? You aren't thinking of checking out?'

Fischer smiled wanly. 'Not yet. And probably not at all, if I haven't to date. It's something else.'

'Well, I'm bored *and* worried, so distract me.'

Fischer told Holleman about Frau Siebert and her broken Hettich, her daily visits and brutal death. It required less time than the upstairs tour, but it was one of those things that couldn't be laid to rest with a bare description. For a while after he'd finished, Holleman considered the facts. As the former commander of East Berlin's Criminal Investigations Directorate, this was still bread and butter business, a matter of facts and conjecture that might have stood at a remove from the hurt it gave, had the hurt not been worn by a friend.

'Do you know what your problem is, Otto? Apart from being Otto, that is?'

'I'm too attractive?'

'And from that. It's the armour, the stuff that coddles a policeman's soul as the pageant of shit washes past him.'

'What about it?'

'You took it off.'

'I doubt that I ever had it.'

'You were good police, weren't you?'

'I hinted that I was. You never had proof of it.'

'I've watched you out-think generals, method murderers and the Intelligence agencies of several nations. It's a testimonial of sorts.'

'You didn't see me before, when I *was* police; when had to do it for a wage-packet. It seemed a depraved transaction.'

'Done properly, it's honourable work.'

'It rarely was, though. Not under National Socialism.'

Holleman considered his friend carefully. 'I don't mean to be a cold bastard, but why does a single death mean that much? We've come out of a time – hell, I hope we have - that Ewers couldn't have written with a hangover. Switzerland aside, there isn't a place on this continent that hasn't seen corpses shovelled like coal into pits, and mostly for no good reason. I feel for poor Frau Siebert, but …'

'You're right, Freddie. She wasn't anyone, just a woman who'd lost most of her mind and all of the rest. But for God knows what perverse reason that makes it worse. There was no cause to it, just an evil mood finding easement by erasing her. It weighs more than it should.'

'Do you know what she is? She's all your bad cases, come to sit on your shoulder.'

Surprised, Fischer nodded. 'You've felt that too?'

'Not about any one of them in particular. They tend to visit as a crowd, in the small hours. I call them the What Fucking Ifs.'

'I tell myself that I mend clocks now. And sell them, sometimes.'

Holleman glanced around once more at the modest stock of retail items, the untidy trays of parts, the watchmakers' instruments placed in no discernible order and the fine collection of dust upon which they sat (or sat upon them).

'Is it satisfying?'

'It isn't the other thing. And it's useful. I mend broken bits of Germany.'

'It's good that someone does.'

Despite his words, Holleman's face stayed where it was, imitating that of a slightly deflated parent whose son has ditched university for a career in juggling. He had no greater awareness of time-pieces than what their dials told him, so the craft – art, even – of resurrecting a dead mechanism belonged to that great edifice of human knowledge marked Not Freddie's Business. He completed his perfunctory survey and sighed.

'Where *is* she?'

The sound of the rear door opening lifted him off the bench he had settled upon, but Dietrich's entrance dropped him once more.

'I have good news. Your son Franz is over the line. He went into a *SchuPo* station in Moabit, and they 'phoned it through to the *Rathaus.*'

'Did he say anything about …?'

'No. He hasn't spoken with his mother today. I'm sorry.'

What had been high anxiety moved up another notch. 'I have to go back. She must be …'

Fischer touched his shoulder. 'You can't, Freddie. Take one step over the line and they'll use you for a football. By now there'll be bulletins out all over East Berlin, and with that tin leg you won't pass as part of any crowd.'

'But …'

'And where, exactly, would you look for Kristin? If she went home, or to Ulrich's, they'll have her already. If not, where then? Your secret rendezvous was here, not there. Sticking pins in a map won't help.'

Dietrich offered the afflicted husband a cigarette, 'Herr Fischer's talking sense. With what's happening in the city today there could be a hundred reasons why she's been delayed. It's hard, but be patient.'

'Fuck patience …'

'Listen, I've dealt with defectors before, so allow me to generalize. You hope that everything goes to a plan, one that has to negotiate a swamp of circumstance you couldn't have seen coming. When it doesn't, you panic, or you wonder why it is that you've lost control of events - or, most often, you wish that it were yesterday once more. The analogy of sailors caught in heavy seas out of sight of land doesn't occur to you, not until it's too late to be useful. For the moment, patience is all you have – unless you're a pious man, that is.'

This was all good sense, and Fischer knew that it wasn't going to work. Neither fortitude nor God could shift Holleman on the matter of other Hollemans, even when guilt wasn't adding a further layer of torment. For the moment he said nothing more, but the anguish bubbled like something about to escape the pot. Fischer glanced at Dietrich. There was something in his expression, a dark cast that hinted at larger preoccupations than Kristin Holleman and her whereabouts.

'What's wrong?'

The agent said nothing a few moments as he struggled with his intelligencer's reluctance to reveal more than was necessary. 'We've had reports from field agents. There are two Soviet columns approaching Berlin. One's coming in directly from Wünsdorf, the other's swinging eastwards to the south of the city, probably from Schönebeck. The intelligence is several hours old, so they may be within the city limits already.'

'How many?'

'It's hard to say, but several battalions of motorized infantry at least. Possibly tanks, too. Certainly enough to put down anything that brews.'

Fischer looked at Holleman, whose face was colouring towards a seizure, and desperately sought a bright side.

'If they were on the move hours ago, it was before they could know how this might turn out. It's cautionary, surely?'

'Probably, but …'

'But?'

'We're hearing that several police stations in East Berlin are burning now, and there's been at least one killing, of a local SED councillor.'

'The strikers did that?'

'It's not clear. They've been joined by many ordinary Berliners, from east and west. And the demands have changed. It isn't just about working conditions anymore. They're calling for free elections.'

'Christ. Have you any idea how many people are involved?'

'In Berlin, it's confused. But in the rest of the DDR, it looks like several hundred thousands. Whether that's enough to make the Soviets react heavily, we don't know yet.'

Fischer was just old enough to recall Germany's last revolution, in 1918, and how brutally the government had come down upon its own people. It was hard to imagine that the Red Army would be less rigorous. The DDR was the Soviet Union's most important client state by far, and if it was lost to the West the others would surely go the same way. What they might do to prevent that would depend upon more than Fischer could guess at.

He looked at Dietrich. 'That southern column – it's probably heading for Adlershof, to coordinate with the *Kasernierte* police.'

'Yes, we think so.'

'That might be bad or good. Either they want to involve German personnel so that any level of response can be considered legitimate, or they'd prefer this to remain a policing action and not a military pacification.'

Dietrich nodded again. 'It would be useful to know what Moscow's saying to Semyonov.'

'They'll be falling over themselves to seem rigorous. At a time when everyone's under the glass, who would want to be seen as the weakling? On the other hand …'

'Is there one?'

'A bloodbath wouldn't be the best advertisement for Fraternal Socialism. It would give the Americans a beautiful propaganda coup, one that could be rubbed in the faces of all the other suspected dominoes.'

'Well, at least we know now that they're going to do *something*.' Dietrich checked his watch. 'There's almost eight hours of light yet. Time enough for a revolution to be nipped off smartly, the easy or hard way.'

Holleman was cursing under his breath, and even Fischer had to make an effort to seem calmer than he felt. 'The telephone lines – are they open still?'

'In the East? Not the public exchanges. Ministry and emergency services lines appear to be.'

'Freddie, what if you call Müller again? He should be able to tell you if Hoeschler and Kristin have been picked up.'

'If they're expecting my call would he tell the truth? Wouldn't he be told to say that they had, to lure me back?'

It was likely. Not having much experience of defection, Fischer hadn't considered its protocols.

'Müller knows me. What if I make the call? Apart from him, no one at Keibelstrasse can connect my name to yours.'

'You don't have a 'phone.'

'The *Südwest-Berliner Zeitung* does, three doors away.'

Holleman considered this. 'Alright. You'll tell me the truth, if it's bad news?'

'What point would there be in lying? Give me the name of Ulrich's employers.'

'Why?'

'It might matter.'

'*Handel Metallbearbeitung.*'

'I won't be long.'

For the next fifteen minutes, Dietrich, who wanted very much to be back at Schöneberg's *Rathaus* to make yet another report to Pullach (where the Organization's hierarchy appeared to be having a collective seizure about the day's events), attempted to describe to Holleman the de-briefing and re-location routines that defectors typically underwent in the weeks following their flight to the West. He might have as usefully chosen one of Fischer's clocks and offered it the same information, but he persisted in the face of iron indifference if only to be able to say later that he had ticked all the process's boxes.

A peel of time-pieces announced the front door precisely on the half-hour. Red-faced, Holleman lurched forward as quickly as his metal leg permitted, but had to wait as Fischer cleared a space on a worktable and put down bread and a newspaper.

'Well?'

'Calm down, Freddie. It isn't bad news.'

'What did Müller say?'

'That he's sick of getting 'phone calls, that his nerves are shot through and what the fuck were you thinking, going over the line and kissing goodbye to your pension? And stop calling.'

'I mean, about Kristin!'

'I didn't ask.'

'You …?'

'I didn't need to. I led with another question, and things sorted themselves. I asked him if companies whose workers were involved in the strikes were obliged to report it. He told me yes, of course, and what the hell was it about? So, had the proprietor of *Handel Metallbearbeitung* called in? I expected to have to wait while he checked, but he was surprised, and said that he'd been asked precisely that question less than an hour ago, by some *wachtmeister* at a local police station'

Holleman deflated visibly and dropped his arse onto the edge of the table. 'Rolf Hoeschler asked it.'

'I would seem so, yes.'

'What was the answer?'

'Yes, also.'

'Christ. She's given Rolf the swerve and gone to get Ulrich.'

'I can't think of an alternative.'

Fischer watched Holleman struggle not to call his beloved wife names that would have had him evicted from a trench. His spur-of-the-moment 'plan' hadn't merely gone wrong - it had been taken by the hand, led into the woods and clubbed. Somewhere in Central-East Berlin, a mortified Rolf Hoeschler was desperately trying to re-acquire his charge amid a termite-maul of peeved citizenry, while the architect of all their destinies was losing his head in a suburban shop, helpless to do more than absorb scraps of half-news as they blew in through the door. The situation would have snipped at the wires of the most serene temperament, and it had set itself upon one that had hardly ever known the restraint of wires.

Dietrich had listened to the exchange carefully. This was the moment at which a sensible handler would make a decision to let go of the leash or wrap it tightly about his fist and brace for the struggle, which meant that by sunset Holleman could find himself in an MfS prison or detained at Pullach, in either case with a good chance of not knowing what the hell had happened to Kristin. Over the past three years, Fischer had taken no more interest in the East German Government than to wonder occasionally how far into it his good friend had wandered, so he couldn't assess Freddie's potential value to General Gehlen; but it was an iron truth that assets became much less so the more of a drag they caused.

No one was speaking, and the pause pushed Fischer into a gap he might have thought more about avoiding.

'Jonas hasn't gone back yet.'

Holleman frowned, as if a fart had interrupted a profound reverie. 'What?'

'He's still at the *Zeitung* office, trying to persuade Herr Grabner that all the news that's worth writing can be cribbed from RIAS broadcasts.'

'So?'

'He's spent the past two days talking to strike committees. He'll know something about the routes they're planning, and who to speak to about other trades that might join the cause. Metal-working comrades, for example.'

'Not if he won't go back across the line. And even if he does, he can't do anything with the information. He's not storm-trooper material, is he?'

'No. But he might be persuaded, and I …'

Dietrich coughed. 'That's probably not a good idea.'

Holleman's face was suffused suddenly by a glow of earnest, naïve hope. 'Would you, Otto? You're a *mensch*!'

21

The longer that Colonel Voloshyn peered at the map, the more his stomach clenched. It was, ostensibly, a survey map of central Berlin, ominous in no sense other than the mild feeling of claustrophobia it might excite in a man used to nothing more crowded than village life. It was up to date, showing previously bombed out areas half-filled with new blocks and the occasionally re-routed major road, given the opportunity by Armageddon to have an historic stretch of meander straightened. It would have tugged at the heart of any Berliner to see the changes that bombing and shelling had wrought upon the old city; but Voloshyn was a Red Army officer and at least partly responsible for those changes. It wasn't the bare prospect of what he was examining that moved his gut.

The policeman – he was dressed like a regular soldier, other than for the *KVP* badge on his arm - was marking the map with wax crayons: blue to denote his intelligence on the present deployment of armed *VolksPolizei* units, black for the approaching Soviet and *Kasernierte* paramilitary forces, and - this was part of what was giving Voloshyn his bad feeling - a sanguinary shade of red to indicate where strikers and other civilians had congregated in Mitte. The latter was a moving feast, obviously; but the shaded areas around Stalin Allee, Unter den Linden and the blocks surrounding the *Neues Stadthaus* were likely to remain so until someone did something about it.

Much of the rest of the bad feeling was being supplied by the policeman's conversation. With as smart a salute as Voloshyn had ever seen off a parade ground, he had introduced himself as Commander Weigl, and though his armband said KVP the rest was standard-issue *Stasi*, a breed always anxious to prove that they were as rigorously doctrinaire as Iron Felix himself. Voloshyn had expected to be briefed about striking workers; what he was being given instead was a manifest of fifth-columns, western agitation and incipient counter-revolution. Clearly, Weigl was a man expecting – even hoping for – a nice little civil war.

Germans wanting to kill each other wasn't something that worried Voloshyn, but he had an aversion to being led by the nose. Though his orders had been broad, they were unequivocally weighted towards not inflicting Hell if at all possible. This fellow – and, for all he knew, his bosses who were presently besieged in the *Neues Stadthaus* – had a millenarian's urge to do something decisive about the numerous pits they had dug for themselves in the cause of what they'd grandly called 'constructing socialism'. A quagmire'd economy, food shortages, arbitrary imprisonments and a human exodus that was making the Israelites look like slug-a-beds amounted to a deal of grief, and there had to be a reason for it that didn't involve taking the blame themselves. Ergo, an enemy was required, and Voloshyn was being offered a leading role in the fiction.

The map was spread upon the bonnet of his GAZ, which was halted on Pushkin-Allee at the northern edge of Treptower Park. In front of them the road dog-legged sharply to the north before resuming its north-western progress into the heart of Mitte (a necessary adjustment to prevent it wandering into the American sector). The column was therefore a matter of only some two to three kilometres from where it could begin to do serious damage to the citizenry should things become ugly, and Voloshyn realised that decisions were looming.

Weigl had asked something, and he'd missed it. 'I'm sorry, Commander?'

'Do you want KVP to deploy with your units, or should we wait until your troops break up the mobs and then put in extraction squads?'

'Ah, yes.' Voloshyn thought quickly. His men were well disciplined, but if they were shoulder to shoulder with someone wanting a fight, they'd call it a *fait accompli* and go in hard. He didn't want to give them an excuse before it was absolutely necessary.

'Keep your men in reserve until I see know we're up against. I'll make a further decision then.'

Weigl looked slightly deflated but he nodded. KVP were deployed strictly under Soviet supervision – or had been, until today. Voloshyn had a suspicion that new rules were going to try to write themselves in the coming hours. He turned and waved to Pankov.

When his adjutant arrived he spoke to him in Russian. It was discourteous, but he didn't want Weigl to get a hint of what he was thinking.

'How many marksmen do we have?'

Pankov seemed puzzled. 'I don't know, Comrade *Podpolkovnik*. But Kyril Kabanov won the Divisional trophy last year and the one before.'

'Bring him here, please.'

Kabanov was a young *efreitor* with ginger-hair that, even cropped, tried to go its own way. He wore his Excellent Marksmanship badge prominently on his tunic and a wary expression on his face, which Voloshyn tried to ease with a smile and a nod.

'You're the best shot in the division, I hear.'

'In the competition I was, Comrade *Podpolkovnik*. But there are others as good as me.' He reconsidered that. 'Almost.'

'Are any of them in the column?'

Instinctively, Kabanov glanced down the stalled line of vehicles. 'I think … four.'

'Good. Go and fetch them, would you?'

When the man returned with his comrades Voloshyn excused himself to Weigl, and, with Pankov, drew them aside. He looked each man in the eye for several seconds as he spoke, to further hammer in what he was going to tell them.

'You'll each deploy with a separate platoon, where you'll identify and pair with one other good rifleman. When we find trouble, I want you to regard yourselves as being in a combat situation. Your targets will be anyone carrying a fire-arm. In each case, don't shoot unless he - or she - raises the weapon as if to use it. If they do, I expect a clean kill. Otherwise, point them out immediately to your platoon leaders and they'll be watched. Pankov, give strict instructions to the commanders: no other men to use their weapons unless a general order is given.'

'What if the mob attacks?'

'That's unlikely. Memories of what the Red Army did can't have faded in most Berliners' minds. A few provocateurs may attempt something in order to goad the rest, which is why I want Kabanov and his friends to be alert. If some collective stupidity grips the crowds and they advance upon you, fire above their heads. If that doesn't disperse them immediately, encourage them with feet and rifle butts. Permission to use deadly fire against multiple targets will only be given by myself. Under no circumstances will you accept orders from KVP officers, no matter how senior - not even if they do something stupid and need to be rescued. Is that understood?'

Everyone, including Pankov, nodded. Voloshyn, satisfied that he'd driven it into their skulls, waved the marksmen away but stayed his adjutant with the other hand.

'Get on the radio to Karlshorst. This is probably our final opportunity to have them agree to deployments before they become reactions. The units from Wünsdorf should be on the northern outskirts of Prenzlauer Berg by now. Say that we'll establish an initial north-south control line on Andreastrasse, and then, advancing into Mitte, extend the line northwards to link up with them, probably at or near Schillingstrasse. If we encounter protests before that point, they'll be contained and allocated to KVP personnel, to permit our manoeuvre to continue.'

Pankov was scribbling furiously, but he paused and looked up at Voloshyn's mention of the German paramilitaries.

'Won't they find a reason to over-react?'

'Possibly, but we can't keep our hand on every situation. If they let loose on isolated pockets of protesters, the damage will be limited. It's a general massacre we'd rather avoid.'

'*If* possible?'

Voloshyn sighed. 'We can only hope. For the first time in years, some part of the German people's destiny is in their own hands. It's just that the choice is narrow – being sensible, or being dead. Send the message, get the column moving.'

22

Hoeschler was getting angry, more so than was sensible, but he was saved from its consequences by a short, thick-set fellow with a prominent tattoo of a woman who probably wasn't his mother. The arm upon which she lived swung its fist-end into the face of an *anwärter* who had been attempting to use Hoeschler's balls as footballs. He had been about to risk his camouflage and mission by reacting in kind, but his new comrade's intervention was so decisive that the unconscious man's comrades hurriedly grabbed him and executed a text-book withdrawal from the line of strikers they had attempted to break up.

'Dedrik.'

It was offered with a short nod (probably all that his massive neck could manage), and Hoeschler returned it. 'Rolf. Thanks.'

'That's alright. It's what the bastards understand.'

Only twenty-four hours earlier Hoeschler might have argued the point; but then he would have been on the other side, urging his men to go for the balls if they couldn't swing their *schlagstocks*. He was man enough to admit now that there might be other points of view.

They were stood in the middle of Gendarmenmarkt, roughly equidistant from the German and French Churches, arrayed with other strikers in what had been a processional formation but which now looked like a line of battle. Hoeschler hadn't intended to be here of course, but the events of that day were unfolding without apparent reference to human agency. He wasn't even sure if he was in the middle of the correct group of metal-workers.

On another day, a normal day, the counter-charge by a small group of *VolksPolizei* might have worked. They represented Authority, and Germans being Germans it was likely that some hard thinking would have ensued about whether an about-face and return to the workplace wasn't the most sensible course. Today, the encounter seemed only to have re-charged the already electric atmosphere that propelled the workers; today, Germans of a certain class were looking for someone's nose to wipe with their grievances.

Hoeschler didn't share the general enthusiasm, but it was hardly politic to say so. He had joined the back of a group of marchers, having been nodded towards them by a trade union steward after asking the whereabouts of staff from *Handel Metallbearbeitung*. Whether he'd been heard correctly, or waved away, or given the wrong information, he couldn't say. He only knew that he hadn't see Ulrich yet, or the lad's infuriating mother.

He would have needed a higher viewpoint to judge accurately, but there seemed to be a least a thousand workers crowding into Gendarmenmarkt, and their number was growing quickly. It was a good point at which to converge – open and spacious, with too many access roads for the authorities to block off, should they decide to make the attempt. From here, the *Neues Stadthaus* – surely one of the strikers' primary goals, if being noticed was the purpose of this – could be reached quickly along one or more of several parallel roads, making their interception a further problem. Whoever organized the march had thought it out carefully, with maximum attention to making things difficult for the enemy.

The police operation against Hoeschler's testicles appeared to have been an isolated manoeuvre. He could see more several units scattered around the edges of the square, but none of them looked as if they wanted to throw themselves into the fray Without exception, rifles were slung over shoulders, and cigarettes were bring passed around and smoked. He recognized several of the men as being staff from Keibelstrasse, none of whom were known shirkers, cowards or time-serving traffic-directors. Clearly, the scale of the protests was far greater than their numbers could handle effectively, but for the first time he wondered if there was an element of sympathy to what was keeping them quiet.

His shoulder was nudged roughly, and he took the bottle of flat beer offered by Dedrik. He was marching with strangers in a cause that didn't move him, but the air carried a very familiar sense of camaraderie. Whatever happened would happen to them all, indiscriminately, and only luck would separate the still-upright from the fallen. It was the same sense that a looming battle encouraged; that gave men the nerve to do stupid things despite what their heads told them. It was a dangerous place to be, and Hoeschler wished himself at least five kilometres away, preferably to the west.

He hadn't stopped examining the crowd around him, but it was time wasted. Unless Ulrich climbed onto a police van, or the mob separated to admire Kristin Holleman's extraordinarily well-kept looks, he wasn't going to find them. And that was assuming they were here, of course. They might currently be in an entirely different press of aggrieved bodies, or a police station (whatever Albrecht Müller had said), or arguing in an alley somewhere as East Berlin fell to pieces around them. He was following a hunch, and hunches without information were as much use as tea-leaves.

'Come on, mate. We want to be at the front.'

No, we damn well don't. But the moment the thought came to him he changed his mind. Presumably, Dedrik knew where the crowd was going from Gendarmenmarkt, and if they were at its head when it moved, Hoeschler could break off, stand aside and watch as it funnelled into one of the streets (if it *was* only one). He told himself it was something, a chance at least.

He and Dedrik began to move, excusing themselves through the mass of men. When they reached its edge, Dedrik pointed himself eastwards. To Hoeschler's surprise, there were dozens of people joining the perimeter of the protest who clearly weren't strikers – men in office-wear, women (some of them with children) and a clutch of young people, who, from their almost uniformly over-long hair, he took to be students from the Humboldt. A few chants were trying to get a head of steam going, one of them about Pharaoh (Ulbricht really should have thought more about his birthday celebrations), and a number of hastily painted slogans on sheets of cardboard were being held at waist height, as if their owners had yet to decide how far they were all going to go. To Hoeschler, who had seen this sort of thing before (most notably in '48, during the City Council coup), it seemed that the fuse had burned almost to the charge. Whatever time he imagined he had, it would be wiser to halve it.

He shifted to the right, departing Dedrik's company while the man was shaking his fist and shouting (something about Pieck's tongue and Ulbricht's arse), and took a position across Markgrafenstrasse. Though it had yet to move decisively, the head of the crowd seemed to be inclining that way – specifically, towards the section of Taubenstrasse leading down to Hausvogteiplatz. His conviction strengthened when a group of policemen who had been standing at the corner of Taubenstrasse moved casually northwards, out of harm's way. He pressed himself back into a doorway and waited for the flow to begin.

Less than five minutes later, a man wearing a trade union sash took the lead and crossed Markgrafenstrasse. A line, some eight to ten strikers wide, formed behind him in reasonable order and followed. Hoeschler scanned them carefully as they passed by into Taubenstrasse. Ulrich Holleman was tall, perhaps 1.8 metres, and his mother only a little shorter. He was fairly sure that he would see them if they were here.

Perhaps he watched too closely; seemed too much like someone with a purpose. The voice, so close that he felt the breath on his ear, made him almost leave the ground.

'What's your business here?'

The young *anwärter* frowned severely, perhaps trying to burnish the tough image that *VolksPolizei* elsewhere had abandoned that day. Hoeschler realised that his false identity wouldn't explain anything – that if he wanted to be rid of his problem quickly he had to take a risk. To his knowledge he'd never seen the man before, and the chances were that today's turmoil had slowed the circulation of what, on any other day, would have been a singularly important bulletin. He pulled his *kriminalkommissar*'s warrant card from a breast pocket and handed it over.

The *anwärter* examined it for a moment, and the frown disappeared. He returned the card, stepped smartly back and …

Don't.

…saluted. Hoeschler had no choice but to return it. It hardly mattered; he had been noticed already by several marchers on his side of their line. A woman – respectably dressed, hardly in the Defarge tradition – pointed an accusing finger. Hoeschler turned to the *anwärter*.

'Get out of here. Quickly.'

As the man obeyed, three strikers – all hearty, square-built types - broke from the crowd and converged upon Hoeschler's doorway. He had just identified himself as the very worst, most unfortunate sort of creature – plain-clothed and therefore almost certainly *Staatssicherheitsdienst*, and horribly alone. It was too late to run, too late to think of something that had a chance of making them change their minds. He tried to smile, held up his hands in the universal expression of *let's be calm, shall we*, and failed to avoid the first punch.

After that, he concentrated on keeping his head covered and let his belly and groin lead the counter-attack.

23

For several moments following his return to German soil, Zarubin checked his extremities to reassure himself that they were fit for duty still. He found it ironic that, having never won the Siberian lottery during all his years of service with NKGB and MGB, the Americans were now offering him a second chance.

In a way, he was grateful. Few former Soviet Intelligence personnel could boast that they were familiar with the principal delivery system of the enemy's nuclear arsenal, but he had just experienced the full measure – nine hours in the capacious fuselage of a B36 Peacemaker with a wholly inadequate flight-jacket over his summer-weight suit. He didn't know to what altitude its ten engines had delivered them (he might have asked, though none of the fifteen-man crew seemed eager to *chew the fat*); but for all the alleged pressurization he imagined that a naturist's winter holiday on Severny Island would have felt humid by comparison.

His on-the-ground-once-more recuperation wasn't helped by the fact that he wasn't on the ground for more than a few minutes, and that his next delivery system – from RAF Lakenheath to Berlin – was an ageing C54 whose pilot preferred to fly with the windows open (Zarubin couldn't swear to this, but the draught was of a magnitude that poor welding could hardly have explained). When they landed at Tempelhof, the co-pilot helped him out of the 'plane and told him to stamp his feet a few times. When he complied he almost fell over.

He had anticipated – dreaded – an open jeep, but Berlin Operations Base had sent a well-insulated Buick which managed, during the eight-kilometre drive to Föhrenweg, to raise his body temperature despite the icy indifference of his mute driver. At the CIA Station he was momentarily disappointed to be met by someone who was clearly junior staff (the shaving cuts and too-large shirt collar made him seem more a tenth-grader than a spy), but he was bundled into the building with impressive speed and offered a sofa in a warm office. Remarkably, he was then asked if he might like breakfast. In less than twenty minutes, eggs, bacon, bread-rolls, butter and black coffee were displaying themselves wantonly in front of him, and in the time it took to eat them he thought nothing more of his two missions.

The tenth-grade spy waited until the coffee was drained before delivering the bad news. 'I'm sorry, Sir. The Chief of Station can't meet with you.'

Of course not, it's nine am. He's either too drunk or can't be extracted from a female member of your secretarial staff. Zarubin had heard the rumours about William King Harvey and was more than ready to believe them. Self-consciously larger-than-life types seldom advertised themselves with quiet application, rigorous observance of protocols or attention to what their clocks were telling them. He allowed himself to be gracious.

'Never mind. I'm at your service.'

'Thank you. Mr Abernathy, our assistant Chief, will be here soon.'

Zarubin didn't know Abernathy either by sight or reputation, but assumed him to be at least as competent and well-informed as his boss. He nodded, as if this were entirely acceptable.

'In the meantime, might I ask the use of a typewriter?'

All hints of industry being pleasing to CIA operatives (with the possible exception of Harvey), he was obliged and then left to himself for the next ninety minutes. By the time the office door reopened he had committed his *magnum opus* to paper, having ordered it precisely in his head during the idle hours in which freezing to death provided the only other distraction.

The gentleman who disturbed this fertile passage was, to Zarubin's mind, the most *American*-looking American he'd ever seen. His jaw was enormously wide, and seemed wider still on the thin neck that supported it. His Adam's apple was more of a melon, and had it slumped would have hidden the bow-tie immediately beneath. The man's entire weight (not added to greatly by a severe crew-cut) could hardly have exceeded Zarubin's own, yet he stood a good twenty centimetres taller.

The apparition held out an enormous, fleshless hand. 'Abernathy. You'll be Major Zarubin.'

Strange, how they accorded even an enemy his former military rank. He smiled, nodded and let his own hand be mangled briefly.

'Thank you for coming. Obviously, we have a fairly good understanding of what's been happening with labour relations here in the GDR recently. What we'd like from you is an idea of what the Soviets might do.'

'Do, Sir?'

'About the uprising.'

'The …?' Zarubin had been in the air for most of the past twenty-four hours. The last he'd heard, the East German Politburo had about-turned on their economic policy, no-one had believed them and some construction workers in Friedrichshain were making a noise about their working conditions. It hardly seemed to constitute an uprising.

Abernathy's eyebrows headed for the crew-cut. 'I'm sorry, you haven't been briefed. As best we can tell, what started as a single industry dispute is spreading across the country. Ulbricht's been in lock-down with the Party since yesterday, the police are on the streets but doing nothing, State Security's been reinforced from outside Berlin but ditto, and the Soviets … well, we don't have numbers yet, but Red Army units based at Karlshorst have been deployed at post offices and telephone exchanges already, and we think that at least a further two or three regiments are converging on the city from Wünsdorf and Schönebeck. What we want to know is, what next?'

Shit. Even as he tried to absorb the news, it was obvious to Zarubin that cleverness would be counter-productive. He had no need to be other than valuable to them - in fact, being a genuine asset would help his other business enormously. It would make what was hugely inaccurate seem credible until it no longer needed to be.

He cleared his throat. 'As you know, the most powerful Russian in East Germany is Vladimir Semyonov, who, if he hasn't yet had precise instructions from Moscow, will have agreed preliminary deployments in Berlin and elsewhere with the Soviet Control Commission and transmitted these to Marshal Grechko. However, it's inconceivable that the Kremlin remains uninvolved in the process. Almost certainly, they'll send someone to be their eyes here, and Semyonov – if he's not a complete fool, and he's not – will be submitting every one of his orders back to Moscow to cover his arse.'

Abernathy raised a hand. '*Their*, you said. Who's *they*?'

'A very good question. Obviously, everything is issued in the name of the Praesidium, but precisely whose is the dominant voice *at this moment* is difficult to say. Malenkov, Beria and Krushchev have been circling like wrestlers, but in a crisis …'

'Yes?'

'They're equally likely to go to one of two extremes – either take their chance that this is the moment to seize the initiative, make the big decisions and earn the gratitude of the decision-stampers, or make a show of consensus to avoid the perception that any one of them is pushing his own narrow interest rather than pulling on the oars with everyone else.'

'What's your feeling on it?'

Zarubin took his time answering that. He wanted to give the impression that he was thinking about it, because he really was thinking about it. He had no idea, of course, being neither in the confidence of the men at the top nor corresponding with anyone who was. If the Americans weren't so uncharacteristically humble about their ignorance of Soviet politics they'd realise that they could have flipped a coin as well as he. He took a deep breath.

'I don't have one. I have an opinion on who may and who should win the struggle for control of the Praesidium, but you're asking me about a moment during that process, and anything I say may equally be accurate or entirely wrong.'

Zarubin hated certain kinds of honesty. He'd seen men patted on the back for admitting that they were fallible mortal creatures and then been given postings to places where camel-fucking was Saturday night's premiere entertainment. So he took another breath.

'But … if either Malenkov or Beria are leading the discussion right now, I'd expect the Soviet response in Berlin to be measured. The former won't want his swan-song to be a massacre and subsequent alienation of the entire East German civil population, while the latter, frankly, doesn't want a result that will require a long-term Soviet presence here to stabilize and maintain.'

'And Krushchev?'

'Impossible to say. As an impulsive man he may do impulsive things. As a relative newcomer to the highest level of power he may wish to show that he can be as rigorous as any of his peers, and certainly, he'll want people to know that he can and will stand up to an American-arranged provocation – which, of course, is how this incident will be painted. On the other hand, would he want his first major achievement to be a slaughter of an ally's citizens?'

Abernathy nodded. 'You seem to be saying that it's more likely that the Soviets won't shoot first and think later.'

'It's more likely, yes. I wouldn't say *probable*, because I don't know what circumstances will face the units entering Berlin. If this *is* an uprising, the only thing we can say is that anything can happen.'

'I take your point. Thank you, Major.'

Zarubin tried to parse the expression on the assistant Station Chief's face. He was troubled, certainly, and that could either be about the situation itself or the fact that the flown-in special advisor had been utterly unhelpful. It was a moment at which a wise man might hint gently at his indispensability.

'I've been preparing a report for the Director which analyses the Kremlin power struggle. I'm sure he'd be happy for you to see it in draft form, given the situation here.'

Gratifyingly, Abernathy seemed impressed. In fact, Zarubin had no idea whether the CIA Director would ever set eyes upon his little tome, but as it had been requested by Washington who could say otherwise?

'You have it with you?'

'I'm finishing it at the moment.' Zarubin waved at the typewriter. 'Perhaps another half hour?'

'That would be extremely useful. Excuse me.' The door opened, and another besuited teenager entered with a sheet of paper. Abernathy took it and waved away the messenger. His face darkened as he read.

'Is it bad news?'

'It's … unexpected. We have a contact at the *Neues Stadthaus*. He writes that in the past hour the entire SED leadership – *all* of it - has been rounded up and taken to Karlshorst.' He looked up from the paper. 'For consultations, right?'

Zarubin had long practised what Americans called a poker face. It was a necessary technique in the Intelligence business, where bad news usually arrived when one was half out of the bath-tub and the towel lay out of reach. Even so, he couldn't be sure that he entirely disguised his surprise.

'If it were that, why not just summon Ulbricht? This is to keep them safe. Someone's decided that the situation could go very badly, very quickly. May I revise my opinion, please?'

Abernathy shook his head. 'That's not necessary. We're all going to be changing our minds as the day goes on. We've put the word to *Rathaus* Schöneberg to have all West Berlin's hospitals on stand-by.'

'And the Allied response?'

'Won't be much. We're trying and failing to seal the border between us and East Berlin. The British are considering imposing martial law in their Zone but haven't done it yet. All military units are on alert but not deployed. The initial delivery of food packages for the Eisenhower Project have arrived; we're ready to distribute them to East Berliners if they're needed.'

'Blood plasma may be more useful.'

Abernathy almost winced. 'Yeah.'

'Technically speaking, if there's a breakdown of civil order anywhere in Berlin, each and all of the Occupying Powers have the right to intervene, regardless of which Zone is affected.'

'And if we want a war, we'll exercise that right.'

'I meant, why not ask the Soviets if they need help?'

The Assistant Chief looked at Zarubin as if he were mildly deranged. 'They'll say no.'

'Of course they will. But the nature of the 'no' might hint at what they're intending, and at what point they're going to regard it as unavoidable.'

'They might just tell us to go fuck ourselves.'

Zarubin shook his head. 'That would amount to admitting they're panicked. Maintaining face is very important when dealing with the Enemy, particularly one who's sitting back and enjoying the spectacle. They'll want you to know that things are under control, and they can't do that without saying *something* about the situation.'

Abernathy pursed his lips. 'I'll put it to the ACC, but don't hope for much. I've spoken to them several times today already, and their reaction's been pretty much the same to every issue.'

'What's that?'

'That of a deer in headlights.'

24

'You'd think that the German *Volk* had got to the point where a bit of peace and quiet would strike them as slightly more attractive than a fart in a U-boat.'

Kleiber watched the small crowd with disgust. They were all *wessies*, arguing indignantly with a half-platoon of unarmed *SchuPo* personnel who were standing between them and a new little war.

Fischer regarded the little scene through the viewfinder of the *Südwest-Berliner Zeitung*'s only camera. He had been issued with a Luftwaffe Leica during two reconnaissance missions in Belgium back in '40, but this was his first time with a Contax. He caressed its body, longing to disembowel and examine its secret intricacies, and all the while tested the cadence of *Fischer's Time-piece, Gramophone and Camera Repairs* in his head.

'They're showing solidarity with their oppressed brethren, Jonas. Don't be a *miesmacher*.'

The younger man snorted. 'Eight years ago they were cowering in cellars, praying that Soviet bullets and cocks would pass them by. Now, they've come looking for some.'

The heat in the crowd was beginning to dissipate. Some two hundred strong, it filled the width of Adalbertstrasse, but loosely. While the small group arguing with the policemen was tightly compacted, its rear-guard was spreading out, breaking up, bored with being in the same place. Fischer noticed something, climbed onto the base of a nearby lamp-post and waved a hand at Kleiber.

'Look.'

The demarcation line was some two hundred metres behind the *SchuPo* patrol. Across it, flanked by an armoured personnel carrier at each extremity, Soviet soldiers were deployed. Their automatic rifles were unslung and pointing into the air, but Fischer didn't suppose they would remain there if the situation changed.

'I thought you said the line was open?'

Jonas shrugged. 'It was, two hours ago. They can't have covered every access point. Let's find another way in. I mean, if we really have to.'

'They'll have enough men to block every road.'

'I know. I wasn't thinking about roads.'

Ten minutes later, Kleiber raised his head tentatively over a fence separating two half-ruined warehouses in the block between Wrangelstrasse and Köpenickerstrasse. On its other side a patch of cleared ground extended to Bethaniandamm. It was a potentially treacherous stretch, a two hundred metre sprint to negotiate, offering a fine field of fire from three directions if someone in a brown uniform decided to liven his dull day.

Fischer sighed. As they'd moved north and east he'd suspected that the young journalist had in mind a fraught swim across the Spree, but this was hardly better. Even if they reached it in one piece, Bethaniandamm itself was a broad, sweeping boulevard, one of a number of perfect routes that a military advance into Mitte might – and probably would - utilize.

'I'll go first.'

'Really?'

'My right shoulder won't lift me. You'll need to help.'

Kleiber made a stirrup with locked fingers and crouched. After only a little frantic clambering, and almost as quietly as a tin can falling onto cobbles at midnight, Fischer put himself on the dangerous side of the fence. He straightened, took the camera that a disembodied hand passed to him and glanced around. The view was substantial but almost empty of human activity. To the south and west, about four hundred metres distant, he could see the Red Army barricade they had circumvented, but the soldiers' attention was directed firmly towards the threatened infiltration of part-time agitators. Directly west, across Bethaniandamm and its twin sister Engeldamm, Melchiorstrasse ran straight away from them, and down its entire length he couldn't see a single soul. He doubted that the daytime view had been so empty since the Surrender.

Kleiber landed heavily next to him and gasped. For a moment Fischer assumed the pale, frozen expression on his face to reflect an aversion to exercise, but then the pale became paler and the expression frostier.

'What's wrong?'

'I'm standing.'

'You are.'

'On a nail. Actually, *around* a nail.'

He lifted a foot, and piece of wood upon which he'd come to rest rose with it. Fischer winced.

'It'll have to come out.'

'I know. Please be …'

With a swift tug, Fischer separated man and nail. To his credit, Kleiber stifled a whimper and immediately tried to put weight on the foot. He winced too, but his foot remained on the ground.

'It'll do.'

He limped slightly as they crossed Bethaniandamm and Engeldamm. They had almost reached the eastern extremity of Melchiorstrasse when he grabbed Fischer's sleeve, pulled him to a halt and stood, stork-like, on his good foot.

'Just a minute.'

It wasn't an unreasonable request, but as they occupied the gutter on Engeldamm two Soviet armoured vehicles tore around the corner of

Köpernickerstrasse as if chased by a Shock Army. It was too late do anything that wouldn't make two idling Germans seem guilty of something; Kleiber was glancing around wildly for somewhere to hide his camera, but Fischer stayed him with a hand on his shoulder.

'Wait.'

As the lead personnel carrier drew level, he stuck out a hitcher's thumb. Several soldiers were squatting on its roof; the one at the front stared down furiously at this cheek, but his comrades laughed, and one of them wagged a finger of his gun-free hand. The second vehicle swept by, its passengers oblivious to the audience. In a few moments the road was clear again.

Kleiber looked impressed. 'That was clever.'

'Desperate is what it was. Come on, let's see if we can get across the river the dry way.'

'The Schillingbrücke's closest.'

'Good. It's one of the two luckiest bridges in Berlin. Some of it may wear off on us.'

The matter of *luck* pressed upon Fischer as they crossed the almost deserted bridge. He was trying to decide why he had volunteered to do this - to attempt to find a single person in the middle of a city on a day that no-one would be where they should be. He had no clues, no inspiration and no deep intuitive itch about Kristin Holleman's motives in wandering from a very simple plan. It was, in every sense, a forlorn hope – a desperate gesture, undertaken for no more sensible reason than that he couldn't bear the plaintive, pathetic cast to his friend's face. For almost eight years now, Holleman had been the embodiment of the guileless, tactless school of policing, his propulsive forward energy reanimating a smashed, demoralized, equipment-free police force; but now he was adrift once more, the same man who had crept back into Berlin in December 1944 under cover of darkness, fearfully hunting for a first clue as to where the Reich had misplaced his twin boys. Fischer had volunteered then, too; but he'd had the help of others, an intelligence department to misuse and the unmistakeable traces left by a behemoth that didn't care to disguise its passage. All he had now was a honed sense of his own impotence and Jonas Kleiber's magic notebook, a confused, scribbled summary of which striking workers might be heading for where (but not when), subject to the whims of *VolksPolizei*, *Staatssicherheitsdienst*, the Red Army and whether or not it rained.

Once over the bridge and onto Holzmarktstrasse, the human traffic increased immediately. Ominously, most of it was heading westwards towards trouble, and very little of it seemed to comprise workers. Though he'd been warned already, the total absence of a police or security presence struck Fischer forcibly.

'Have police withdrawn to barracks and stations?'

Kleiber shook his head. 'As far as I can tell, they have orders to protect certain sites, but otherwise not to try to interfere with the crowds. They cordoned off the House of Ministries this morning, early.'

Fischer revise his opinion of the luck of bridges. Compared to one building on the corner of Leipzigerstrasse and Wilhelmstrasse they were as good as cursed. As the Air Ministry, it had survived almost unscathed the aerial and actual battles of Berlin as everything around it was pulverized; now, reassigned to serve as East Germany's largest wen of politicals, it was allocated a bespoke security force while the rest of the city was allowed to fall to the mob. Perhaps it should always have been a hospital; he couldn't imagine that anything bad could happen under its roof.

'What about the strikers? What are their routes?'

Kleiber peered at his appalling script. 'The construction workers are gathering at Stalin Allee, Block 40. I met some chemicals folk at Lotharingstrasse, but they didn't seem to know where they were supposed to concentrate. The miners don't appear to have turned up at all ...'

'Metal workers?'

'Um, they were going to gather with their comrades at the Invalidenpark ...' Kleiber paused and frowned. 'No, that's the steel workers. Other metals trades were looking to rendezvous at Gendarmenmarkt.'

'Shit.'

'What's wrong?'

'There's no single, obvious route from there to the *Neues Stadthaus*. They could go one or more of half a dozen equally logical ways.'

'Then why don't we head for the *Stadthaus* and wait for them to come to us?'

'Have you seen the crowd scenes in DeMille's *Ten Commandments*'?

'Oh. Yeah.'

'There'll be, what, a hundred thousand converging on that point, if the battles haven't started already. How would we find Frau Holleman in that maul?'

'Hold on, Otto.' While Kleiber clutched a lamp post and examined his wounded foot once more, Fischer noticed something ominous. A few Berliners were moving against the predominant flow, escaping the pull of looming trouble. Some carried household items, appliances or baggage, and for a moment he assumed them to be from the intelligent end of the City's gene-pool. But if that were the case they wouldn't have been looking back as much as forward; wouldn't have danced around their fellow citizens as if rumours of a plague were circulating. Once more, he revised his hopes for how much time remained to do something useful. If looting had started, the Ivans wouldn't concern themselves with the political implications of going in heavily.

His diagnosis gained legs moments later, when he caught sight of his first casualty. Across Holzmarktstrasse, a woman and a man were making slow progress eastwards. She was trying to support him but his legs were playing games, and a makeshift bandage around his head hadn't prevented blood from seeping into his shirt.

'We have to move, Jonas.'

'Alright. But to where?'

Fischer thought quickly. If the metal workers were moving eastwards from Gendarmenmarkt to the *Stadthaus* by whatever fairly direct route, they would need to cross the island. On its west side, south of the museums, three bridges had been repaired or rebuilt. Should they take a guess as to which one was most likely to be traversed by Ulrich Holleman and his workmates? Probably – *probably* – he could rule out the Schlossbrücke; it was too far north of Gendarmenmarkt to make it a first choice for the marchers unless they had advance warning that one or more of the other bridges had been blocked by security forces. Which left the Gertraudenbrücke and the small bridge at Werderschermarkt. As to which of the two might be more likely, casting runes would tell him as efficiently as any further effort to weigh odds …

The idiocy of what he was doing struck him suddenly. The best information he had was already two to three hours out of date, so unless the strikers had decided to halt for a picnic and a few rousing speeches they were probably over the bridges already, across the island and facing whatever the police and MfS had managed to put in their way. *Or*, the Soviets had done the sensible thing, let the marchers onto the island and then blocked its eastern bridges, effectively corralling and putting a moat around the problem. *Or*, a dozen other incidents might have got in the way of plans, strategies and intentions, making any predictions as sound as a horoscope. The *Neues Stadthaus* might be burning at the moment; it might equally be as quiet as a church, with just a few cleaners out on Molkenmarkt, shovelling away the dropped slogans and cigarette butts. He couldn't know until he went there, and going there might be both dangerous and pointless.

Bloody Freddie. A few hours ago, Fischer had only a few ailing clocks, a sparse lunch, and, hopefully, the odd sale to ponder: a peaceful schedule coloured only by a little sadness whenever Frau Siebert's brutal death came to mind. The rest was now under armistice - his wife's passing, the world as it presently was, the prospects afforded to a war veteran well into middle-age – all of them wrapped now in the soul's blanket, deadening what had once kept him from sound sleep and waking peace. A physician might have called it all half-anaesthetized rather than healed, but he was content with that - that, and the steady predictability of a life finally dialled to mundanity.

And now he was where he shouldn't be once more, a familiar sense of looming disaster returned from its long holiday. He loved Holleman every bit as much as he would an irritating brother, but he often came as would a well-filled, loosely-aimed chamber pot, its most liberal daubings reserved for those closest to him. Were it possible to turn back time it might have been wiser to hand him over to Germany's enemies at the start of the last war, and have him blow up in their faces instead.

He sighed, rubbed his face and turned to Kleiber. 'We have to find some police.'

'Why?'

'So I can get arrested.'

25

As always, Pankov's handwriting was beautifully regular, a pleasure to read. It certainly wasn't the message's legibility or lack of it that confused Voloshyn. He handed back the paper.

'What do you make of it?'

His adjutant frowned. 'It's … difficult to say. Perhaps the situation's becoming worse.'

Ostensibly, message's content was clear enough, though it had no relevance to Voloshyn and his men. It contained no orders for them – in fact, no orders whatsoever. It stated simply that four Red Army soldiers had been arrested over the course of the past hour for refusing to fire upon demonstrators. It was a warning: to no-one in particular and to every Soviet formation involved in the pacification of Berlin and other German cities today.

He had departed his base that morning with orders to avoid killing strikers if at all feasible, but the meaning of *feasible* seemed now to be in question. His initial assumption had been that deadly force was only to be used if his men were threatened physically, yet the message implied that the threat was considered rather to be to Soviet authority. It was understandable, of course. The last thing that Comrades Semyonov and Grechko would want was for their men to display any hint of sympathy for the protesters' cause – to give them a Potemkin moment that the Allied media could milk like a prize herd.

This changed things. He was in the process of deploying his men in six units, each column led by a tank, to cover all east-west axes from Holzmarktstrasse northwards to Mollstrasse as they advanced westwards to converge on Molkenmarkt. Having given orders that unarmed civilians were not to be shot at will or whim, he could be reasonably confident that no incident occurring out of sight of his command car would escalate to something unmanageable. But if he now told his men to put one in a few of the noisier protesters to set an example to the rest he might have half a dozen little wars on his hands and lack the means to prevent them becoming bigger ones. He had been here in 1945 with 1st Ukrainian Army, moving slowly through the rubble-scape, flushing out the last forlorn hopes, and recalled how difficult it had been then for senior officers to exert tactical control. Left to themselves, individual units had made their own policy on taking prisoners, depending on how much shit they'd had to face already that day. He didn't consider himself excessively sentimental for not wanting to repeat the experience.

Of the two majors he had with him, he trusted one not to allow over-reactions. The other he wasn't too sure about. Even his name – Suvorov – conjured too vivid an image of how the man might react to what he considered to be adequate provocation. In any case, both of them would need to rely too much upon their junior officers, none of whose minds he could read or tempers judge. It therefore required that Voloshyn … what? He turned to his adjutant.

'Are the marksmen allocated to each of the six columns, Ivan Petrovich?'

'They are, Comrade *Podpolkovnik.*'

'And their officers understand the use to which they'll be put?'

'Perfectly. I distributed orders in writing.'

'Good. Ammunition?'

'Sixty rounds per man. Forty to the marksmen.'

'God forbid it isn't enough. The tank commanders know not to put one in the breech unless instructed?'

'They do, Comrade *Podpolkovnik.*'

Even to think of it turned his stomach over. He couldn't draw in his deployments sufficiently to monitor them effectively without leaving large holes. But to leave them to their own initiative … he didn't want to be the means, however indirectly, of making more orphans, not when his tally was already greater than a soul should bear. It left him with the single option: to pretend that he hadn't seen the message; to continue as before, leaning upon the hopeful assumption that crowds confronted by Soviet personnel would disperse rather than be willing to take casualties in the name of looser work quotas.

He was about to give his adjutant the bad news when a burst of static from the radio car dragged the man back to it as if a rubber band connected them. This message was longer, and Pankov's careful script slowed things; Voloshyn was agitated already, and the pause almost made him forget his carefully-pretended insouciance, hurl himself across the road and snatch the damn thing from the man's hands. He breathed deeply, and counted the vehicles in that part of his command remaining on Lichtenbergerstrasse.

Pankov's face said almost everything he needed to know. 'Tell me.'

'Demonstrators have concentrated at several points. The situation is bad. Two district police stations have been burned out, Gedenkstätte's been stormed and prisoners released and official paperwork has been thrown onto bonfires. SED officials are being attacked in the streets, and some have been hospitalized. Our first objectives are Molkenmarkt and then Monbijouplatz. Orders are to move forward immediately, connecting our right wing to the left of units from 144th Motor Rifle, to disperse anti-social elements.'

'Who's commanding the 144th group?'

Pankov fumbled in his pocket for his notes from the early morning briefing. '*Polkovnik* Geladze: Anikoloz Geladze. Do you know him?'

'No' Voloshyn swore to himself. He was outranked, and therefore had to move quickly. 'Contact him. Tell him that out right wing is already extended along Holzmarktstrasse towards Molkenmarkt.

Suggest that we take responsibility for the first objective while our right wing and his group push directly west. Then, tell our column deployed on Schillingstrasse to move steadily once they've joined with the 144th, taking care not to allow protesters to infiltrate through side streets as they advance.'

'That will slow them.'

'Possibly. But we need to be thorough. Tell Major Suvorov that he's to be our liaison with Comrade Geladze. He's commanding out on the left; tell him to lead the Schillingstrasse column personally.'

Pankov stared at his notes. Voloshyn couldn't say whether graphology had any scientific basis, but his adjutant's passage through life's mine-field was as careful as his handwriting. He was good administrative staff, a man born for paperwork, as natural a fighting soldier as any priest or poet. Conscripted too late for war, this victorious peace was all he knew of Army life, and he seemed perfectly content with its mock military exercises and occasional review. Today, he looked out of balance, ruffled by more than the prospect of confrontation with a disgruntled proletariat. Voloshyn had said nothing to him that ignored or contradicted Karlshorst's orders, but it wasn't the Red Army way for a Lieutenant-Colonel to take the initiative in a potentially delicate operation, not when he could sit back and let a full Colonel shoulder the responsibility. Nor was it usual for an officer with hopes of advancement – or of treading water, even - to display symptoms of reticence when his orders contained the word *immediately*. Pankov wanted to ask questions, but that wasn't allowed. He probably wanted to be somewhere else entirely, and that was doubly out of the question.

'Pankov?'

'Yes, Comrade *Podpolkovnik?*'

'Get on with it. Tell the officers we're moving in five minutes.'

26

Hoeschler wanted to thank someone, profusely. He had felt himself losing consciousness, which meant that he had probably been about to die. *Someone* had found the balls to wade into a group of big bastards with bigger feet and extract him.

Curiously, no one seemed to want to take responsibility for it. He recognized them - they were the same four-man *VolksPolizei* patrol than had seen trouble coming and backed away from it, but the prospect of a colleague getting the shit kicked clean from his body had brought them back, and at some cost. There wasn't one of them who wasn't a sight fit for an admissions room – bruises, cuts and an eye that was already turning Imperial purple were proud badges of diligence, as were Hoeschler's bloodied assailants, encouraged back into their demonstration by heftily-swung *schlagstocks*. At least one of the victors should have been pumped up, eager to make the point that it was his idea, his initiative and his fitness for more than just pounding Berlin's streets that had delivered a superior officer from a hospital bed.

'Good job, lads. Who do I kiss?' Hoeschler did his best to make a face of it, but his head was doing tight, swift laps. It took some effort to focus, and when he managed it dizziness almost toppled him once more. One of the *anwärters* steadied him with a hand while he gulped air and tried to locate his balance.

'We didn't notice the fight, comrade. It was your mate who pointed you out and sent us in.'

'It wasn't a fight, believe me. Which mate?'

'The blond one, looks and talks like Stasi.' The *anwärter* glanced around. 'He's ... gone.'

Stasi. Hoeschler had heard it a couple of times at the station – newly-coined slang for an old problem, dressed up in slightly different clothes. He had no friends in *Staatssicherheitsdienst*, though at that moment he would gladly have made the man's acquaintance, bought him a drink and said nice things about whatever parts he hailed from. No doubt the euphoria would fade and his enthusiasm for the breed with it, but he knew of no rule that said guardian angels had to be decent types.

The crowd had almost gone by now, siphoned down Taubenstrasse without him having the faintest idea whether Kristin Holleman and Engi were with it. He had no more inspiration, no better notion than to go west, pick a crossing at random and wait there in the hope that they would appear magically. It was surrender, and he almost surrendered to it.

'Where are you based, comrade?'

The *anwärter* had his notebook out. Of course he did – an assault upon a man he believed to be a *kriminalkommissar* still needed to be reported. For a moment Hoeschler tensed, but even as it rang his head told him not to be stupid. He was gone, fled, or soon would be.

He could give them the full biography, and they were welcome to make of it what they wanted.

'Keibelstrasse.'

'Ah, top men.'

'You haven't been there, obviously. We have as many cocks as anyone else.'

The policeman grinned, flattered by the intimacy. 'We're based at Friedrichshain, the park station.'

'Nice location.'

'It's not bad. We used to have a lot of trouble with cigarette tsars, but that's dropped off a lot recently. And we had some child murders a few years back.'

'I remember that, in 47. A bad business.' Hoeschler could recall every detail of it, though he hadn't been involved – wasn't even police, at the time. But the 'murders' had been something else - just a tragedy, brought on for all the best reasons. Perhaps this fellow had heard only the polished version, the one about fearless *VolksPolizei* triumphing over depravity. Come to think of it, there hadn't been a Park station back then, only …

Hoeschler glanced at the policeman's mates. They were having a smoke, probably debating whether their battered faces and uniforms were a good enough reason to call an early end to the shift. He lowered his voice.

'Is your station on the telegraphic network?'

'Of course.'

'Can you use the nearest radio van to call in? I need to know if there's been an arrest.'

'Yes, comrade. Name?'

She wouldn't offer Beckendorp of course, and he doubted that she'd admit to Holleman either. It didn't matter; she was in the company of a teenage boy, and Hoeschler already knew precisely which name he'd give, if asked. It was one which could ring no bells whatsoever, yet in a crisis it would put up a small flare. He had agreed it with Engi long ago, when neither of them had trusted the world about them.

'Engelbrecht Preis. Aged approximately seventeen, red hair.'

'He's starting young.'

'Yes, a bad one. It's quite urgent.'

'Give me five minutes, comrade. Here.'

Hoeschler took the handkerchief and dabbed at his mouth while he waited. Gendarmenmarkt was emptier now than on normal days, when East Berliners ate their lunches here surrounded by more God and Culture than the rest of the city could hope to offer. Even with one of its two great churches half-wrecked it was a pleasant space, one that he had walked through often without ever appreciating. Gifted a second life, he took care now to give it a chance.

The dutiful *anwärter* returned within the promised five minutes. He was holding a piece of paper, but - to Hoeschler's relief - looked disappointed.

'No-one by that name, comrade. At least, he hasn't been processed yet. He could be in a van at the moment.'

'On his way to a prison?'

The other man pulled a face. 'Not today. What would be the point, if his mates or the guards freed him ten minutes later? No, we've been told to hold all arrests at one of five principal stations. Didn't you see the orders?'

'I didn't go in this morning.' Keibelstrasse would be one of those designated, and of the major East Berlin stations it stood closest to the *Neues Stadthaus*. The tiny distances and large odds frustrated him. If Kristin and Engi *had* been arrested he could almost have strolled to intercept the police van, waved his warrant card and extracted them, a manoeuvre requiring only preternatural powers of anticipation and timing, or the luck of his Uncle Karl, who never met a pack of cards or a horse that hadn't made money for him (unfortunately, luck and Karl had parted company somewhere on the long road to Ypres), or perhaps sight of his own giblets – a treat he'd been spared by the intervention of this lad, his mates and ...

The blond one. He had a saviour, and now that relief was fading he began to wonder, hard, who would expose himself to do that good turn. *Stasi* and *Volkspolizei* mixed like wine and bleach, so even had he recognized Hoeschler for who he was (or had been), would he have risked the crowd's mercies in the same stupid way the victim had done? If it wasn't that, he could think of only one possibility. He was being followed.

Beckendorp and he had discussed their defection on two occasions: the first a week earlier, and then again the previous evening. The past few weeks' turmoil within the Party, its clashes with the Kremlin, had convinced his boss that there was no future for him in the SED. For Hoeschler's part, his ties to the east were as flimsy as to anywhere else. He had a safe, reasonably well-paid job, but if the other Germany had opportunities he was ready to look for them. They hadn't argued about the principle of their betrayal.

Beckendorp had far more to lose, professionally and personally, so he wouldn't have spoken to anyone else - not even his family - until the last moment. Hoeschler hadn't told a soul, and taken care not to seem distracted or semi-detached at work over the past days. No one could have known before that morning, so how was it possible that he was being hunted already?

The answer occurred even before the question had fully formed in his head. The DDR had lost hundreds of thousands of its citizens over the past year, an exodus that constituted a rolling humiliation for Ulbricht and his administration. For the first time since the Ming

Dynasty, a barrier was being built to entirely separate a nation from its enemy – in this case, capitalism. It was as good as an admission that the other Germany was winning the battle for the affections of their common folk.

With the fence incomplete still the haemorrhage continued, the 'friendship' with the Soviet Union was looking increasingly like a chronic dependency; and now the SED, the sole legitimate authority, was set at its own throat. The last, bitter embarrassment would be a major defection – someone the West could hold up to the cameras and say *If this man ran, who wouldn't, given the chance?* Hoeschler had no illusions about his own worth, but Beckendorp? A senior SED official and one of the most senior policemen in East Berlin, a man long known for the cardinal socialist sin of cynicism – the prospect of his crossing the line would hurt like flame on a gouty foot.

Staatssicherheitsdienst weren't much yet, perhaps ten thousand fervent paranoiacs in search of an enemy; but they were breeding fast, a necessary foil to the inclination of people to think wrong thoughts. Beckendorp had crossed their precursors K-5, and enough of them had made the jump from one to the other for a race-memory to put down roots. The State could spare the manpower to keep its problem children in view.

But Beckendorp had left his house in uniform that morning, so it must have been Hoeschler, turning up at Gartenweg 16 with bag and boy, who had severed the trip-wire. Hell, it might not have required

Stasi personnel to be present – the street was practically an apparatchiks' colony, its many net curtains factory-set to *twitch*. What he had imagined was the opening phase of a subtle extraction could have been an unwitting public admission of guilt.

If he was correct – *if* he was correct – then finding Kristin would be the worst possible sort of success. It would lead *Stasi* to her husband, and they probably weren't intending to hit him with a lecture on betrayal. By the same token, Hoeschler couldn't just give up and save himself, hoping that she and Engi would come in their own time. Either course would deliver a traitor to a fate the Regime would publicize to the heavens. What better, cheaper way to quell a stampede of their own kind?

The Blond wasn't going to just step out and hold up his hands, and *VolksPolizei* hadn't yet added clairvoyance to its training programme. Absent an inconceivable piece of luck, Hoeschler wasn't going to find the man before he could do damage, which left a single, appalling option. He was going to have to re-write his own recent history.

The Good *Anwärter* stood patiently still, waiting for instructions or dismissal. Hoeschler patted his shoulder.

'I owe you lads a lot, but can I ask one last favour?'

'Certainly, comrade.'

'I need to clean up and report. Could your van give me a lift back to Keibelstrasse?'

27

When Mr Abernathy had departed to brief his superior, Zarubin was led to a much smaller office containing only a chair, desk and typewriter. Once alone, he opened his small briefcase and removed the intelligence report. Contrary to what he had told the assistant station chief the product was entirely complete, even to the exuberant signature above his name. All it now required was the most important ingredient of all - immutability.

He took the time to re-read his work carefully, to satisfy himself that its many inaccuracies rang true, or at least held their own against flashes of reason. Even so, he wouldn't have dared submit it to an organization that had more than a rudimentary understanding of Kremlin politics.

Actually, that wasn't quite true. His fastidious nature that had refined the paper's content to a point at which it had come to be almost convincing, thoughtful shit. It didn't hurt to *go the extra mile*, as the Americans would say; after all, it would almost certainly be examined to its minutest detail afterwards, and he wanted them to think well of his abilities even as they considered sending assassins to track him down.

After the second re-reading it took an effort not to go looking for someone, but he diverted himself with thoughts of Maxim Shpak, ploughing his Pennsylvanian fields, throwing up the occasional barn, milking his cows, and, given a spare five minutes' loose time, impregnating his willing young wife. The prospect might have been more attractive had not the delightful irony of it all pressed so strongly. Shpak's career in Soviet Intelligence had fitted him as a frock would a bear, his lack of viciousness and guile an affront to the sacred task of thrusting knives into backs, fronts and faces. All logic said that he should have found a firing post, or a posting so far from Moscow and civilization that not even goats would notice his passing. Instead, he had leapt entirely from the present, ugly world into a different sort of oblivion, a cocoon of safety among souls for whom a flushing toilet represented depraved indulgence.

Half an hour passed, and idle thoughts of the farming life had begun to drift towards structural alterations that might have transformed that damn plain church into a fine country residence when the office door opened and the young fellow he had earlier mistaken for a schoolboy entered. Zarubin frowned (as if the disturbance had distracted him from vital geo-political considerations) and lifted his report from the desk.

'This is urgent. Two copies are to be made immediately, one for the Director in Washington and another for your Station Chief. Please don't staple those or the original until I've had the opportunity to ensure that the copies are good and the pages are in their correct order. All three must be stamped *Most Secret* and franked by the Station Clerk. Thank you.'

The young man disappeared with admirable promptness. Zarubin sat back and stared at the wall in front of him. It was bare except for a barely discernible (and certainly unintended) interruption of the dark cream decor caused by a careless painter who had overladen his brush at some points and starved it at others. It was mildly distracting to find shapes and likenesses in the several irregular patches, and Zarubin badly needed to be distracted. It was all that was keeping his heart from exploding through his rib-cage.

His unofficial secretary returned in less than twenty minutes, with a pile of paper (stacked into three sections) and an office stapler. Zarubin nodded his thanks in the manner that tells someone to bugger off without quite offending, and when the door had closed and the footsteps receded, opened his briefcase and removed a single sheet of paper. Separating the original report from the two copies he extracted its concluding page and inserted the other, which bore a different name but equally illegible signature. He stapled each of the three copies (without checking either the quality or order of their pages), placed the two photocopies side by side on the desk and the original with its orphaned sheet into the briefcase.

His heartbeat had slowed slightly, but only because the next part required that he move, and the mechanics of moving distracted the mind from consequences slightly. Still, it was difficult not to be overly cautious - to open the door slowly and peer timidly through a half-centimetre crack into this little piece of American Berlin. Instead, after forcing himself to breathe deeply several times he strode confidently out of the office, down the corridor and into the small general office. At the desk nearest to the door a male typist clattered busily, his eyes on a document to his side. Zarubin walked up to him, coughed and smiled pleasantly.

'Would you let Me Abernathy know that I've left the report and a copy in room 36, please?'

The man looked up. For a moment he frowned as his head went from one mundane thing to another, but the pause gave him the cue to lift a half-smoked cigarette from an ashtray by his side. He returned the smile and nodded.

'Thank you.'

He purposely hadn't said goodbye, because when Abernathy, or his secretary, or whoever was in charge of security began their frantic searches he didn't want the man to be able to say whether Sergei Aleksandrovich Zarubin had left the building. It would slow things a little, and things most definitely needed to be slowed – not least because this was going to be the most measured, nonchalant flight he could manage.

Briefly, he visited the men's room, and then, wishing good morning to each (thankfully preoccupied) member of the Station staff he encountered in the corridor and stairwell, descended to the reception area on the ground floor. As when he had entered the building earlier, two US Marines flanked the narrow wooden stile through which all personnel were required to pass when entering or leaving the premises. He placed his briefcase on the small table next to it and waited while the larger specimen examined it. The book he extracted was Wouk's *The Caine Mutiny*, and the frown suggested that he disapproved strongly. It being many of his compatriots' read-of-the-month he had no grounds for objection, however, and as the case contained no other items it was returned within seconds. Zarubin nodded his thanks and walked out on to Föhrenweg.

West Berlin bus services leading away from the demarcation line were still running, and he had to wait no more than five minutes at the first halt he came to. Disembarking at Steglitz station, he showed an address to an elderly man and was directed to the correct bay. After that, he needed only to ask the driver of the second bus to let him off at the halt closest to the address. The report he had already transferred from beneath his shirt and back into the briefcase, and he allowed himself to sit back and relax as the service negotiated streams of people marching north-eastwards, all with the increasingly vain hope of crossing the line to show solidarity with the striking workers.

It had worked, all of it, as he had hoped. A few years ago he might have congratulated himself and added a further centimetre's worth of mortar to the edifice of his self-regard, but exile in a strange land works on a man's self-confidence. He had been scared – scared of missing something, scared of chance, scared that he wouldn't summon the courage to turn *what if* into *when*, and *how*. And now that he had done so without apparent cost he felt only a small measure of relief, the chemical release that comes when one expects the worst and gets something less.

Of course, the *worst* wouldn't have been quite that. He imagined that US prisons were terrible places, over-stocked with bad people who would be happy to express their patriotism in quite unpleasant ways. Yet having now succeeded in avoiding that fate he faced an even more brutal prospect, and he needed no imagination whatsoever to see it clearly. Perversely, this clarity was what anaesthetized the fear, if only for the moment. For the first time in a long while, he could see the path ahead with some degree of certainty. It had very few likely detours, though quite an abundance of thorns.

The bus slowed, the driver turned and shouted 'hoy!' and Zarubin stood up. The halt was so close to his destination that for a few moments after alighting he remained there, not wanting a casual backward glance to give him away. It was prudent, perhaps too much so. The street was quite empty, and if any curtains were being pulled back he couldn't see them. He walked up to the door and knocked smartly.

It opened almost too quickly. Surprised, he took a step back, and his mouth dropped open. He hadn't spoken his native tongue for some years now (except to his typewriter, to Maxim Shpak or to poor Yuri Sheremenko), and didn't realise that he was doing it now.

'Fuck your mother! How…?'

The other man didn't speak for the moment. His own surprise seemed greater still, but it was tinged (and quickly became more so) with something else, something close to anger. He thrust forward a large hand, grabbed an expensive lapel and dragged Zarubin inside.

'Christ on the water!'

28

Fischer's previous experience of law enforcement in what was now the DDR had led him to believe that it would be easier than this. He had assumed that approaching and admitting to a *VoPo* patrolman – on today of all days - that he was a *wessie* would have done the job, but the ones they had encountered all had other business on their minds. The first one had shrugged and told him to fuck off (though not with any real heat in it); the second had taken a minute to lecture him on the irresponsibility of adding to what was already an extremely difficult situation, and then told him to fuck off; the third had informed him that there were far more pressing things to worry about than sightseers, and wished him a safe return to parts west.

Kleiber was using their latest pause to rub his wounded foot once more. 'Tell them you were Himmler's favourite back-door boy.'

'Is homosexuality an offence over here?'

'I've never thought to ask. I suspect it's the *Himmler* bit that would count.'

'They wouldn't believe it. Not this face.'

'A spy for the Americans, then.'

'I want to get arrested, not shot. Some minor infraction, that's all.'

'I still don't see why.'

They had reached the corner of Stralauerstrasse and Littenstrasse, just two short blocks east of the *Neues Stadthaus*. The occasional Colosseum-roar from that direction hinted either at trouble or an injury-time goal.

'Look, Kristin has been arrested, or she hasn't. She may yet be arrested, or she may not. If she hasn't or won't be, then fine, she'll cross to the west at some point today and the thing's done. But if she's arrested, we – I - need to know. I also need to know where she's been taken. The only way to do this is to have access to *VolksPolizei* records.'

'They'll do that, will, they? Book you in on the charge-sheet and then open their file-room door?'

'Don't be obtuse. I know one man – Albrecht Müller – in the East Berlin police force. We spoke on the 'phone about an hour ago. He might do me a favour and say what's happened. He can hardly do more than that.'

'But then you'll be in the shit. How does that help?'

'We'll know something, at least. And I can't see the majesty of socialist justice being wielded too savagely against a war-veteran clock-repairer with half a face. They'll probably kick my arse and dump me over the line this evening. You'd better get rid of the camera and notebook, though. They won't be too gentle with the capitalist Press.'

Kleiber shook his head. 'Bollocks. If you're arrested I want a record of it in case they try to disappear you. Just promise to give me your bad side.'

'I will if I can *get* arrested. Seriously, what might do it?'

'Shouting something wounding about Ulbricht.'

'I doubt that anyone in East Berlin's not doing that right now. They've probably suspended the offence for the day.'

'What about '*Socialism has failed! Come west, comrades, where we eat cake every day*?'

'Again, being able to go home afterwards would be preferable.'

Kleiber sighed. 'Well, I don't know, Otto. Police everywhere take objection to citizens waving their cocks in public places. Perhaps you could infiltrate the demonstrators' front-line, whip it out smartly and wink at whichever poor bastard gets the eyeful.'

'He might return the wink.'

'Yeah, there is that.'

Fischer scanned Stralauerstrasse to the west. 'Jonas, would you mind being arrested, too?'

'I would, though Herr Grabner would consider it a proper reporter's baptism. Why?'

'I'm rethinking the capitalist Press thing. We could be open about it - approach a policemen, tell him that we're both journalists and ask if we might have the official view on the current situation. You can show him your Press card.'

'He'd … arrest us.'

'Hopefully, yes. But doing it like that we could hardly be accused of subversion, or working to undermine the Regime. The DDR likes to pretend that its own Press is free, so they'd look bad if we get more than a slap, overnight administrative detention and a very public release the next day. With luck, they might even give us – you - a quote about how all of this is an Allied provocation.'

'And having me arrested too helps … how?'

'My brilliant plan relies on me not being recognized, but I've got an unforgettable face and too much history in this city. I may be unlucky, in which case I need you to get back and let Freddie know what we know, if anything. You *are* the Press, and you're too young to have built grudges.'

'I know a farmer in Lancashire who'd disagree with you.'

'Not the farmer's daughter cliché?'

Kleiber grinned. 'Thur's nowt else to do of an evenin' on t'moors.'

'I didn't get a word of that.'

'It was English, of a sort. What if the story doesn't work on the next one we come across? Can we go home?'

'No. We'll pick one who looks like he's having a bad day. Come on.'

'Otto, look.'

In front of them, Stralauerstrasse, which had been almost empty when they paused, was filling rapidly with humanity, all of it about twenty abreast. For a moment Fischer assumed that he and Kleiber were in the way of a march, but the men – and they were all men – didn't have the coordinated step or momentum of trouble pointing itself at something. Nor was anyone shouting, which, given the number and weight of grievances workers were bringing to Mitte today, seemed strange.

Kleiber was moving sideways, into Littenstrasse. 'Let's get out of their way.'

'You're a reporter, for God's sake. Go and ask them what they're doing.'

'Fuck. Hold the Contax, then.'

Kleiber removed his notebook and pen from a pocket and edged nervously forward. In less than a minute the head of the loose procession had reached him. The first man he spoke to tossed his head in a manner that Fischer hardly needed to interpret, but a second spoke out of the side of his mouth as the *Südwest-Berliner Zeitung*'s industrial relations correspondent shuffled along beside him. Carried by the flow almost as far east as Dircksenstrasse, his return journey was a crab-like flit around several hundred pairs of shoulders, all of them thicker-set than his own. At one point he stumbled, but several hands lifted him back upright and slapped him out of their way. To Fischer it seemed good-natured enough, though no less bruising for that.

When the intrepid correspondent had returned, he let him catch his breath. 'What's happening?'

'They're construction workers, from the Friedrichshain hospital site. They marched into Molkenmarkt, shouted their piece at the *Neues Stadthaus* and now they're going home.'

'To work?'

'No, to do more sitting-in. Their strike committee liaised with those from other industries, so everyone gets a chance to turn up here and have a go without causing congestion.'

Fischer was impressed. 'They sound well-organized.'

'Yeah. That fellow told me that most of his union's committee members are former *Wehrmacht*, and I assume the others are the same. People tend to trust ex-soldiers to get things done, don't ask me why.'

'He didn't know when the metal workers are turning up?'

'I asked, but he said not.'

'A pity.'

'Look, there's a patrol.'

Further up Littenstrasse, a small group of police were watching the flow of marchers. Two were smoking, while a third took his ease on a low wall and the fourth fingered his *schlagstock* with hopeless longing. It was this last one that interested Fischer. He looked as if hours of inaction were beginning to gnaw at his self-worth.

'He's our man. We'll ask his opinion of the situation, and whether he thinks the strikers have a point.'

'You don't think he'll use that stick on our heads?'

'Not if we seem earnest. Can you be earnest, Jonas?'

'I can be Lillian Gish, if it keeps me from a beating.'

29

Lieutenant Pankov's fondness for the DDR and its attractions survived the first fragment of brick lobbed at his head, but only just. His eyes had been on his commander (whose own eyes, more sensibly, had been upon the trajectories of several incoming projectiles), and he noticed it only when a centimetre of his scalp was scored by its passing. The wound was shallow, and, like most injuries that men of iron weren't allowed to notice, intensely painful.

'Ow! Fuck! I ... beg pardon, Comrade *Podpolkovnik.*'

Voloshyn was fairly certain that he had spotted the stone-thrower, but the man was surrounded by his workmates and couldn't be dragged out without a full platoon being committed. A fist-fight was the last thing this unlawful assembly needed - in any case, he wasn't quite sure that it *was* unlawful, the SED having made several quite contradictory statements regarding the validity of workers' grievances over the past few days.

'Move back, Lieutenant.'

Rubbing his head, Pankov re-joined the foremost of three ranks, deployed at forty-five degrees to the front of the vast neo-classical façade of the *Neues Stadthaus*. Voloshyn nodded at the major commanding the unit. A whistle blew briefly, and the rear line of soldiers lifted their rifles. The single volley hushed the cries of the crowd momentarily and forced it back into itself, a defensive ripple as the bullets passed harmlessly into the sky over Molkenmarkt. The major blew his whistle once more, and the front rank levelled their rifles directly at the protestors. As a hint, it lacked ambiguity.

For almost a minute the two sides, German and Soviet, stared at each other. Then, a few of the braver souls at the rear of the crowd restarted a badly-rhyming chant about workers' rights and Ulbricht's mother. With a better view of the ordnance, the group of stone-throwers at the front maintained their open-eyed innocence for a little longer, but within a minute rocks began to fly towards the *Neues Stadthaus'* lower storey windows. Voloshyn turned to the major and shook his head. He had no problem with damage to German property; in any case, the men that these people had come to insult were elsewhere by now, safe from the consequences of their bugger-ups.

A little while earlier those rocks might have found *VolksPolizei* heads on their way through, but the police cordon around the building had withdrawn when Voloshyn's men arrived, leaving the field clear for military units - as agreed, apparently, between the DDR Government and Soviet Control Commission. That was what continued to bother him, the *field* part. Logically, he should have deployed his men quickly in combat formation and cleared Molkenmarkt with two or three well-aimed volleys. A few dozen protesters would have died, about the same number dragged themselves to hospital and the rest – the majority – fled to their homes, changed their soiled underwear and never, ever again thought of doing anything similar. But his instructions complicated things. He wondered who it was at the Commission here in Berlin or at the Kremlin who wanted things done short of a sizeable body count – who, in effect, had replaced his size 46 Army boots with ballerinas' slippers.

That was his inner optimist, he decided. When had there ever been just the one dog in the pit of Soviet planning? The day's events had already hinted at a cast that could fill an apostles' table Why, if he was to proceed carefully, had news about soldiers arrested for refusing to fire on protesters been disseminated? And why, at that moment, was he hearing desultory gunfire to the north, just about where units from 144th Motor Rifle Division were similarly doing their bit for Soviet-German relations? He had been briefed that the SED hierarchy couldn't agree a strategy to deal with their irate masses; what if the Control Commission and Kremlin were similarly torn? He had no idea whether the decisions he made here would be considered correct, wrong, both (by different parties) or neither. As a loyal and effective member of the Red Army, he preferred to do what he was told, but today he was in the worst of places, gifted – cursed with – a degree of latitude in a situation where initiative might be fatal.

He wanted desperately to talk about it, but he had only Pankov and the other officers of 248th Motor Rifle Regiment. A six months' peacetime acquaintance didn't bring nearly enough intimacy to risk expressing an honest opinion, particularly if it didn't turn out to be entirely the right one. And he had recognized the expression on Pankov's face whenever he asked *what next* – the guarded, correct sort of look that a man practises when requesting orders from a man he'd diagnosed as going places he'd rather not see. In Pankov's boots, he too would have wanted them to put distance between himself and such a wretch.

It was in moments like this that Russians prefer their vodka at metal-scouring strength, but Voloshyn was that rarest sub-species of his race, a teetotaller. A keen, sober mind was an excellent tool with which to plot the right course, and to suffer the full sharpness of it turning out not to be. He was proud that he had been considered competent to deal with such a delicate matter; but a glance into the cold tunnel of recent history gave him a clear view of what happened when powerful men's trust was found to be misplaced. He thought enviously of his fellow regimental commanders back at Schönebeck, who would be putting on an almost convincing display of frustration, cursing their poor luck not to have been chosen for this mission. He would gladly have wished any one of them here, and he there.

He looked out into the crowd. It almost filled Molkenmarkt, but he had already sensed its lack of fervour, the death-wish that would have forced him to make a decision. It was beginning to thin already, to dissolve from its rear extremities around the Nikolaikirche; but his lookouts on the *Stadthaus* roof had confirmed that a new set of protesters was advancing towards them down Grunerstrasse, along the flank of the north-south perimeter created by the 144th and 248th.

It might be the final wave, or it might be only the first of a dozen more; and each time he did nothing his inaction would be taken for impotence, never restraint.

He turned and hooked a finger at Pankov, who was having a field-dressing applied to his head. The lieutenant scurried over, trailing an unsecured bandage.

'Your orders, Comrade *Podpolkovnik*?'

'The Regiment hasn't had riot-control training?'

'No, Comrade.'

'Well, there's nothing like practice. I want six squads, twenty men in each, in front of the *Stadthaus*. Place three tanks, supported by a heavy machine-gun unit, to their right – I want them to be the first thing that protesters see as they enter Molkenmarkt from Grunerstrasse. The rest of the regiment will deploy at right-angles to the front of the building - that will put them on the flank of the crowd as they face it. It'll also allow us to move to block the Mühlendamm if more protesters try to cross the Spree from the south.'

Pankov was scribbling in his notebook. 'Understood. The squads …?'

'We brought staves in the personnel carriers - arm them with those. From now on, stone-throwers at the front of the crowds are to be identified, pulled out and arrested immediately. If a few heads have to be broken in the process, fine; that should deter anyone who's thinking of joining the party. If it doesn't, the flanking troops will fire high, but only just – make them think we're trying to part their hair. Alright?'

The question was quite unnecessary, given that the Red Army had long since decided that discretionary lines of commands were bad ideas, but Pankov was familiar with his commander's curious way of putting things.

'Yes, Comrade *Podpolkovnik*. No killing unless we absolutely need to. Haircuts are permissible.'

Surprised, Voloshyn glanced at his adjutant. Pankov wasn't known to have a sense of humour; perhaps the blow to his head had loosened something and allowed the absurdity of their situation to shine through. Killing Germans was all they'd been taught, and now they were to think of it as a possibly good, possibly bad, possibly necessary-but-regrettable thing. Half a kilometre to the north, Colonel Geladze and his 144th were facing the same conundrum, and the fact that he hadn't yet tried to direct or even coordinate his efforts with the 248th suggested that he was similarly confounded by it. It might be that across the entirety of the DDR, Soviet commanders were trying at that moment to second-guess what their leaders were thinking, if anything. So perhaps Pankov was suffering the effects of perception rather than concussion. The situation – insofar as anyone could understand it - was enough to make a dog laugh, or hide.

'Tell the squad leaders ...' Voloshyn paused. He had been about to urge caution, but that was ridiculous. They had some sort of a fight on their hands now, however the many authors of today's standing orders wanted things to fall out. The best they could do now was hope to keep the bodies from piling inconveniently.

'Tell them that the squad making the most arrests for the fewest fatalities gets a crate of the Purveyance Board's finest.'

30

His capacity for novelty having been tested sorely that day, Freddie Holleman could think of no combination of circumstances that might have put this man here, now, in front of him. The question, therefore, didn't do justice to the fine investigative mind behind it.

'How the sweet fuck are you here?'

The other man glanced down at his lapel, frowned and carefully smoothed out the crease that a large, tightly squeezed hand had inflicted. Being a particularly fine wool-silk mixture, the cloth responded well.

'The number twelve bus. Before that, the Schöneberg – Steglitz service. I'm afraid I didn't notice its route number. Hello, Inspector.'

'I'm not, anymore. Not since this morning.'

'Ah. Hence your presence in this other country. I assume that Comrade Beckendorp has been laid to rest with his career?'

'Yes. I don't know what to call you. Will Major do?'

Zarubin shrugged and glanced around 'I don't mind. Where's Herr Fischer?'

Holleman was about to deny everything, but *Fischer's Time-piece Repairs* above the door had rather done for that strategy. 'Out, at the moment.'

'Is he likely to be long, do you think?'

'He ... might be. Shall I take a message?'

The delicacy of the conversation was becoming farcical. Each man knew enough about the other to have him executed at least twice, yet neither had the power to effect it. Having much the coarser temperament, Holleman felt his impotence more keenly and broke first.

'How the hell did you find him?'

'You're aware that I work for the CIA?'

'I expected so. It isn't as if you had much choice.'

'Well, I was able to utilize the might of US Intelligence.'

'How?'

'By 'phoning Camp Grohn in Bremen, requesting the number for *West Side Records*, calling Adolph Kuhn and asking where I might find our old friend Otto Fischer.'

'He just *told* you?'

'Why shouldn't he? I was enjoying my new life far away in America, so there was no risk. Perhaps he assumed I was having sentimental thoughts for our desperate days back in Stettin.'

'Christ! What do you want with Otto?'

Zarubin's eyebrows rose. 'Nothing at all.'

'Then …'

'It's here, this place. *This* is what I want.' His hand swept the panorama of shabby walls, untidy benches planted haphazardly on the pitted and scoured wooden floor, the spilled watchmakers' tools and thin display of repaired clocks.

Holleman considered the siren lure of a dead-end business for a moment only. 'A hiding place?'

'Where no-one would ever think to find me. For a few days only, until I can arrange passage.'

'To where?'

'Ah.' Zarubin smiled and said nothing more. It was a familiar smile, one that any reasonable man would want to wipe with a fist, and for Holleman the feeling returned now like a lost friend. It made giving the bad news that much more satisfying.

'But *I'm* here. That changes things.'

'It doesn't matter. I doubt that you'll be advertising the fact.'

'What *I'll* do isn't the point. Everyone at Keibelstrasse must have been told by now that I'm a traitor, and at least one of them knows that Otto's a good friend. He might not think to make the connection, but then again he might. They'd have to trace this address of course, and that will take time. Hopefully I'll be gone by this evening, but an MfS squad may find their way here in the next day or two. I suppose a previously-defected MGB Major would count as compensation, of sorts. Your old bosses at Karlshorst would certainly think so. Oh, and there'll be a Gehlen Org man returning for me soon.'

The smile died slowly. 'That's all … unfortunate.'

'You chose a bad day.'

'It rather chose me. I was brought to Berlin to advise on what the Soviet reaction to the workers' unrest might be. Until now, I'd thought it a happy coincidence of my plans and the CIA's needs.'

'You'll have to improvise.'

Zarubin pulled a face. 'You mean stumble forward blindly, hoping for the best? No, thank you. I have too many bear-traps to avoid.'

The shock of seeing his old boss was fading, and Holleman began to think about what it meant. 'This city's a dangerous place - the scene of your crimes, so to speak. Whatever you're doing, why do it here?'

'Actually, it's probably one of the safest places in Europe, if only for today. Everyone who's likely to recall me has plenty to deal with already. Where better to hide, than in a monstrous shit-slide?'

'And tomorrow?'

'Tomorrow, or very soon, I need to make a decision.'

'About what?'

'About who'll want me dead the least.'

'Then I take it the defector's life's not what you hoped for?'

'America is America. You either fall enraptured into the life or you don't.'

'What persuades you that you haven't?'

Zarubin pursed his lips and examined the floor's rough grain. 'It's hard to put into words. Perhaps it would have been easier if I'd fled oppression, or starvation, or had a family to provide for. The US is a land of immense opportunity, no doubt about that.'

'I can hear a *but*.'

'It isn't a society that welcomes nostalgia. Immigrants are accepted almost without reservation, but the price is surrender.'

'All societies require conformity.'

'That isn't enough. One has to *believe* in the American Way; the alternative is to be a drop of oil in a great expanse of water, carried along but never belonging.'

'You never belonged much to anything.'

The Russian laughed. 'I thought it would be an advantage in a new life. It turned out to be anything but.'

Holleman's head was too full of its own business to be sharp today, but the implication of what he was hearing finally penetrated. 'You're coming *all the way* back? Why? Why not go to … fuck, anywhere that neither the Americans nor Soviets can touch you?'

'I miss what's usual. Siam or Patagonia wouldn't fill that hole.'

'There isn't *anyone* among your own people who doesn't want you dead. It's their patriotic duty to fill another sort of hole with you.'

Zarubin nodded. 'It's a risk - alright, a strong possibility. Whether it happens is down to what I can bring home with me.'

'You have American secrets?'

'No, something better.'

'Bullion? A formula for enlarging cocks?'

'A tissue of lies, very carefully wrapped.'

Holleman shook his head. 'Lies can be found out. And then you're cacked.'

'Not these. Or rather, if they are it doesn't matter. It's the timing that's critical.'

'How?'

'Better that I don't say, for the same reason that I don't want to know too much about *your* business - in case one of us doesn't get out of Berlin. Now, for the love of God, would you know where Herr Fischer keeps his tea?'

31

Even considering his short but sanguinary career with *Fallschirmjäger* 1 Regiment, and the subsequent interlude as a puppet of Soviet Intelligence, Hoeschler wondered if this was the most courageous or stupidest thing that he had ever attempted. It stood or fell upon a single precaution he had taken soon after dawn that morning, and for which he had mocked himself as a coward, or at best a belt-and-bracer.

Keibelstrasse's front desk officer this shift was *wachtmeister* Melchior Cordt, an imminent retiree whose skills as a policeman extended to, but no further than, an encyclopaedic knowledge of *VolksPolizei*'s official football team (though even this faculty had been dulled by disgust at its recent name change to BFC Dynamo). Today, he looked preoccupied - upset almost, which for a man hoping for distractions might be good or bad. Hoeschler took two deep breaths to steady himself and walked up to the desk.

'Hello, Mel. What a business, eh?'

Cordt's mouth dropped open at the prospect of this apparition. After a few moments his hand began to move glacially towards the telephone, as if he was dreading the moment it made contact. Hoeschler gave him the slightly quizzical look of a man who had done no wrong.

'What's the matter?'

'N … othing. Just a minute.'

Cordt lifted the receiver, dialled three numbers and placed his other hand over his mouth as he whispered into the receiver, a performance that would have shamed a first-time extra in a crowd scene. Hoeschler's role as an oblivious innocent required only that he keep the slightly idiotic expression on his face, and then allow it to shade subtly to exasperation while he waited for what he knew perfectly well was coming.

It arrived within three minutes, gang-handed, down the main stairs - Beckendorp's immediate subordinate, *VP-Kommandeur* Petersen, and three junior officers, all looking like they'd drawn straws to drag a lucky winner to the scaffold. In a moment Hoeschler was surrounded, and it took no effort to give them a sense that he had started to feel very bad about how the day was going.

He was bundled into the ground floor's only interrogation room and pushed into a seat. Petersen, his face a dying camp-fire hue, leaned on the table directly in front of him.

'Where is he?'

'Where's who, Comrade?'

'Don't be obtuse. Beckendorp – where is he?'

Hoeschler glanced around, trying to glean some revelation from the grim stares that surrounded him. 'In his office? The House of Ministries? What's happening?'

'You're saying that you've not been with him today?'

'I haven't seen him since … yesterday afternoon I think, when he and the other Party men went out to calm the construction workers. Why?'

It convinced none of them, as he'd expected. He was known to be the fled man's closest friend at Keibelstrasse – taken on by him, in fact, without any of the formal recruitment procedures that other police were obliged to endure. They had no reason trust him, particularly as he was almost six hours late for his shift.

'Where have you been? All leave and training was cancelled yesterday, you knew that. Why are you in that state? And where's your uniform?'

'I *did* know, Comrade Commander. But my boy was sick, I had to get him to the doctor. I called in this morning at about 6am, and told the duty *meister* that I'd be here as soon as I could. I didn't take the time to return home for my uniform, given the circumstances of the day. My *state* is due to some demonstrators I came across who decided they didn't like *VolksPolizei*. I shouldn't have waved my warrant card.'

'Check that the call was registered.'

One of the junior officers left the room. Petersen's scowl hadn't moved an inch. 'When we cancel leave and everything else, it means just that. You should have been here at dawn.'

Hoeschler had hoped desperately that the far lesser crime of dereliction might be noticed. Petersen was a by-the-book man, someone whose domestic life was a necessary intrusion. His sort could be pushed, goaded into distraction.

'I know, Comrade. But my son was ill, and, with respect, this is just a job.' He said it cockily, which wasn't difficult, because if Engi *had* been sick he might well have punched off the mouth that implied it was of no concern. He had the satisfaction of seeing Petersen pale slightly, but before the conversation could brew further the officer returned to the interrogation room.

'He called in. It was logged at 6.07.'

For several seconds, four *VolksPolizei* officers glowered at the errant fifth, who returned it with interest. In that faintly absurd impasse, Hoeschler examined the logic he didn't trust once more. They could have no proof that he knew of Beckendorp's flight – it was hardly likely that a man contemplating the ultimate betrayal would have chatted about it to a friend beforehand. If Hoeschler was a collaborator he would have run too; but here he was, walking into Keibelstrasse like it was (almost) any other day. They might have suspicions but his story was sound, and if they wanted the doctor's telephone number to further check the truth about Engi's malady, that was fine – he doubted very much that the Soviets would reopen East Berlin's civilian exchanges just for them.

He waited, holding his breath until Petersen scratched his head and gestured at him. 'We can't deal with crap like this today. *Kommissar* Hoeschler!'

'Yes, Comrade?'

'You'll remain in the building until we can speak again. Don't even think of leaving without permission, however ill your son is.' He turned to one of the other officers. '*Kommissar* Müller will answer for him. At least *he's* proved his loyalty beyond question.'

'Excuse me, Comrade?'

'What is it?'

Hoeschler paused, though this was the part he was most likely to enjoy for its own sake.

'May I ask something?'

'Can you be brief?'

'Yes. What's all this about Inspector Beckendorp? Has he done something wrong?'

Petersen's face went through the spectrum once more. 'He's … gone west.'

Hoeschler reprised the wide-mouthed performance he'd given *wachtmeister* Cordt. 'Surely not?'

His superior's mouth, in contrast, parted only so far as to spit out what must have been poisoning him. 'He's admitted it. In a letter, to *VolksPolizei*-President Schmidt.'

'Shit! You just can't tell with some people.'

Any response to this wise observation was interrupted by a thunderous knock on the interrogation room door. An *anwärter* lumbered into the room, thrust a paper into Petersen's hand and saluted clumsily. 'Comrade Inspector, a message from a colonel of Soviet troops.'

Inspector. They hadn't waited until Beckendorp had gone cold in their hearts.

'Which colonel? What unit?'

'I … didn't ask, sir. He said he had prisoners, and wanted to know where he could put them.'

Petersen glanced at his junior officers. To Hoeschler they seemed to share something … he would have called it a sort of wariness, or apprehension, but that didn't make sense. The Soviets were making arrests, doing *VolksPolizei*'s work for them, taking the blame for whatever excesses were seen to be necessary. If the men at Keibelstrasse were required to do no more than arrange the secure accommodation, what was there to be worried about? He would have called it dodging the falling brick.

Petersen swallowed visibly and straightened up. 'Tell him that we don't have room for them. Our cells are taken. Give him a list of the other stations that have the facilities. He should try those. If he argues, refer him to VP-President Schmidt … no, to the Soviet Control Commission.'

Hoeschler had been absent without leave for several hours, now – a would-be traitor, though they didn't yet know it. He couldn't therefore know what had been happening here and elsewhere in East Berlin since dawn; but if the cells were full, someone had been busy. The previous evening he had seen the duty sheet before leaving for home. Then, they had hosted their usual complement of cockroaches, mice droppings, lavish fixtures and a grand total of three human souls, one of whom was due to be released under caution about an hour later. If they were now all 'taken', between forty and fifty further citizens had become guests of the state in the intervening hours. However lethargic the response of other *VolksPolizei* units to the day's upheavals, Keibelstrasse at least was pulling its weight, and some of that effort might have swept up Kristin and Engi. He needed to see an arrest list. If it contained bad news, he needed to conceive the means of getting them out and across the line before someone put a face with a name. Above all, he needed to start thinking beyond the moment.

That morning, staring down at his splayed uniform, he had imagined all of what might go wrong. *This* had been first in line - the disaster, the worst of all possible worlds (other than a bare, unimaginative vision of himself, Engi and Kristin lying on the line itself, riddled by police ordnance), and now he was inhabiting it, but not alone. He was to have the company of Albrecht Müller, a decent bloke whose career, if this situation could be rescued, might be caught in the crossfire. The potentially disastrous twist was that he was one of the few men working at Keibelstrasse who had met Kristin Holleman – or rather, Frau Beckendorp. A man's loyalties could only be tested so far before something gave, and Hoeschler was about to turn the rack's wheel.

Petersen had him escorted to the fourth floor, the Criminal Investigations Department. Between the interrogation room and there, the corridors echoed as if it were 2am in one of the less popular attractions on Museum Island. He saw plenty of his colleagues, but they were sitting at their desks waiting, hardly speaking to each other. There wouldn't have been much for them to do today in any case – industrial disputes weren't the natural habitat of criminal investigators – but a mood hung as heavily as sodden curtains. They had lost control of their city, either to the protesters or the fraternal comrades who pretended not to be occupiers, and a fading reality had re-impressed itself. For years now they'd been allowed to pretend that things were improving, slowly but gradually; that having a German government meant something. But the Soviet Control Commission was called that for a reason, and today they were being reminded of it.

Müller was at his desk, looking about as gay and carefree as everyone else. His eyebrows rose when he saw Hoeschler, and they were fixed in that elevation when one of Petersen's men, an *Oberrat*, gave him his instructions regarding the not-quite-prisoner. It wasn't his way to argue with Authority, and he didn't try now. In fact, all the officer got for his trouble was a mute nod and a good view of a chewed lip.

When he had gone, Müller examined his colleague as if he wore his lawyer's robes once more, and was having a first view of the cannibal-rapist he'd been appointed to defend.

'What's going on, Rolf?'

'Nothing, mate. I took my lad to the doctor's this morning, but everyone seems to be jumpier than a punishment battalion today. I don't think Petersen believes me.'

'You've heard about Beckendorp?'

'Yeah.'

'It's hard to believe. He called me this morning before the lines died, from West Berlin. When I asked about it, he just admitted that he'd defected. All those years, we never knew him.'

'It's all to shit, then?'

'It is. They've made Petersen head of Criminal Investigations, pending confirmation from Schmidt. Things will be different now.'

'They will. The man's never looked sideways at a rule, much less bent one.'

Müller almost smiled. 'I don't think Beckendorp ever met one that he didn't try to bugger. Still, he was good police. I wish he hadn't run.'

Hoeschler was almost beginning to wish the same. He felt no connection to East Berlin, no love for Ulbricht's brand of socialism or the ever-present press of Soviet power; but he could have lived in peace with all of them, if it were just a matter of himself alone. But Engi made it complicated. His life had been so blasted by war and loss that he deserved more than just the necessary minimums – at least, his surrogate father entertained the same vague hopes for a son that any biological parent might. He had lived through Weimar, so he didn't swallow the pap about capitalism's glorious bounty, much less the American promise of riches for everyone who made the effort; he just wanted Engi to be able to take his time, make his own choices and see a bit of the world, even if at the end of it he came straight back to what he was most familiar with. In the old days, Germans used to see the world, and not always with the intention of spoiling it.

But this wasn't what he'd expected when he tied himself to the Beckendorp exodus. Living in a socialist paradise was far preferable to dying prematurely on the road to capitalist heaven. *What ifs* were for fools, but he couldn't help thinking that if he had called in sick the day before and taken Engi out to Müggelsee for a swim and picnic, he'd be sitting here now with Müller, shaking his head, pretending not to believe the news, and his present life's passages – grey, mundane but safe still – would have carried on almost as before.

Müller was staring at him, trying to glean the truth about what he'd heard. Hoeschler knew that he couldn't just repeat the story he'd given Petersen; they knew each other and Beckendorp too well. He shrugged.

'I'm sorry, Albi, I lied. He told me, yesterday, that he was going. I didn't waste breath trying to argue him out of it. And I couldn't betray him, you know that.'

'But *why*?'

'He wouldn't say. It's probably the politics. He's on the wrong side of the SED, seen some of his friends fall recently. A man can get jumpy about things like that.'

'Christ!' Müller ran his fingers through his sparse hair. 'Why do sensible people get into politics? It's a fucking cesspit.'

'You know the truth about him, about who he really was. I don't think he had a choice back then, not in '45. They thought he was this great *kozi* streetfighter, it's why he got a job at all. Once the milk turns it's too late to do anything about it.'

'Yeah, you're right. Still …'

Hoeschler hated lying, hated the thought of what Müller would think of him when – if – he managed to find Engi and Kristin and get to the west. The man would probably understand, but that didn't make it any less a treachery. He forced himself to think of why he was here, how little time he had, how a man who was probably *Stasi* might have followed him to Keibelstrasse and even now be thinking of upending the tradition that MfS didn't talk to *Volkspolizei*. Hoeschler had put himself into the pit and doused himself with sauce - someone was going to notice, and probably sooner rather than later.

He tried to smile and seem casual about what he wanted desperately to know. 'Anyway, there's nothing we can do about him now. I hear you've been busy today.'

Müller looked up, surprised. 'Me? How?'

'No, I meant this place, the overflowing cells. You must have been pulling them in like mackerel.'

'What the hell are you talking about?

Hoeschler didn't doubt the sincerity he saw in Müller's face. The man was genuinely dumbfounded.

'Petersen … he refused a Soviet request to take in some prisoners. He said the cells were all taken.'

'That's bollocks.'

'What?'

'We had two men downstairs at midnight, a pickpocket and a wife-beater. They were going to be charged this morning, but someone ordered them released. Since then we've taken no-one. We've got more cells than any other station in East Berlin, and for the first time since I've been police we don't have a single guest. It's empty down there. On a day that the city's catching fire, we're doing nothing, nothing at all.'

32

'Is this what you had in mind?'

Fischer glanced at Kleiber, but the young man's face was guileless, without a hint of a smirk. Then again, incarceration isn't usually much cause for levity.

'No, not quite.'

They sat on a small bench in a cell in Station 19, a largish hamster cage in a by-no-means glorified shed, guests of a resident *wachtmeister* and two of the four policemen who had (after much debate) arrested them. The one with the twitching *schlagstock* glanced at them occasionally with a degree of satisfaction. His mate, by way of contrast, had the appearance of a man living a mistake.

Kleiber sighed. 'No, me neither.'

The *wachtmeister* was having another go at arguing the point. 'They can't stay here. Stations are being attacked, and there's only me. If there's trouble, I'm to call in, lock up and withdraw to Friedrichshain Park Station. I can't take them with me, can I?'

One of his colleagues shook his head firmly, but *Schlagstock* shrugged. 'They're *wessies*, troublemakers. We were told to avoid Keibelstrasse, and this is the closest station. We'll ask for instructions later.'

'Keibelstrasse won't take them, not today. They're not taking anyone. That was the order this morning.'

Fischer frowned. 'That's …'

Kleiber had removed his shoe to examine the puncture in his foot, which, having stopped bleeding, was robbing him of his Ernie Pyle moment. He looked up. 'What?'

'Unexpected. And disappointing.'

'So, your plan's buggered?'

'We'll see.' Fischer stood up and coughed to attract official attention. 'You can't keep us here. We're the Press.'

Schlagstock grinned. 'The western Press. Lying fuckers to a man.'

'We don't need to lie about the DDR. It's in the terminal ward, kept alive by the Ivans for no good reason.'

'Shut your mouth.'

'Yeah, Otto', hissed Kleiber, tugging at Fischer's jacket. 'Fucking hush.'

'Why? I'm only saying what everyone knows. I find the truth and I write it, that's why I get the top stories. Governor Timberman gave me an interview last month, and Charles Coleman the one before that. *And* I had two hours with Adenauer last year. You don't know what you've done, arresting me. There'll be hell to pay.'

Kleiber groaned softly. *Schlagstock* laughed. 'Here that, Detmar? We've got royalty. Who's your friend? Ed Murrow?'

Fischer sneered down at his alleged accomplice. 'The kid? Nobody. We took him on last week – we had to, he came with the editor's second wife. You can keep him if you want, but me, I'm a problem. You've caught a bigger fish than you can land.'

'A top fellow, eh? Can you smell it, Detmar? I'm soiling myself.'

Detmar looked considerably more convinced than his friend. 'I don't know, Emil. We'll have to let them go eventually. What if they write bad things, stuff that gets us in the shit?'

'But we had to arrest them! They shouldn't have been here.'

'I know, but we need to pass them on – I mean, *up*.'

'You heard the orders. We can't send them to the Praesidium, for Christ knows what reason.'

'No; but *wessies* are different, particularly if they're someone. We should call in, now, and ask what to do. It's safest to let Rank deal with this kind of stuff.'

The *wachtmeister* was nodding emphatically. Emil, whose carefully-nurtured hard-man persona was amenable still to the occasional pull of common-sense, thought about it for a few moments. The day was already beyond any kind of strange, and a diplomatic incident with the name Emil Busch pinned to it was not going to improve things. If these men were nobodies it hardly reflected well that he had pushed his comrades to arrest them; if they were something more than that he was certain that the same comrades would ensure their bosses knew who had done the pushing. It wasn't as though he wasn't known for it already.

'Alright. Who do we call?'

Detmar shrugged. 'Does it matter, as long as it's logged?'

The *wachtmeister* was already dialling the Keibelstrasse exchange number. He listened until the connection was made, and then, without saying a word, handed the receiver to Emil.

The *anwärter* spoke for just under a minute, but his face managed to change colour twice during the time. Clearly, the duty officer at Keibelstrasse didn't want to know what the news was, however important it might be. Eventually, Emil raised his voice and managed to say *western journalists* with sufficient force to make the other end draw breath. Even Fischer and Kleiber, several metres and a line of bars from the telephone, heard the silence that followed.

A different voice spoke, briefly, and Emil replaced the receiver without replying. His colleague Detmar scratched his chin nervously, aware that his suggestion had pushed him somewhat into the zone in which flying shit came to rest.

'What did they say, Emil?'

Emil rubbed his face. 'That we bring them in.'

'Oh. Good.'

'I don't know that it is. We're not to log the arrests, nor talk about it to anyone else. And we take them in via the back entrance, the alley from Liebknechtstrasse.'

'The back door? Why?'

'Why do you think? Because they don't want anyone to know about it.'

'Christ. I wish we hadn't arrested them.'

Emil said nothing, and glanced at the two prisoners much as he might a three-day-unflushed lavatory bowl. Kleiber, head down, was scowling at his punctured foot, while Fischer examined the near-distance, trying to translate the bilious feeling in his gut.

The only bright face was that of the *wachtmeister*. He had picked up his cap and station keys and was gesturing towards the shed door.

'I'll lock up, shall I?'

33

Pankov saluted smartly. The occasion – it had become one, quite quickly – seemed to demand formality. It was an analgesic, a means of dealing with what soldiers did.

He held another communique in his other hand. '*Polkovnik* Geladze wants to know how many dead we have, Comrade.'

Voloshyn took it and put it into a tunic pocket unread. 'You counted them carefully. Has the total changed?'

'No. It's still two.'

'Good. What about the 144th?'

'He reports sixteen.'

'Were they armed?'

'He didn't say.'

Voloshyn's marksmen had dropped their two when pistols came out from under coats, and neither had managed to get off a shot before moving on to a gentler world. Molkenmarkt cleared with gratifying speed after that, the demonstrators scattering through a dozen streets. That had been twenty minutes ago, and neither they nor the next appointed wave had since reassembled. In that pause, Voloshyn redeployed his men and took the time to examine the bodies personally. They didn't carry union cards, or look as if they toiled much for a living. They were young, too, in their early twenties – probably nihilists revolting against whatever caught their attention. Both pistols were antiquated Belgian FNs, without ammunition. Presumably the deceased had studied the art of revolution in an art gallery, their exemplars the weapon-waving heroes who, in a more prosaic reality, usually directed the cannon-fodder from several kilometres to the rear.

Stupid little bastards. He tried and failed to pity them. It wasn't as though the world had yet settled back into those safe, prosperous times that made folk long for a life on fire. A good education, a decent job and children who had a reasonable chance of growing up – why the hell wasn't that enough for now?

He was rifling their pockets when Pankov returned once more from the radio car. 'Two messages. Comrade. We have orders to complete our move towards Monbijouplatz and then Unter den Linden. The 144th will break contact with us, reverse and move east to Stalin Allee to clear the Block 40 site.'

Voloshyn rubbed his head. 'Very well. Send our prisoners under guard to Keibelstrasse …'

That's the second message, Comrade. Keibelstrasse says no.'

'They say what?'

'They're full, apparently. Can't fit any more.'

'Did you tell them we have almost forty of their citizens?'

'I didn't get as far as numbers.'

'Keibelstrasse is one of the designated stations for arrests, yes?'

Pankov nodded.

'If they've too many prisoners they can stack them in their courtyard. Tell them we're sending in what we have. No arguments.'

'They said …'

'What did they say?'

Pankov swallowed. 'That if we have a problem with it we're to take up the matter with the Control Commission.'

Voloshyn stifled a curse. If someone at Keibelstrasse dare give that message it was because their backs were covered – by Comrade Semyonov himself, perhaps. Which meant that the Talking Heads were jabbering to everyone but the units charged with restoring order in the city – the ones who really needed to know what was going on. He glanced around Molkenmarkt. The 248th couldn't take their prisoners with them, not if more trouble loomed at Monbijouplatz or Unter den Linden – regarding which, of course, they had no information one way or the other.

'Let them go.'

'Go, *Comrade Podpolkovnik*?'

'All of them. Confiscate their identity papers and tell them they have half an hour to get home, lock the doors and shut the curtains. After that, if we find them in the streets we'll shoot them in their fucking mouths. And make sure you march them past these two on their way out. It might make them thoughtful.'

Pankov turned to give the orders, but Voloshyn stayed him. 'We'll be leaving a large gap between the 144th and 248th. Contact Geladze; request his permission for us to bring up the rest of the Kasernierte Police Regiment. The ones we have with us already, tell them that they're to remain here to guard the *Stadthaus,* and, as they're reinforced by more of their own, to extend their line on to Museum Island and close all bridges from there to here. Tell them they're allowed to fire on any further trouble.'

'Right.'

When Pankov had scurried off, Voloshyn glanced around the brick-strewn space in front of the *Stadthaus*. His instructions to his adjutant had been precise, yet he didn't much care how precisely they would be followed. He'd issued them for form's sake, for his own peace of mind. It was what a good, cautious commander would do; it made him feel a little better about a situation which gave him very little cause for satisfaction.

Why were they being redeployed so clumsily? Were there no available forces to move in behind them as they advanced logically, in a coordinated fashion? It seemed hard to believe, given that half the Red Army (well, half of its most effective units) was based in East Germany. Was the situation so fraught elsewhere, that only two partial regiments were available to hold down two million potential insurrectionists? Or was Moscow as clueless about the situation as its Berlin puppets?

The Kremlin had been distracted for three months now, the leadership circling each other, searching for a good, decisive grip, dodging nervously before one could land upon them. To minds concentrated by the prospect of victory or annihilation, an uprising in Germany might, at worse, be regarded as just another lunge to avoid. Until Stalin's death the reaction from Moscow would have been entirely predictable – go in hard, bloody hard, and decide afterwards what came next. The Boss would have sorted it out, even if the bodies had to be buried by bulldozers afterwards. The men who applied now for the vacancy he'd left didn't want to bugger their chances with a wrong decision.

Voloshyn was a professional soldier, in for life, and a solid chain of command was his fundament. He feared now that it was shifting beneath his feet. Semyonov, the Kremlin's principal man in the DDR, would be seeking instructions frantically, and getting … what? Were the Kremlin Hopefuls arguing a dozen possibilities beneath a heavy chandelier at that moment, or shrugging and glancing at their wristwatches, hoping that things - assisted by a couple of regiments here and God knew where else in the rest of the country - would sort themselves out?

He wanted a cigarette, but his men's eyes were on him. They trusted a mere lieutenant-colonel to know what came next on a day when generals appeared to be paralysed. He had three sets of orders in his tunic pocket now, and one thing had struck him forcibly about each of them – they had been issued in the name of the Control Commission, not Grechko, their ultimate military commander in the DDR. He was a new man to the job, the seat in his Wünsdorf office not yet fully warmed. Was he as confounded as everyone else, or playing safe, dribbling out units only as requested and letting the Commission tie its own noose?

As shrewd as they might be, these were not appropriate thoughts for an officer, and Voloshyn's bowels squirmed. He reviewed his actions, tried to recall anything that hadn't been strictly in accordance with the paper in his pocket. Certainly, he'd erred on the side of not shooting Germans too promiscuously, but his original orders had hinted heavily that a bloodbath was to be avoided. Geladze seems to have interpreted them somewhat differently, but even sixteen fatalities in an urban mob-control situation could hardly be considered a massacre. And they had both …

It had been nibbling at the edges of his attention, but he was reminded now how readily Molkenmarkt had cleared. Presumably, Geladze had secured the area north of Alexanderplatz just as quickly, otherwise he wouldn't now be shifting to Stalin Allee. It shouldn't have been this easy, not unless they were dealing with something less than a full-blown insurrection.

Stones had been thrown (principally at the *Stadthaus*) and two empty pistols waved – it hardly amounted to the advance up the Odessa

Steps. Voloshyn glanced around, found one of the leaders of his extemporary riot squads and waved a finger. The man – a corporal - trotted across from where he and his colleagues were guarding a small, forlorn group of protesters.

'Have you spoken to any of them?'

'None of us know German, Comrade *Podpolkovnik*.'

'Bring one to me.'

The corporal returned with a thick-set, middle-aged fellow whose mouth was almost entirely hidden by a thick, shaggy moustache. His clothes hinted at employment at the rough end of some process, a hands-dirty job whose evidence was gathered thickly under filthy fingernails.

Voloshyn nodded at the man. 'Where do you work?'

'Not saying.'

'Alright. What sort of work do you do?'

'Processing.'

Voloshyn sighed. That narrowed it down to a role somewhere within roughly three-quarters of heavy-industry. 'Why are you here today?'

'The quotas.'

'The new ones? But they've been suspended.'

'That's what they say. But what does that mean? They change all the time. Next week they'll be unsuspended, or we'll get new, new ones that are even worse.'

'What do you want, then?

'A fair wage for the work we do. And decent housing for all of us, not just the ones up the Party's arse.'

'You're not intending to bring down the government?'

'Eh? Why? They're all the same. Why would we swap one set of useless bastards for another?'

'Go on. Get out of here.'

Pankov had instructed the squads by now, and the man's fellow protesters had begun to disperse. He followed them, glancing back twice as if unsure of what he had just said and heard. Voloshyn felt much the same. In the ideal socialist society, industrial strife was by definition an act of sabotage against the workers themselves, but the Germans hadn't had much practise as yet either with socialism or ideals. Even a non-economist could see that Ulbricht's administration had fucked things in a manner that embarrassed even the Kremlin (whose own experience of economic fuckery was profoundly deep and wide). Some members of that same administration had proclaimed – several times in the past fortnight alone – that the workers had both a point and every right to make it, which made a man charged with clearing them off the streets feel ambivalent.

He didn't regret the two corpses at his feet. They were suicides (or as good as), and he'd given them what they must have expected. But the rest of it felt like a game, a manoeuvre on some board whose layout he couldn't see. What was needed here was little more than crowd control, and *VolksPolizei* supported by *Kasernierte* forces should have been dealing with it, not a front-line Red Army formation. Either someone had panicked monstrously, or …

Voloshyn couldn't make out *or*. Why would someone who wanted a situation to go away goad it into becoming something bigger than it was? Every civilian fatality would be a gift to Western propagandists, their 'proof' that socialism didn't work. Every image of Soviet tanks churning up Berlin streets would cast minds back to '45 and remind Germans that bitter enemies didn't and couldn't become brothers overnight. Yet Ulbricht relied entirely upon his Soviet allies. To alienate them – or worse, turn his own people against them – would be a particularly effective form of political self-murder. None of this was logical; at least, not to a lieutenant-colonel's mind.

But orders weren't conceived to make sense, and that was the start and finish of it. The indefatigable Pankov had returned and was hovering nearby, waiting for the hooked finger. Voloshyn obliged him.

'What?'

'*Polkovnik* Geladze agrees that the remainder of the *Kasernierte* Police should be brought up, Comrade.'

'Good. Get the battalion commanders here, quickly. And give me your map of central Berlin.'

He was examining the routes between Molkenmarkt and Monbijouplatz that would have to be covered as he advanced, when he noticed that his adjutant was hovering. 'What?'

'When I called the 144th I also contacted Major Suvorov, to tell him to bring his men back here.'

'That was correct. What of it?'

'He asked about prisoners, what he should do. I told him that Keibelstrasse wasn't taking any, and that he should let them go with a warning. He said that wasn't what he'd heard, exactly.'

'What do you mean?

'Half an hour ago, two policeman asked permission to cross where his unit had deployed, just north of Schillingstrasse. They were on their way to Keibelstrasse with two prisoners, apparently western journalists they'd captured. They said they'd been told specifically to take them there.'

'Really?' Voloshyn blew out his cheeks. If the Germans wanted to play stupid games with their secure accommodation it wasn't his business, though having taken the trouble to acquire prisoners rather than shoot indiscriminately he felt as if his efforts were being mocked. It inclined him to rethink his orders.

'If there's more trouble at Monbijouplatz, fire above heads as before. If that doesn't work, target a few of the stone-throwers and other idiots.'

Pankov was scribbling once more. 'Deadly force, Comrade *Podpolkovnik*?'

'Aim for their legs. If the rest don't scatter …'

'Comrade?'

Voloshyn returned his attention to the map. 'I'll think about it on the way.'

34

Daintily, Holleman raised the Dresdner china cup to his lips and twitched.

'Fuck.'

Zarubin's eyebrows lifted. 'Actually, you make a fairly decent cup of tea.'

'It's Dietrich.'

'The Gehlen agent? Where?'

In that damn big red *Hansa*. He'll park around the back and come straight in. You'd better get out, quickly ...'

Despite this potentially catastrophic turn of events, Zarubin reacted to it calmly. He put down his cup, went across to where a number of clocks awaited repair and selected a battered Junghan. He placed it on the bench, sat down and continued to drink his tea.

Holleman was impressed. It would have taken him about ten minutes to think of it, by which time he would either have been under arrest or shot.

The back door slammed and Dietrich walked into the shop.

'Ah.' Zarubin laid down his cup once more and stood. 'Herr Fischer? I have a clock that needs ...'

'No.' Dietrich frowned at this unexpected intrusion, but without suspicion. Zarubin's excellent German was tinged with a hint of Russian usually, but now he spoke with an entirely convincing Danziger accent.

'Oh dear. I'm afraid I can't wait much longer. Do you know when he'll be returning?'

'I'm sorry, I don't.'

Holleman coughed. 'Perhaps you'd like to leave the clock here? We could take your details.'

'Would you? It's Eichhorst, initial P. My address …'

'Just a minute.' Holleman found a pencil and a blank specimen of the cards that Fischer attached to each of his broken flock, and wondered why he was conspiring with part of his old, bad world to confound those whose goodwill he desperately needed. When he looked up and saw Zarubin's deeply serious, guileless face he almost laughed - a symptom, he was sure, of his present frailty of mind.

'… Kilstetterstrasse 92, apartment 14, Zehlendorf. I'm afraid I don't have a telephone.'

All Dietrich needed to do was demand to see Zarubin's papers, and everything would fall to shit; but that would be to admit that he was Authority, and admissions weren't what made spies. In any case, why should he? Herr Eichhorst, P. was a well-mannered, well-dressed gentleman with a broken clock in a clock repairer's shop, which was about as sound as anything short of a dollar bill.

Holleman finished writing out the card and placed it inside the clock's glass face. 'I can't give you a receipt. I don't know where Herr Fischer keeps them.'

'That's alright. I know where he lives.'

Zarubin picked up his briefcase, smiled at Dietrich and strolled out of the front door. Holleman could hardly wait until it was back in its jamb.

'Kristin …?'

'Nothing yet.'

'That's it, then. She's been arrested.'

'You don't know that. Your side of the city's in chaos. There could be many reasons why your wife's been delayed.'

The reassurance was familiar, and beginning to pall, and even in his distraction, Holleman could hear the lack of conviction – or possibly indifference - in Dietrich's voice. No doubt Pullach was pushing him ever harder to get their new defector to a place where he could be useful. It was a day in which everyone wondered what the hell was happening in the heads of the DDR's missing Government, and a man who knew every one of them was – or could have been – worth his weight in pieces of silver. Yet instead of spilling his soul, Friedrich Holleman was cowering in a small commercial premises in southwest Berlin, desperately hanging on for word of his spouse. He had imagined that he had very little time remaining. Perhaps that had been over-optimistic.

He needed to keep Dietrich's attention, and the only way he could do that was to give him something.

'What are the Politburo saying?'

The agent shrugged. 'Nothing. They haven't issued a statement for several hours now. We have fairly robust intelligence that Soviet troops have engaged the demonstrations, and that shots have been fired. How many, and in what direction, we can't say.'

'You think the Red Army's taken over?'

'It looks that way.'

'But it isn't.'

'What do you mean?'

Holleman picked up the clock that Zarubin had used as a prop. It was an art-deco piece, a squat, square item that must have seemed out of fashion even before it found its first owner. He'd always hated the style, which was probably the best of testimonials. He and aesthetics were at best glancing acquaintances.

'You have to understand what went on yesterday.'

'Where?'

'At the House of Unity, the Politburo meeting.'

'You mentioned that Hermstadt, Brandt and their friends demanded a reversal of the work quotas.'

'I did, and Ulbricht agreed. But it was the manner of it, the way they stood up to him and his allies.'

'How do you know about this?'

'Erich Honecker, he told me.'

'The head of the FDJ? Isn't he an Ulbricht man?'

'Yeah, one of the few who didn't spend the war in Moscow. Him and me don't have much in common, but he's been kicked a bit over the past year for putting his cock in places it shouldn't be. He got a colleague pregnant, I showed a little sympathy when everyone else was shaking an outraged head - you know how it is. Anyway, he said that there came a point yesterday when he thought Ulbricht was done for. News was coming in that workers at the Friedrichshain Hospital and Block 40 had marched down to Leipzigerstrasse and demanded that he address them personally, but he refused to go, said he had too much other stuff to deal with. That looked like contempt or cowardice, and Fritz Sellmann ...'

'Who?'

'The Industry Minister, one of the few senior SED men who kept his head yesterday. He 'phoned Ulbricht from Leipzigerstrasse and said 'Walter, for fuck's sake get down here and talk to them'. Do you know what Ulbricht did then?'

'Declined?'

'In a way. He stuck his head out of the window and looked about for a bit. Then, he pulled it back in, picked up the 'phone and said 'don't worry, Fritz, it's raining. Construction workers don't like getting wet, they'll be gone soon.''

'I find that hard to believe.'

'So did the two dozen or so witnesses to it. It was the moment at which our Stalin turned out to be someone else. Even Honecker thought him horribly weak.'

Dietrich frowned. 'I don't understand. You've made it plain that you're on the other side of the SED fence from Ulbricht. If his authority's so shaken, why are you here today? Who's most likely to profit from his fall?'

Holleman shrugged. 'Rudy Hermstadt, probably. He's well in with Zaisser, so State Security have got his back. Moscow likes him, and though Semyonov's told him to ease off on criticising Ulbricht, the Control Commission's now more or less saying what he's been writing on the subject for months.'

'And you're a Hermstadt man?'

'I wouldn't say so, no. Being a newspaperman as well as a politician, he has a feel for what makes the common man itch; but his experience is much more about telling others what's wrong than doing what's right himself. And I don't think he's got the iron to topple Ulbricht. Yesterday passed, and today is …'

'A disaster for the DDR.'

'Yes, but disasters aren't always bad. If you look at the bare prospect of it – the huge crowds and burning police stations - you could think that it was all up for Ulbricht; but given that his administration's been trying to douse a dozen fires for months now, perhaps one big explosion's what he needs to suck the oxygen from them all.'

'You're talking about Moscow?'

'It's *always* about Moscow. If Stalin's death caused heart attacks in the Kremlin it's been the Black Death here. Berlin wants desperately to know who's going to win the succession struggle, because it's our future as much as theirs. We hear promises of eternal friendship and support from some mouths; from others, it's why the fuck do we keep squandering our hard-earned roubles on a death-ward case like the DDR? Now, what if there's a way for Ulbricht to move things along in Moscow, in a direction that favours him?'

'By failing? With weakness in the face of industrial unrest? It doesn't seem likely …'

'By failing utterly - by making the loss of the DDR too big a fucking disaster to risk even contemplating.'

'You're saying Ulbricht's arranged today's events purposely?'

'Of course not. I expect that if he could turn back the clock a year and go fishing instead he'd do it in a moment. Everyone's lost faith in him - the SED, the man in the street, the Kremlin – even MfS can't be trusted not to sit on their hands as long as Zaisser's the Security Minister. All he has left in his corner are the *Kasernierte VolksPolizei*, and twelve thousand loyal automatons aren't nearly enough. What would you do, in his boots?'

Dietrich looked to the ceiling and considered this. 'Reconsider the fishing trip?'

'It's too late. He's made too many enemies recently to contemplate retirement. So, what else?'

'Tell me.'

'First, he calls Semyonov and says that he can't trust *VolksPolizei* not to either run or join the protests if it comes to a street confrontation. Then, probably, he twists the facts a little and claims that his opponents in the SED are all pale pink and would prefer to slow or even reverse the push to a truly socialist economy – Christ knows, given the bugger-up that the Party have made of the process over the past year it's hardly conceivable that they wouldn't. To give Semyonov the final nudge, he throws in a hint to remind him that if it all falls to shit the Kremlin won't have the option of revisiting Stalin's idea of negotiating a reunified, neutral Germany. The West will absorb the ruins of the East on its own terms, and they'll probably include full membership of that fascist military alliance, the Atlantic thing.'

'NATO.'

'Yeah, that. So, Semyonov calls Moscow and says look, we have no choice. If Ulbricht falls, his successors – whoever they are - will need to make so many concessions that their authority will be shot to pieces. The fellows on the other end of the 'phone hear this and think fuck, he's right - do any of us want to be remembered as the *muschis* who lost Germany?' Holleman paused and shrugged. 'I'd bet my ex-salary that the authorization to deploy Soviet troops was unanimous. And for what? It isn't to keep order on the streets – it's to keep Ulbricht where he is. The really ironic thing is, the fellow in Moscow who comes out of this best will probably win the succession race, and he'll have Ulbricht's failures to thank for it.'

Dietrich was nodding slowly. It made sense of at least part of the near-chaos they were seeing across the line. Holleman pushed while he was ahead.

'Call Pullach and explain it to them. Then ask if I can have a few more hours to wait for my wife.'

35

KriminalKommissar Albrecht Müller was edging towards a degree of calmness about the fled Beckendorp, the unexpectedly not-fled Hoeschler and the several irruptions of a day he would happily have wished away, when his desk telephone rang and tore the skin off the pudding.

It was Keibelstrasse's very own Talthybius, *Wachtmeister* Cordt, from the reception desk, 'We've got a couple of arrests, *wessie* journalists. *Oberrat* Busch ordered them to be brought in.'

'Aren't westerners the business of MfS?'

'I suppose so, but like everyone else today they're not answering the 'phone.'

'So why are you telling me? It's hardly a Criminal Investigations matter.'

One of them, he's got half a face. He claims to know you.'

A blade pushed through Müller's tunic couldn't have been less welcome. He glanced anxiously at Hoeschler, who was sitting at the next desk, speaking quietly but urgently into another 'phone. It couldn't be a coincidence. Otto Fischer hadn't been at Keibelstrasse for more than five years, and now he'd turned up on the very day that his best friend Beckendorp (or whatever his name really was) had fled west, probably to bring the final spade-full of filling for the hole that Müller was presently surveying.

And as a journalist, too. If Ernst Reuter himself had walked in, asking if his good friend Alby Müller could take an hour or two for lunch, it wouldn't have looked worse. He'd spent his entire moral collateral that morning persuading acting-Inspector Petersen that his prior association with the traitor Beckendorp was unstained by collusion, and now the western Press had come begging an audience – had actually given his name at reception! What the hell was he going to …?

'I've never heard of him. Fischer, you say? Put him in interrogation room one.'

At the next desk, Hoeschler twitched as if his arse had taken a live wire. 'Not …?'

'Yes. Why is he here, do you think?'

Because Plan A fucked itself so badly that the poor bastard's been flung in to try his famously shitty luck. 'I don't know. It's remarkable.'

'It's beyond remarkable. Something's going on, a plot to put Albrecht Müller against a wall.'

Hoeschler swallowed and tried to speak casually. 'Would you prefer that I spoke to Otto?'

Müller sighed. 'Yes, Rolf, I very much would. But he asked for me, and everyone heard it. In any case, I'm supposed to be watching you for signs of traitorous intent. You'd better come downstairs too.'

Wachtmeister Cordt, pleased to scrape the matter entirely off his hands, had put both prisoners into the interrogation room by the time that Hoeschler and Müller descended to the ground floor. One of them, the younger man, was staring at the table in front of him and chewing a fingernail. The older, half-faced man glanced up as the two policemen entered. He frowned slightly, but a casual observer could have read nothing into it. Hoeschler, who'd had the better part of five minutes to prepare himself, nevertheless managed to seem as edgy as a cat on a bacon slicer.

'Hello, Otto.'

'Hello, Rolf. You look well.'

'You don't.'

Fischer smiled. 'And *Kommissar* Müller, now. Well done on your promotion.'

Müller tried to smile, and failed. 'Thank you. You're a journalist these days?'

'No. My friend here, Jonas - he's the journalist. I claimed to be because I needed to be noticed.'

Kleiber nodded gloomily. ''Ow do.'

'What?'

'He says hello. Müller, may I ask you a question discreetly? I mean, without it being recorded?'

'It's a bit late for discretion. Why did you have to use my name at the front desk? Why not Rolf's ...' Müller's mouth opened as he looked from Fischer to Hoeschler and back again.

'You didn't ask for Rolf because you assumed he wouldn't be here today.'

On the way from the Friedrichshain sub-station to Keibelstrasse, Fischer had wondered how he might address the matter of Kristin Holleman without ringing too many bells. The unexpected presence of Rolf Hoeschler, her intended Siegfried, had half answered it but complicated things horribly.

Hoeschler swallowed hard. 'She isn't here. Nor at any of the designated holding stations.'

Müller was still trying to absorb the shock of being an unwilling accessory, but the pronoun grabbed his attention. 'Who?'

Fischer looked at Hoeschler, who wasn't going to say anything more if he could help it. 'You don't know her. Someone we're both worried about.'

'From the west?'

'Yes.' Fischer eased his conscience with the logic that, if everything had gone as planned, it would have been only a half-lie.

Müller sighed. 'It's her lucky day, whatever she's done. We aren't arresting anyone, apparently. Well, except you and your friend. I assume you encouraged it?'

Before Fischer could answer the door opened and a short, thick-set man with savagely cropped hair strode in. Müller and Hoeschler came to attention.

'Are these them?'

'Yes, Comrade *Oberrat*.'

The newcomer offered the objects in question his most contemptuous face. 'Come to gloat, have you?'

Kleiber assumed the earnest, sincere expression he deployed at all his sources. 'Not at all, comrade. As you can imagine, the *Zeitung*'s readers are very concerned about events. We want to get an accurate picture, rather than hear everything from American radio. A statement from a high-ranking – though unnamed - *VolksPolizei* officer would of course feature prominently in our report.'

Fischer's admiration for the young man's nerve rose considerably. Butter applied to a wound couldn't have soothed more effectively. The *Oberrat* relaxed visibly.

'It's a difficult time, what with Allied provocations.'

Kleiber nodded violently. 'That's what my editor says. He's from Silesia originally, and still misses his old *heimat*.'

Kleiber's employer hadn't set a foot east of the river Spree in his life, but the statement was admirably difficult to verify. The *Oberrat*'s brutal features softened further.

'Where in Silesia?

Kleiber didn't blink or miss a beat. 'Breslau. His house was a few yards from Feniks' department store.'

'Ah! Me and the wife rented holiday rooms in the Old Town, back in '38.'

'Small world.'

'It is, it is.' The ugly head nodded for a few moments, its attention firmly fixed upon picturesque pre-war Breslau. 'Which *Zeitung* is it that you're from?'

'The *Südwest-Berliner Zeitung*.'

The *Oberrat* stared at Kleiber for several moments and then closed his eyes. 'Get them out', he said quietly.

'Comrade?'

'Find an *anwärter* – two – and tell them to escort them across the line; make sure they don't come back.'

'They're free …?'

'It's a district rag! What's your circulation? Twelve?'

Offended, Kleiber drew himself up to his maximum sitting height. 'During last year's Flower Show Week it was almost three thousand.'

The *Oberrat* looked around. 'Hear that? Press Barons are beating a path to Keibelstrasse. Let me know when the London Times arrives and we'll issue a fucking statement!'

The interrogation room door slammed with unnecessary violence as he departed. Of the four men who remained, only Kleiber seemed pleased. He stood up and rubbed his hands.

'Come on, Otto. Even Herr Grabner can't say I didn't try.'

Fischer shook his head. 'This doesn't help. Müller, what did you mean, you're not arresting anyone?'

'Exactly what I said. *VolksPolizei* aren't confronting the crowds, and someone's told us not to make arrests. We're to leave everything to the Ivans.'

'That's …'

'Mad.' Hoeschler shook his head. 'Why would anyone want the Red Army on the streets? Shit!'

Fischer caught the slight hint of frantic in his voice. 'What is it, Rolf?'

'My boy, Engi – he's with her.'

'Christ.'

'We have to do something, Otto. And I've no idea what.'

'Well, we know that they haven't been arrested yet. Have there been shootings? Müller?'

'Some. About half an hour ago you could hear shots from here. It sounded uncoordinated. Perhaps it was just a warning. Rolf, you … '

Hoeschler couldn't hold Müller's dumbfounded gaze. '… didn't mean to come in today, did you? You went with Beckendorp.'

'Albi …'

'Don't.'

Fischer thought quickly. It was all in Müller's hands now. If he did the correct thing and shouted for help, half a dozen lives would be over, or as good as. If he said nothing and allowed them all to go about their urgent business it would be professional (perhaps even actual) suicide, and his family would suffer the consequences of it. He deserved the truth, or something close to it.

'Beckendorp had to leave.'

'Why?'

'I'm not sure yet, but it was a desperate act. He had a good life here, and prospects for a better retirement. There's nothing across the line that he wants, believe me.'

'What about you. Rolf?'

'I promised him that I'd get his wife out.'

'Then what? You'd just come back, as if from a day trip?'

'Obviously not. I want my boy to have a better chance than me. In the West we don't owe anyone.'

'It's not because you're a capitalist, then?'

'Hoeschler snorted. 'I'm not anything. I believe sincerely in getting to and from my bed each day with the least fuss. And having enough to eat in-between.'

'Then why do you have to …'

Fischer put a hand on Müller's shoulder. 'We all have our histories. They might never jump up to bite us in the arse, but they're always there, the dark bit on the horizon. For me the last straw was Sachsenhausen. After that, I'd had enough of staring at ceilings I couldn't see when I should have been sleeping, working odds, hoping for better. So, I went west. It isn't paradise over there, or even particularly better than here. It's just somewhere without a memory of *me*. I can't speak to Rolf's motives, but a blank page is a wonderful read.'

Müller shook his head. 'I could never go there. My girls love their school, and Anna's happy with her life as it is. Besides, what about *my* history?'

'You were a defence counsellor in the People's Court, just about the best of a bad system. They've hanged the judges, called it quits and closed the book.'

'You were soldiers, honourable men. You don't understand the shame.'

Fischer looked at Hoeschler. 'Did you know that Rolf and me met on a day when soldiers of our glorious, elite regiment lined up about forty Greek men and shot them? Their crime was to own guns. All Greeks outside the cities have guns, they need them for birds and rats, but that didn't matter – an armed man was a partisan and orders were orders. There was plenty of shame and precious little honour in it. Let the past lie. It isn't as if we want you to run too.'

'What *do* you want?'

It was a good, extremely difficult question. To turn a blind eye? Go for a piss, take time shaking out the drops and return a roundabout way?

'I want you to denounce Rolf. To your new boss, Petersen.'

'*What?*'

Hoeschler nodded. 'I'm deep in it with Beckendorp, Tell him that.'

'They'll put you against a wall!'

'I'll be gone with Otto, across the line before they find us.'

'But how could you get away?'

'Quietly, out the back. Who would notice, with everything else going on?'

'But if I don't try to stop you, they'd think I was …'

Hoeschler caught Müller and laid him gently on the floor. Fischer peered down anxiously. 'Is he breathing?'

'He's fine.'

Kleiber took the Contax from Fischer's hand and examined it. 'You know that it's me who pays for any damage?'

The corridor housing the interrogation rooms led directly to the rear of the building and then, at the top of a short flight of stairs, divided to the car pool or exit. A solitary *anwärter* sat on a chair, guarding the door out on to the access alley. Hoeschler waved his warrant card, his other hand gripping Kleiber's collar. The policemen opened his mouth, but a glance at Fischer's plain clothes and mutilated face killed any query, and before the three men had turned the corner his mind was back upon the ache of his empty stomach and the shift's end.

Fischer stopped before they reached Liebknechtstrasse. Escape had been easier than he had expected, but they were no closer to solving the mystery of Kristin Holleman's disappearance. He looked at Rolf Hoeschler, whose blank expression mirrored his own lack of inspiration.

'Did you find out where the trouble is?'

'All over, but the main concentrations seem to be where there's the most space to gather - Wilhelm-Pieck-Strasse, Unter den Linden, Molkenmarkt and Stalin Allee, though I think the Reds have closed down the protests outside the *Neues Stadthaus* already.'

Fischer considered this. 'Stalin Allee's a construction site, so I assume it's occupied predominantly by its own workers. The crowds outside the House of Unity – well, they could be from anywhere, but if it's true that the Politburo's fled to Karlshorst they may be dispersing already. That leaves Unter den Linden – long, wide, straight and easily accessed from any direction except west. It has to be where the most protesters are concentrating.'

'You think Kristin and Engi are there?'

'Rolf, I have no idea. It's the best of several faint hopes – I think. Anything or nothing could have happened. All I can suggest is that we go there, each of us take one side of the road and move westwards slowly. If she and your boy *are* there and not at one of ten thousand other possible location, it's the best, and probably the only, chance we'll have of spotting them.'

'If they've found Ulrich ...'

'Then they'll probably be on their way west, whether or not she's managed to persuade him to go.'

'She's a hard woman to refuse. And she has help.'

'Who?'

Hoeschler told Fischer about Kristin's visit to the Pankow bakery and her drafting of Ulrich's pregnant girlfriend. 'It gave me hopes that if they found Ulrich before trouble started he wouldn't dare lead the girl into any harm.'

'But we don't know if they did, and harm seems to be just about everywhere today. My gut tells me there's more to this than we're seeing.'

'What do you mean?'

'So little seems to make sense – the withdrawal of most police from the streets, the effort to get the Red Army involved and now the unwillingness to fill cells with arrests. I'm beginning to sense something of why Freddie thought he had to make such a drastic decision.'

'He didn't say more to me than that it was *time*.'

'I don't think he was lying about that. Come on, we need to be in Unter den Linden. Jonas? Are you …?'

Kleiber sighed. 'A sensible man would run home, but this camera appears to be working still and there's half a roll unused. Shot or pestered to death – what a fucking choice.'

They set a brisk pace down Liebknechtstrasse. Had any of them cared to glance back they might have noticed the light-haired man who walked in the same direction but some eighty metres behind them. His face was half-buried in a newspaper, yet he seemed to lose no ground as they approached and then crossed on to Museum Island. Twice they were held up by Red Army patrols and managed to get through only when Hoeschler argued and punctuated it with his warrant card; but the man who followed said something to the soldiers that moved them smartly out of his way.

Once over the Spree canal and on to the eastern stretch of Unter den Linden the world began to fill with Berliners. Most of them were men in work clothes, trying to order themselves into ranks but struggling with the inertial force of too many trades squeezed into too small a space. There were civilians too, some of whom had thought it wise to bring children, as if the coming trouble would be catered and then distracted by Kasperle shows. A few young men whose hair was too long for a workbench hovered at the crowds' peripheries; most of them had rolled up their shirt sleeves, which to any self-respecting security forces would be as good as a prior admission of intent to throw stones.

Approaching this melee, the three men's blond tracker grew confident. Assuming that he wouldn't be noticed he lost the newspaper and closed the gap to less than fifteen metres. It was almost intimately close, yet necessary - when they found the woman he wanted to be sure that he could bring down all three before they could react. The magazine in the pistol beneath his arm contained twelve bullets, but if the job required more than one for each man he knew he'd feel bad. It may have been something handed down in the blood from parents he couldn't remotely recall, or a lesson unconsciously absorbed during his hard youth; but either way, he had never liked waste.

36

For a while after leaving Fischer's delightfully *en détresse* little shop, Zarubin wandered the streets of Lichterfelde. It was a part of Berlin he hadn't previously visited, even in those glorious, too-few days after the city fell but before the Red Army grudgingly handed over the districts that would fall under the administration of their alleged Allies. Back then, he had been too busy suborning fearful Berliners, inviting them – for a pittance hardly worthy of the name – to be the eyes of the Soviet Union in what would become the Western Zones. Many had agreed, either to avoid the heavily hinted-at price of not complying or because they feared the Allied presence in the city would be all too brief. It had fascinated him at the time, how swiftly the white flag had transmuted the most remorselessly martial nation on earth into a vast pool of passive collaborators.

His defection had freed a great many of those unwilling employees. At first they would have been puzzled, wondering why Karlshorst wasn't on their backs but grateful for the silence. Six months later, they might have begun to allow themselves to exhale, to hope and even make plans for a future free from the less-than-brutal but horribly troublesome Major Zarubin. Did they still think of him with no fondness whatsoever, he wondered, or had he been consigned by now to the best -forgotten cupboard, like so much else in the German psyche?

He passed between shaded areas, trying to remain cool in the early summer afternoon. After a half hour's perambulation he decided that he had pinned Lichterfelde, a place as pleasant as any of middle Europe's much-depleted urban spaces. There hadn't been too much heavy fighting here – even *Liebstandarte SS Adolph Hitler*'s old *kaserne* (and that of the Kaiser's Prussian Guards' before them) had been skirted so completely that the US Army had been able to move straight in without having to apply even a lick of new paint. This struck him as particularly unjust. All across Germany, a generation of honest, hard-working folk had seen their houses and factories lit up like candles or crushed like beetles, while this crucible of militarism remained wilfully intact, its generals' villas pristine still, flaunting their Wilhelmine staidness. Only the area's median waistline told something of *now* as opposed to *then*, and had it been a slice of France even that would have been dismissed as merely fashionable.

His personal *Baedeker* tour ended at a small café off Drakenstrasse, where he sat down with a black coffee and allowed his pressing problem some air. His plan had been too extempory, too reliant upon everything moving like one of Fischer's repaired mechanisms, and now he was in every sense exposed. The search must have begun already, and if any advantage remained to him it was in the very probable reluctance of the CIA to admit anything of their blunder to the US Army, who alone had the manpower to chase him down swiftly. Even so, West Berlin's one hundred and eighty-six square kilometres was nowhere near enough to provide adequate cover. He was a man with a deadly virus in his briefcase, a growing price on his head and absolutely no time or resources to fashion a workable means of staying alive beyond sunset.

Bloody Fischer. How like the dolt to allow himself to be pestered by old friends when an old tormentor needed him more. What was a man with a fine brain doing, wandering the streets of East Berlin on a day of disintegration, a day in which Schiller's statue couldn't have found its own plinth beneath its arse? Is that what friends did for friends, he wondered, toying with his coffee and avoiding the gaze of the girl who had served him.

It was the suit - and his pretty features, of course. No doubt she thought him a potential deliverance from her drudge's life, a lifeline requiring only the small investment of her unvalued virtue. He wished now that he hadn't smiled when he placed his order, and even more that he hadn't affected an American accent as he did it. Camp Andrews was only a half-kilometre distant, and the young ladies of Lichterfelde must have regarded it much as the wandering Israelites did that first hint of a sea breeze.

Seduce her; go to ground until you have a new plan. He flushed the thought before it could put down roots. She lived with her parents, or a large, jealous boyfriend, or a dog that MGB considered one of their best agents in West Berlin – his luck being the way it was, nothing bad was improbable. In any case, the memory of his Philadelphia heiress was too freshly stinking for him to want to return to the cold fornication business. That sort of thing was best reserved for when it couldn't be avoided.

So, what were his options? West Berlin had become – he had made it - too dangerous; East Berlin remained as deadly as it had been since the day of his defection. He had no friends in Germany, no means of testing black waters before he plunged any more deeply into them. The logical, sane answer was flight, but he had a grand total of forty-five US dollars in his billfold, which would get him as far as trees.

Forty-five dollars; it was enough to buy supplies, find a cheap hotel and keep to his room for the next week. If he could pass as an American he might not need to produce his papers – the implication – if not reality - of deep pockets could bend rules, keep his name off the lists that hoteliers were required to send to local police stations …

Idiot. His description would circulate more quickly than dysentery in a T34, and the week would pass as an extended torment of expectation, each knock on his door the click of a hammer on an empty chamber. Hiding was of no utility; he had conceived a bold, decisive (for good or bad) plan that wouldn't go anywhere if he was cowering under a bed or twitching curtains each time he heard footsteps below his window.

Which brought him back to Otto Fischer, whose half-face couldn't be read, or moods parsed, or inclination to flush away one of the least sufferable reminders of his tortured past gauged. Zarubin wished fervently now that he had a greater hold upon the man's loyalties than having once saved the life of the woman he loved (only for the ungrateful sow to die anyway, barely two years later) and not having had him shot on a couple of occasions since. On paper it all looked impressive, but even now he couldn't quite decide if he hadn't been useful to the man in ways that might be considered offensive.

He would be throwing himself upon the mercy of altruism, and even thinking it made him queasy. To a former officer of Soviet Intelligence, innate decency was much like the interaction of Jovian moons - a thing known to exist but far beyond experience. Ironically, his plan both fed and relied upon an absence of trust, yet its success required that he have faith in a man's reluctance to be other than himself – or at least, the self he had been almost six years earlier.

So there it was – a choice that, being desperately alone on an empty plain, wasn't a choice at all. He would go back to the shop and wait. Governments might fall today, an oppressed people rise up and slay their tormentors, a new war blossom for fear of what might be lost if less than *something* was done; and all the while he would be sitting on a workbench, sipping tea, examining dead clocks and checking the live ones every minute or so. He almost hoped that Friedrich Holleman was there still (though of course without his Gehlenist minder); at least the unresolved tension in the air between them might help kill time until their mutual saviour returned. And if he took along some small token of goodwill, perhaps Fischer might think less than sourly of his unexpected Russian guest than he had every right to.

'Excuse me?' He lifted a finger, and his admirer caught the movement instantly. She swayed seductively rather than walked to the table, and it occurred to him much too late that his question might be entirely misinterpreted.

'Could you tell me if there's anywhere close by where I might buy flowers, please?'

37

Almost two metres off the ground, Fischer had an unimpeded view of Unter den Linden's western stretches.

'Can you sense it?'

Balancing precariously on the same section of rubble, a few metres south of where Frederick II had once glared at the Linden trees, Kleiber sniffed the air. 'What?'

'The unified purpose - the common will that moves citizens to rise up against all the crap they've been obliged to endure?'

'No.'

'Neither can I. It's just a lot of folk with their own grouses, come to where they can shout them in company.'

Hoeschler looked up anxiously from street level. 'Can you see anyone that might be them?'

'No. There are plenty of women here, though. Christ, some of them are pushing prams, like it's a day out.'

The stretch of the road west of the Humboldt had been hit heavily by the Allies in the final months of the war, and even eight years later, much of the ground awaited new building work. Consequently, the largest proportion of the crowd had gathered here, where it could spread beyond the boulevard's natural confines (though prudently, it avoided the new Soviet Embassy, whose two visible guards were quite enough to keep it safe). Picking individuals out of that maul would have been impossible even with high-powered binoculars and a static citizenry.

'We'll have to wait until they start moving as a mass. *If* they do.'

Kleiber shrugged. 'What if they turn west, towards Tiergarten?'

'Why would they, unless it's a planned mass escape? Their gripes are with what's east of here, not west.'

'Oh. Yeah.'

Fischer scratched his head. 'Mind, some of them might think to head for Wilhelmstrasse. There are more than enough SED windows to smash down there. Shit, this is like combing sand for … sand.'

Hoeschler shook his head. 'If Kristin's found Ulrich, he won't dare be anywhere they're throwing stones. She'd spank him with a paddle. He can't even use bad language when she's around. In any case, the House of Ministries is one of the few places *VolksPolizei* had the sense to secure today. Müller told me.'

'It doesn't surprise me. That building's going to survive the End of Days.'

Hoeschler tugged at Kleiber's trousers. 'Did Otto tell you what he did in there?'

'The old Air Ministry? No.'

'He lied, and called it reporting. Then he was promoted, to lying and calling it Intelligence. This is a man without a moral core.'

Kleiber looked at Fischer with great respect. 'Yet you didn't make the General Staff.'

'I had too much competition. And they were all prettier than me - except Bürkner, obviously.'

The crowd was noisy but incoherent, its many preoccupations chanted or shouted with no effort to coordinate. Fischer preferred it like that; a mob with no single purpose was much less threatening to men charged with dispersing it. He heard the names of senior SED politicians called out too many times for comfort, but most of it seemed to be insulting references to their genealogy, rather than too-direct demands for their heads. Berliners had always been good at digging away the foundations of a politician's inflated self-regard – even Adolph hadn't been spared – and their leaders usually allowed them a little leeway when releasing the valve. He just hoped they wouldn't try to test the limits of where their mouths could take them.

He no sooner had the thought than an ominously audible phrase began to emerge from the drone of its competitors. It was concise and guttural, more an expletive than a slogan, all definite advantages over the more laboured 'end the new quotas' and 'the workers demand decent housing.'

Ulbricht Out! Ulbricht Out! Ulbricht Out!

The demand wasn't amenable to negotiation, only rejection or surrender, and Fischer had a feeling that the latter wouldn't be an option. Which left only the question of whether the authorities would let the demonstrators tire themselves out or apply some active discouragement. He glanced around. As far as he could see, there wasn't a single policeman either on Unter den Linden or in the side roads that bisected it from north to south. That didn't mean, of course, that the Security Ministry hadn't sent out their plain-clothed thugs to mingle with the crowds and goad insolence into something more; but the lack of a visible deterrent to what was happening was remarkable. He could almost imagine that …

'We should get closer.' Hoeschler was straining his neck, willing to see his boy and Kristin Holleman among the thousands of souls in front of them.

Fischer nodded and climbed down from the rubble, followed more gingerly by Kleiber. 'Let's move to Friedrichstrasse and then separate. You'll take the south side, Kleiber and me the north.'

They walked westwards across Opernplatz, converging upon a mini-horde streaming southwards into Unter den Linden to swell the protest. Very few of them seemed to be workers; there were suits and other office wear, a broad selection of practical *hausfrau* styles – all of it more in the nature of what filled the city's green spaces whenever lunch-breaks could be taken *al fresco*. A better-organized but purely industrial demonstration wouldn't have excited a fraction of the heartburn that this must have been giving the Politburo.

Kleiber had been examining his immediate environment like a technician testing a new turret. He reached forward slightly and tugged Fischer's sleeve.

'We're being followed.'

'Who?'

'Young fellow, blond, dark clothes, about twenty metres behind.'

Both Fischer and Hoeschler resisted the temptation to glance back casually. 'Are you sure?'

'I'm a reporter who's prone to anxiety attacks. What do you think?'

'What gave him away?'

'I noticed him earlier, before we stopped, so he must have stopped too. Since we started off again he's been looking everywhere – left, right, behind – but never at us, nor the damn great mass of trouble that he's walking straight towards.'

Fischer nodded. 'Let's stop and talk for a while.'

Facing each other, they had, collectively, a three-hundred and sixty degree view. Fischer took the one directly to the east and saw him immediately - a young, long-haired man, apparently distracted by the architectural detail adorning what remained of the State Opera House. He could understand now why Kleiber had noticed him in the first place. MfS were a heavy recruiter these days, and arrogant. They didn't care to disguise their men as other intelligence organizations did – why should they, when their primary purpose was to intimidate a nation into conformity with whatever came out of the House of Ministries? They were becoming known for their two uniforms – the green, official thing and the louche, street-smart ensemble that kept a lot of leather-workers in employment. This one could have been studying at the Humboldt, but he wouldn't have been here on his own today. Students didn't do demonstrations alone.

If he was right, the man would be armed, a shoulder holster. It wasn't necessary to wonder whether he would use it, only why. Neither Fischer nor Kleiber were threats to the DDR, however provocative their presence in East Berlin on one of its more difficult days. Hoeschler had done his best to persuade his bosses that he hadn't run with Freddie Holleman, but what if MfS were less gullible than *VolksPolizei*? Even if he wasn't a prominent political catch, surely a traitor brought to justice sent a powerful message?

No, it couldn't be Hoeschler. The target was Freddie Holleman, but he was already gone, safe, ready to spill SED secrets to General Gehlen's men. So, if someone wanted him returned unopened they had to find a lure, something that he couldn't help but attach himself to, and that wasn't Rolf Hoeschler. They wanted – they needed – Kristin Holleman, and if they found her poor Freddie would fall off his false leg in the rush to re-cross the line.

'If you see Kristin, don't twitch.'

Hoeschler had got it already. He nodded. 'I was getting a hiding from some strikers earlier. A blond fellow that I didn't see interfered and had me dragged out. What do we do about him?'

'Here? Nothing. We need to get him into the crowd, then take his gun.'

Kleiber held out the Contax. 'I checked it again. I think the shutter curtain's fucked, so you may as well try it on another head.'

Fisher shook his own. 'This fellow's not going to be brought down by a camera. Once in the crowd, we go at him from two sides and shout *Stasi* as we do it. I doubt he'll have many sympathizers on Unter den Linden today, and his gun will prove the accusation.'

Hoeschler had moved around slightly to get a glimpse of their man. 'Right. So, we just walk in and let him follow?'

'You're taller than me. Once in there, I'll move left and wait for him to pass me. Try to keep your head up. You too, Jonas.'

'I have a strong cringe reflex.'

'I know, but do it for Hemingway.'

'When, exactly?'

'After I move sideways, walk slowly for one minute then stop and turn. I'll come up from behind and try to pin his arms. I doubt I'll be able to hold him for long.'

'Mind the reverse head-butt.'

'I will, very much.'

Hoeschler grinned. He seemed to be charged, full of a nervous energy that Fischer recognized from a time before the martial spirit had been quite burned out of him. *Doing* something was always preferably to waiting for the blow. He turned to Kleiber.

'If we struggle with this, it'll be up to you and Carl Zeiss AG.'

Kleiber looked doubtfully at his broken camera. 'I've never actually assaulted someone.'

'You were a soldier, weren't you?'

'For about twenty minutes, until a kind Tommy accepted my surrender. It was the day before my fifteenth birthday.'

'Well you can practise on a German. Come on.'

They moved forward, towards the demonstrators, and Fischer felt every surviving follicle on the back of his neck working double-time, trying to warn him of a descending blow. It was almost a relief to enter the throng - like being part of an army, the herd presence offered a false sense of deflection, of safety amid a press of flesh. Yet what they entered was a strangely uncoordinated affair. Without a visible enemy at which to make a point, the demonstrators were letting off in every direction and none in particular, their fists waving at all points of the compass and most of the skies for good measure. It made for slow progress, but the lack of organization closed down sight-lines and made an easy pursuit difficult.

Some twenty metres into the crowd a small gap opened between two of the demonstration's involuntary divisions. At that point, Fischer touched Hoeschler's arm, and, dipping slightly, moved crab-like to his right, pushing into a group that had coalesced beneath a large sign demanding an end to one party rule. It was done quickly, discreetly, and no one reacted to his presence. Keeping low, he turned and waited.

A minute later, their stalker hadn't yet emerged into the gap. Instinctively, Fischer glanced back at his friends. They were walking on but very slowly, and closing upon the other edge of their small human *polynya*. This one was moving with more of a purpose, eastwards, squeezing the gap, and as Hoeschler and Kleiber collided with it a woman in the front rank took the latter's arm, said something and pointed in what, to her, was the right direction. The significance of it escaped Fischer for only as long as it took him to catch his breath. Wildly, he turned again and from his side of the closing gap saw a gun barrel emerge deliberately, steadily, from among the bodies.

The plan was gone, and with it any clever alternative. He fell rather than pushed his way out of the protesters he'd hidden among, and got an angry shove from a neighbour. It was his only piece of luck, turning him slightly and putting his stronger left arm (the one he wouldn't have used instinctively) closer to the weapon. He chopped down, hard, on the hand that held it and then stumbled into a clumsy dance embrace.

The expected head-butt arrived on time but from the front, and no less painfully for it. He managed, just, to keep the left hand's grip on his right wrist, but the arms he pinned were far stronger than his own. A knee came up into his groin with less force than if it had had distance to play with, and he retained just enough presence of mind to keep his feet moving to make poor targets for stamping boots. This excellent tactic deployed, he calculated (loosely, without the aid of his missing thumbs) that he had at best about ten seconds before he was on the floor, his head conscripted for a kick-around.

His grip had begun to slacken when he found himself trying to hold upright a large sack of coal. He managed to step back before he was dragged down, and the body dropped, leaving a close view of Rolf Hoeschler, wielding what remained of a once-fine example of German photographic technology. He was suddenly, intensely grateful to have been wrong about what a Contax could or couldn't do.

Even the protesters closest to the struggle had hardly noticed it, but as Fischer lifted the gun from the ground they parted like slugs from salt. Suddenly, he and Hoeschler were in free space, the irrefutable evidence lying sprawled between them. He opened his mouth to say something that almost certainly would have incriminated him further, but before it came out Kleiber had rushed forward, waving towards the north side of Unter den Linden.

'The Red Army's here.'

From Friedrichstrasse and Glinkastrasse, tanks emerged noisily, flanked by riflemen. As they did so the crowd's interest in the doings of Otto Henry Fischer dissipated entirely; some scattered frantically into waste ground south of the boulevard, others drew together, forming a denser mass. Between the two reflexes, the gap in which the fight had taken place expanded into open ground

Hoeschler pointed towards the French Palace, whose bulk separated the two streets. In its smashed second storey windows, small shadows moved.

'I think they're snipers.'

Slowly, Fischer spread his arms and lowered himself, laying the gun slowly on the ground. When he straightened he placed both hands behind his head in the universal gesture of surrender. A glint of light in one of the palace windows might have been a reflection from a wristwatch, had it not held too unerringly upon his face. He tried hard to be the statue that no one would ever think to raise in his honour, and hoped fervently that Hoeschler and Kleiber were doing the same.

38

The red Hansa was no longer parked in the alley behind Fischer's shop. For a few minutes, Zarubin recced the block, looking for betraying hints of nonchalance in the demeanour of those citizens who didn't seem to have anywhere to be urgently. Having received only the most cursory, disinterested glances, he entered the shop through its front door.

Holleman was there still, his low mood casting an almost visible pall over the merchandise.

'Are those for me?'

Zarubin placed the bouquet of white roses on the workbench. 'For Major Fischer, to ease anything he may have on his mind still.'

'I don't think he holds grievances.'

'Well, they'll make the place a little prettier. I assume you have no news yet?'

Holleman sighed deeply. 'I haven't got anything.'

'No doubt everyone's been reassuring you, so I shan't try your patience.'

'Thank you. And I'm sorry.'

'For what?'

'For not thinking of a clever way to warn you.'

The loud click immediately behind Zarubin's left ear explained everything. He sagged slightly.

'You moved the car.'

'I had my colleague take it back to the *Rathaus*. He was worried I might damage the paintwork.'

Dietrich moved slowly into view, the pistol steady in his hand. 'I assume that I'm addressing former MGB Major Sergei Zarubin.'

'The Americans moved quickly, then.'

'I think they must be soiling themselves. They don't usually consider it worth their while to tell the Org anything until it's already history. What have you done?'

'Very little, as yet.'

'Then I'm sure they'll be very grateful to have you back.'

'That might be …'

'What?'

'A mistake.'

Dietrich gestured at one of the benches, and Zarubin sat down.

'How? You defected, probably for a purpose, and now you're going home with something the Americans really don't want to part with.'

'A fair guess. But that *something* is nothing.'

'Well, that's not my business. No doubt …'

'Actually, it is. You're German after all, and this will very much affect Germans.'

Dietrich smiled. 'Something that's nothing will affect us, and very much? How teasing.'

Zarubin gestured slightly with a hand. 'It's in my briefcase. Might I show you what I mean?'

'And have me lower this? No. Tell me instead.'

'It contains an opinion, about matters upon which the CIA would like to be better informed. I wrote it at their request.'

'And you don't think they should have it?

'They *do* have it. That is, they have a copy - two, in fact.'

'So, it must be you that they desperately want back.'

'Yes.'

'There's a reason, naturally.'

'Of course. It's because they're Intelligence, and I misled them, and therefore I must have a dangerous purpose. It's a hazard of our work, to judge everything by the risk we think it represents.'

'In what way are they mistaken?'

Zarubin gestured once more. 'What's in there is worthless. It's almost entirely inaccurate in a factual sense, and wholly so in its interpretations. They paid me very little for it, and very little is what it's worth. To them, at least.'

'Ah.' Dietrich sat on a table opposite. Holleman nodded at Zarubin.

'He talks like this a lot. I never met a man more fond of confusing folk.'

'No, I think I understand. This *something* wasn't meant for the Americans.'

'But I needed them to think that it was.'

'Because …?

Zarubin frowned at the floor. 'May I answer that with a question? I promise that your answer will determine what you do today.'

'How fascinating. Please.'

'Do you want to see a re-unified Germany?'

'Of course I do.'

'Tomorrow? Next year sometime?'

For almost a minute, Dietrich stared at Zarubin, saying nothing. Finally, slowly, he shook his head.

'No, of course you wouldn't. It could only happen one of two ways – either the plan for a neutral, disarmed Germany that both Churchill and Stalin endorsed in principle last year will be accepted by the Americans and Adenauer – and it won't, obviously – or the DDR collapses under the twin weight of its economic failures and the Kremlin's reluctance to bail it out further, after which the BDR would attempt to absorb the pieces on its own terms. This, of course, Moscow will never countenance, which would mean war. And you wouldn't want it in any case because West Germany isn't nearly strong enough to assume the burden. The only feasible reunification will come in perhaps five or ten years' time, once you can absorb the shock.'

'So, why are you here and what is it you think I'll do?'

'I'm here because I want to go home, which is almost impossible.'

'They'd put one in the back of your head and laugh while they did it.'

Zarubin grimaced. 'That's very likely. So I need something spectacular to offer them.'

'The *something* in that briefcase?'

'Yes.'

'May I ask ..?'

'For them, a revelation. For you, clarity.'

'Clarity about …?'

'Whether the DDR will be kept on its feet for the next few years, or Germany becomes a battleground once more.'

'What's the revelation?'

'The report is nonsense, as I said. But it carries one very precious thing - the official stamp of the CIA. When they see it, whatever MGB is called these days - and, therefore, the Kremlin - will regard as having a certain credibility. From the horse's mouth, as it were.'

'The what?'

'It's an American colloquialism. The report waffles a great deal about conditions in the Praesidium and the priorities of its various members. But, in concluding, it infers that one of the leading contenders to assume the leadership of the Soviet Union has been in contact with the Americans, who have agree that the Churchill-Stalin proposal will be agreed by them in return for certain guarantees.'

'What guarantees?'

'They're not specified. They don't need to be.'

'You name this man?'

'Yes.'

'You'll be putting him against a wall.'

'It's where he belongs.'

'Who?'

'Ah, well.' Zarubin stood and brushed the seat of his trousers. 'Shall we talk about what you'll do? Your colleague, the one who took the big ugly car – does he know about me?'

'He knows *of* you – he's read the same bulletin as me. I didn't mentioned to him that I'd seen you, because if you hadn't returned I'd be the man who let you slip through our fingers. It wouldn't look good on my yearly report.'

'So you have no reason not to ignore my presence here.'

'Really? Convince me.'

Zarubin lifted the briefcase, opened it and extracted a document. 'I suggest you pass over the dreary analysis and read the last page. It's somewhat different from that of the two copies.'

It took a while because Dietrich read it twice. His eyebrows came down only slowly. When he closed the report Holleman held out his hand. 'May I?'

Zarubin nodded. The former Inspector of Police was used to reading things quickly, and it was only a few moments before he gave his preliminary opinion.

'Fuck!'

Dietrich lifted a finger. 'Tell me how this makes me forget you.'

'With Beria gone, Malenkov will need to make a decision. I state in my report that he doesn't want the job, which is just about the only knowingly truthful thing in it. What he does want, and very much, is a path to a peaceful retirement, one in which he won't be dragged from his bed one night in the good old style. There are two ways to achieve this: he either gives up on an easy life and fights to step into the Boss's old shoes, or he gives Krushchev his active support. I don't think it'll be the former, but that's not important. With either him or the little bald one in charge, Germany gets what she wants – a period of certainty, in which the DDR will be supported sufficiently to prevent the crash.'

'But if the Soviet Union can't afford that cost …?'

'She has no choice, which is why I believe that Malenkov will make his goal of re-balancing her economy one of the conditions of his support for Krushchev.'

'Couldn't you have put all this to the Americans, and asked their help?'

'No. They *want* a collapse – of the DDR, and, in an ideal world, the Soviet Union also. They don't care who'll be standing beneath the falling rubble. That's the thing about having two oceans between yourselves and trouble – they give a very different perspective on what damage does. Would you like to think about this?'

'One more question.'

'I'm in your hands.'

'Why Beria? Why not Malenkov, or Krushchev?'

'Firstly, because Beria is on record as believing that the DDR isn't worth the trouble of supporting further. But principally …'

'Yes?'

Zarubin leaned forward and lowered his voice. 'Imagine a synthesis of Heinrich Himmler's soulless efficiency and the moral foundations of Julius Streicher. Wouldn't you want to do something about that?'

'He's that bad?'

'In MGB I heard things that would curdle soul-milk. Believe me, his recent defection to the human race is entirely tactical, and temporary.'

Holleman was re-reading the report's final page for the third time. He shook his head. 'This could get you drawn and quartered.'

Zarubin shrugged. 'It's why I need time, to think of a safe way to get it into the right hands. Once I'm in Moscow the job's almost done – I have contacts there that I can use without putting my name on anything. It's the space between here and there that's deadly. I have to find a lift home, from someone who won't think to use my corpse as a step-up.'

Dietrich had folded his arms across his chest and was examining his shoes. Zarubin opened his mouth and then closed it again without speaking. He had heard too much pleading to want to be guilty of it himself, so he was almost grateful when Holleman coughed.

'We've had some bad years.'

Dietrich looked up. 'The DDR?'

'Germans generally. It would be … pleasant, if things quieten a little.'

'But I work for Gehlen, who works for the Americans. And they want this gentleman, badly.'

'That's the problem – we all work for someone else. We take sides because we have to, it isn't like we have a say. This ...' he waved the report, '... is having a say, even if it's only by proxy. If it helps to keep our masters from settling their differences on German soil, would that be wrong?' Holleman gestured at Zarubin. 'And what advantage will the Amis gain by getting this one back, apart from the satisfaction of cacking him?'

The arms unfolded long enough for Dietrich to rub his forehead. 'It goes against every instinct.'

'No, just the ones that a defeated people have had to grow. We've kissed arse for so long now that we've forgotten how not to. What does it matter if you put your hand on a bible and swore to help defeat communism? Would God mind if you looked the other way, just for today?'

Zarubin cleared his throat. 'I have it on the best authority that He's an American. So yes.'

It made both Holleman and Dietrich laugh, and Zarubin almost allowed himself a tiny glimpse of a way out of this little shop. When no one said anything more he forced himself to wait – a once-arbiter of German fates, a man who ran small divisions of terrified informers, their sordid little secrets no more than half-safe in his hands, held his breath while two other Germans decided whether or not he had a future in the respiratory business. Strangely, he found it difficult to appreciate the irony.

When the SIG finally went back into its holster, more than his diaphragm relaxed. He loosened his grip on the bench beneath him (though not on his bowels) and unclenched his knees. When he felt that they could be trusted he stood slowly and waited.

Dietrich sighed. 'Well, this Zarubin fellow sounds like a proper treacherous bastard. I certainly hope someone finds him.' He turned to Holleman. 'Do you know this area?'

'A little. Otto and I did some detective work here in early '45.'

'A telephone?'

'The closest? Where Otto went a couple of hours ago - the office of his friend's newspaper.'

'Ah. Yes.'

Dietrich paused at the front door. 'Time's probably run out. I'll ask again about your wife, but they're going to want me to bring you in.'

'Do what you can. Please.'

Holleman watched him disappear down Curtius-Strasse while Zarubin retrieved his report and returned it to the briefcase. When both were safely beneath the white roses he nodded at the door.

'If I were still in the business I might offer that young man a job – a real one, I mean. He thinks more than is usual for his breed.'

'He's not too …'

'Dogmatic?'

'Yeah. But isn't that a terrible quality in a *spook?*'

'It's rare, certainly – too much so to judge accurately. Which, of course, may answer your question.'

39

For twenty minutes, Fischer, Hoeschler and Kleiber sat on the unyielding surface of Unter den Linden, their backs against the massive twin rear wheels of a BTR-152 personnel carrier. To entertain them while they waited, a young man from somewhere far east of the Urals pointed a rifle directly at each of their heads in turn with almost metronomic consistency, breaking the routine only once when Kleiber raised a hand from the ground to scratch his nose. That earned him several minutes' exclusive attention, during which time the soldier mumbled some imprecation that was probably intended to shrivel testes, or perhaps dead mothers in their shrouds.

Fischer used the distraction to half-turn his head and watch the progress of the confrontation. Sensibly, the Soviet commandeer had deployed soldiers across the western extremity of the boulevard, sealing off the protest from access to the Brandenburg Gate and the most immediate exit to West Berlin. More soldiers were reinforcing them, allowing the line to be extended southwards. The tanks had stopped at the end of the streets down which they had approached Unter den Linden, their barrels pointing directly into the crowd; other Red Army vehicles, including several identical to the one against which his back rested, were positioned end-to-end, forming an extemporary armoured barricade along its north side through which dozens of rifle barrels poked. The tiny remaining sliver of Otto Fischer the soldier approved: whoever commanded these troops had put his strength on the crowd's flank and rear, where it could threaten the maximum damage. If anyone moved to make trouble, the burial detail was going to be spectacularly busy.

Chants broke out once more from that courageous element that still faced the Soviet troops, but they were uncoordinated, and thin. Much of the crowd had disappeared already, taking the hint that somewhere else might be the wiser location. Fischer could see very few women now, and most of them were students, their youthful energy not yet sufficiently tempered by an understanding of what bullets did to human tissue. Again, he had little sense that a revolution was in progress. Uprisings were planned, led and intentionally bloody, as prodigal with the lives of their supporters as those of the establishments they intended to overthrow. All of that might be happening somewhere in the DDR, but what he had seen so far was too amateurish and opportunistic - a concentration of grievances, piggy-backing an industrial dispute for the rare chance to be heard.

He hoped the Ivans could see it, too; but then, they might and shoot anyway, glad of the chance for some live-round practise with moving targets. It was always hard to tell with Soviet formations until it was too late to matter. If the crowds were confronting an elite unit, there was an even chance that the Geneva Convention had at least been read by someone, if only for amusement. If they faced some second- or third-echelon rabble it might become another '45, and afterwards a court of enquiry would listen to straight-faced claims that the deceased had brought it all on themselves.

He was still considering the odds when the firing commenced. For a moment he expected the entire front rank of protesters to go down like dropped sacks; but they scattered instead, and the second volley was equally harmless (though several walls on the south side of Unter den Linden took new damage). He heard engines fire up, and the two tanks moved forward, but only by about their own length. It was enough; the last few souls brave enough to have waited to see how this was going to develop turned and followed their more prudent comrades into the streets and waste grounds to the south of the boulevard. In moments, the entire stretch of Unter den Linden from the Humboldt to Parizer Platz had emptied of all but its pigeons, the Soviet soldiers and their tiny group of prisoners.

For some minutes thereafter, the Soviet officers re-deployed their men, securing every corner of the streets that emptied into the boulevard, while the tanks advanced into its central space, occupying an area that once had been shaded by linden trees and positioned side-on to give any further protests a good idea of what they'd be facing. When the movements were completed, two officers approached the carrier against which the Germans leaned. Quickly, their guard kicked Hoeschler's leg and came smartly to attention.

From his fraught collection of Eastern Front memories, Fischer guessed that one of the two men was a lieutenant, the other something considerably more senior. As usual, their initial, cursory glance at his ruined face came back swiftly and took more time about it. The senior man frowned.

'Are you the western journalists?'

Astounded, Fischer could think of nothing more intelligent than 'Why do you say that?'

'One of my majors reported a police patrol crossing his lines with two arrested press men. The one with half a face caught his attention.'

'I'm a journalist.' Kleiber held out his Press card. 'The *Südwest-Berliner Zeitung*.'

The lieutenant sniggered. His commanding officer took the card, read it and turned to Fischer. 'And you?'

'I mend clocks.'

The lieutenant's smile disappeared. 'May I kick him, Comrade Lieutenant-Colonel?'

He said it in German. Fischer stood up quickly. 'No, really. My name is Otto Fischer. I have a small premises, three doors from the newspaper.'

The senior officer appraised him carefully. 'Just clocks?'

'I'm hoping to move into watches. And gramophone players.'

The other man lifted his arm and drew back the sleeve to expose his wrist, though not so closely that Fischer could make out any detail on the face of the watch.

'Where is this from?

'I'd imagine either the First Moscow plant or Tschistopolsky.'

'And what's likely to be wrong with it?'

'Nothing. Typically, it will be an excellent copy of an excellent Swiss watch.'

'But if I pressed you?'

'I'd say it depends. Have you dropped it? The shock-proofing isn't quite up to Swiss standards, probably because your General Staff expects you to steal someone else's in a combat situation. If you haven't been careful it might be running a little slow.'

Voloshyn lowered his arm and forgave the impertinence. It had amused him, and he felt a certain relief at not having to shoot this terribly mutilated fellow – not yet, at least.

'Him?'

Hoeschler stood also. 'Ex-police. Retired.'

'Which police?'

'*VolksPolizei.*'

'Why are you with these two?'

Hoeschler nodded at Fischer. 'He's an old comrade, asked me to help him find someone.'

'You chose a bad day for it.'

'It's the day that's brought it on. We're looking for a young fool who wants to show solidarity with eastern workers. We're trying to get him home before you shoot him.'

Fischer nodded. Had he been asked, he would have said something similar.

Voloshyn turned to him once more. 'Yet you decided to assault someone and wave a gun instead. A curious strategy.'

'It was *his* gun. He pointed it at my friends. I tried to stop him.'

'Why did he do that?'

'I don't know. We haven't met previously.'

Lieutenant Pankov coughed. 'The gun's a Nagant, Comrade *Podpolkovnik*. The man might be State Security.'

'Has he said anything?'

'No. We can't wake him. His papers say he's no-one.'

'Alright. What's the situation?'

'No reports of further concentrations in Mitte, other than the loud but peaceable one that's been camped outside the House of Ministries for several hours now. In Friedrichshain, there's a very large crowd in Stalin Allee – that was from the 144th, before they engaged. No further reports from Colonel Geladze as yet.'

'Right. We stay here until we get new orders. Pass the word to brew tea, rations to be distributed and ate at readiness.' He glanced westward, toward the Brandenburg Gate. 'What are the Americans doing?'

'Watching, Comrade. No attempt to interfere. One of our lads saw them turn back some protesters who tried to get through to the west.'

'Good. If we need to stay here for the night I don't want any provocations – no-one waving their bare arses at them or giving the fist, alright? Each unit commander to be responsible for his men's behaviour.'

'I'll pass it on, Comrade *Podpolkovnik*.'

Fischer hadn't understood a word of the exchange, but the signs weren't ominous. This officer seemed the phlegmatic sort, not to be roused without good reason. He had treated the crowd as a domestic disturbance rather than the enemy, given orders to fire above heads and even resisted the temptation to dole out a few kickings. Most amenably, he hadn't had the sole armed protester shot out of hand, for which the said offender was sincerely grateful.

Voloshyn lit a cigarette and regarded the ruined face. 'Where did you get your trophies?'

'Okhvat, in '42.'

'A hard fight, I think.'

'I don't recall any easy ones. But yes, you surprised us.'

'You seem to have been lucky.'

Fischer smiled. 'I've often thought that.'

'Hardly any of your men got out. You must have been wounded early in the fight.'

'A couple of aircraft used me as a landing strip. I don't recall much after that.'

'And before the war?'

'Criminal Investigations, in Stettin.'

'And now you mend clocks?'

Fischer decided that he was becoming tired of the implied criticism in that observation.

'They don't kill, rape, steal or beat their wives. And if they lie it's only because they're broken. They make excellent company.'

Voloshyn nodded, turned and scanned Unter den Linden. In the early evening light its evacuated length was as tranquil as a small town's main street, the occasional small kettle-brewing fire giving it an almost summer-camp feel. Fischer tried to read the face, but foreign cultures expressed unspoken things differently. He took a chance, wanting to keep this slight hint of good-fellowship moving.

'And you? What were you before the uniform?'

Voloshyn turned back. 'There was no *before*. If you grow up deep in sugar-beet country, the choice is fields or barracks.'

'Ukrainian?'

'A hamlet, near Bokhny. You won't have heard of it.'

'It's a part of the Soviet Union I didn't manage to invade.'

'Don't feel bad about that. More than enough Germans did. And we repaid the favour.'

Fischer nodded. 'With ample interest.'

Voloshyn looked at him curiously. 'It makes me wonder sometimes why you people hang on – in West Berlin, I mean. Isn't the rest of what you call West Germany preferable to this? You can't be making a political point, surely? Or do the Americans, British and French make you stay?'

'It's home. One sees it differently than strangers do.'

'You were born here?'

'No. I first saw it in summer '28, just before the second Crash. Three of my friends and I, cocky little bastards from the Baltic coast, thought we'd have a long weekend in the city to do some growing up. On our last night we fell into a club on Ku'damm, a place where the girls – even the cloakroom staff - were naked except for their pants, and those were completely transparent, with a small piece of silver lamé sewn on to hide their bushes. It was commonly understood that the price of entrance bought the right to grope the passing meat. I noticed that those who did it clumsily got an over-the-shoulder smile, but the girls always went a different way around the tables on the way back. The best I could do was pat the hand of the one who brought our drinks, and then I tipped her ridiculously, the last of my money gone all at once. She came back later, no doubt thinking she could do some private business, and sat on my knee.

'I thought about that moment almost every day for years afterwards, the heat of her arse on my leg, the forthright nakedness of it, her complete lack of shame, her breath in my ear, her smell, her small, lovely breasts. When I met my second wife, the memory had the decency to fade; but I've returned to it a great deal since she died. It holds a lot of what was – what still is - different about this place.'

Voloshyn nodded. 'Who wouldn't want to preserve a memory like that?'

'Preserve? I'd build a church to it, if I knew how.'

The Russia suppressed a smile. 'Well, this particular part of Berlin doesn't want you or your money. I would of course arrest you, but …'

At that moment, *but* sounded more beautiful than Fischer could ever recall. He waited.

'… apparently, every prison cell in East Berlin is full already. It's very strange, but I don't want to be dragging flotsam with me. Pankov!'

'Comrade *Podpolkovnik*?'

'Write out two permissions, for the bearers to pass through our lines.'

'But, Comrade …'

'What?

'The unconscious fellow …?'

'I don't care. Whoever he is, he's paperwork. We have two western interlopers we don't want, so what would a diligent officer do?'

'Shovel them out of sight and mind, Comrade?'

'You're destined for greatness, Lieutenant.'

Voloshyn tuned to Hoeschler. 'You, of course, aren't going west. Where's home?'

'Marzahn, Comrade.'

'Then you'd better start walking. Forget your foolish young friend; if he hasn't been arrested or shot yet then he probably won't be. If he has, you can't do anything about it. You understand that I'm not going to repeat myself?'

'No, Comrade.'

'You two ...' He turned to Fischer and Kleiber, '...will march straight to the American checkpoint at the Brandenburg Gate and pass through it. I'll have one of my marksmen watch you every step of the way, with orders to open fire if you turn back. Understood?'

Fischer glanced towards the gate. It was going to be a back-itching walk between here and there. 'Yes, sir. May I ask your name?'

'Voloshyn, Andrei Mikhailovitch, Lieutenant-Colonel.'

'And this unit?'

'Why? Is it going into the newspaper?'

Kleiber was shaking his head violently. Fischer steadied him with a hand. 'If it does, your civility will be mentioned, together with the fact that you dispersed a mob efficiently, without shooting anyone. It would make a good impression - so good, in fact, that the Americans might suppress it as unhelpful.'

Voloshyn gestured at his men. 'We are elements of 2nd and 4th Battalions, 248th Motor-Rifle Regiment, 10th Guards Division. Efficiency my commanding officer will appreciate; the lack of casualties, not so much. This was a crowd of western fifth-columnists, after all - or it will be, by tomorrow. Now please, remove yourselves.'

Fischer looked at Hoeschler, whose face told nothing. They shook hands, Kleiber retrieved his battered camera and the two West Berliners turned towards their runway-straight exit from the DDR.

They had taken only a single step when something occurred to Fischer. It was the answer to a puzzle that hadn't really puzzled him, but it drew together several of the day's little enigmas – why Freddie Holleman had run, why the East German Government seemed paralysed by events, why they had purposely withdrawn *VolksPolizei* from the streets when every strand of common sense would have urged them to lock the city in an iron grip – and tied them neatly with the same ribbon. It wasn't much, but this Soviet officer had been more decent that he needed to be. Some sort of exchange seemed correct.

He turned once more. Hoeschler was gone already, through the line of armoured vehicles. The Lieutenant-Colonel had been giving orders to his adjutant, who ran off smartly to execute them. When he saw that his problem hadn't departed his eyebrows rose.

'What is it now?'

'You said that the station prisons were full. In fact, they're not. They're empty, and by design.'

Voloshyn shook his head. 'Why the hell would that be?'

'They've been reserved, and not for the decent workers with legitimate grievances who marched today - nor, even, for the troublemakers who joined them later and shouted terrible things about Ulbricht. In fact, I think the gentleman was probably delighted when they turned up.'

'Why?'

'He needed them to scare you.'

'German civilians don't scare me.'

'You, the Soviet Union. Or rather, you, the Kremlin.'

The frown on the Russian's face relaxed slightly. 'Explain yourself.'

'I spoke with a friend earlier today, a good communist and member of the SED. He told me he couldn't see any good way out of what was happening - for himself, that is. I wondered what he meant, but the oddities are beginning to form a line. I don't suppose that you're unaware of the troubles the DDR's been experiencing?'

'It's not my job to notice.'

'No, but two hundred thousand citizens fleeing west leaves some flattened ground, doesn't it? Every major economic target missed, and not by a whisker; wages worse than stagnating; the prospect of western Germany drawing further ahead in the race to reconstruct – and all the while the House of so-called Unity's been at its own collective throat, arguing about what's needed to put things right. In a normal year, they could rely on you – you the Kremlin, I mean – to give them a hefty, helpful shove towards some sort of policy, but you've been preoccupied by a Stalin-shaped hole. And then, a week ago, the work quotas business exploded like a fermenting midden. Half the SED's Politburo wants to shoot the workers, the other half shake their hands and say that an apology's due. So what's a Head of Government to do?'

'Resign, if he has any sense.'

'Or simplify the choices. Better still, remove the prospect of choices.'

'By …?'

'Offering a glimpse of chaos, of what happens when the Party loses its grip on the people. If Ulbricht had been able to follow his instincts there would have been mass arrests and more than a few shootings. He would have cleared the streets in minutes and declared martial law. But he didn't have that particular choice. There aren't enough *Kasernierte* police or State Security stiffs to do the job, and in any case his Politburo might have argued the point until there wasn't one anymore. So, he deflected the problem by letting you shoulder the effort. And take any blame for casualties, of course.'

'He's deliberately removed his hands from the wheel?'

'And prised off those of his political enemies also. He's pushed you into making the only viable choice, if you want the DDR to remain loyal to Moscow. And that choice is Ulbricht.'

Voloshyn shook his head. 'A fantastical theory.'

'Is it? Where do you go when you're desperate, when everything's buggered and there's no clear way forward?'

'To your pistol.'

'You go home. Home, for Ulbricht, is Moscow. You know that – he's an iron-class Stalinist, as pure as the Boss himself. But home's been less reliable lately, too concerned with its own affairs. No-one knows how things will settle, so he's done you a favour of sorts. He's concentrated minds, reminded you that the Soviet world extends further than Red Square, and that you'd better take notice. And you have.'

Fischer glanced back at Kleiber. The twitch wasn't quite visible yet, but a gentle prod might have sent him in an arc over the beckoning bulk of the Brandenburg Gate. It wasn't kind to keep him waiting.

'So, tomorrow the empty prison cells are going to fill quickly, with loyal SED men whose visions don't quite accord with those of their General Secretary. After that, what? Probably denunciations, show trials, executions and a lot more careers in State Security. No doubt the workers are going to get some small concessions – nothing to embarrass the Finance Ministry but enough to show them who their friends are. And at the end of all that, no-one will be troubled by *choices* anymore.'

Voloshyn asked himself whether the mutilations gave the story more credibility than it deserved, but he couldn't find the holes in it. For hours now he had felt like he was being worked by strings, pulled to no logical effect. He had assumed the hands working them to be those of his own people, but if the Control Commission or even Grechko himself were obliging Ulbricht with a show of solidarity, he was worse than a puppet This was a surrender to events, and he was holding the white flag.

He turned to reassure himself that Pankov was well out of hearing range. 'Would you like an opinion?'

'I can hardly say no.'

'To my mind, it's impossible to insult a politician, the German variety least of all. Even when they do something admirable it's only a by-product of self-interest. Patriotism is what they say it is, duty the burden of other men, failure the fault of anything but their own cowardice or stupidity. We should have cleaned them all out several months ago and started again.'

'But that would have required leadership from Moscow, and I think you have the same problem there?'

Voloshyn looked hard at Fischer, weighing the chances of him ever returning to the east and speaking of matters that would have been much better left unsaid – of perhaps forgetting himself and quoting a former, glancing acquaintance. It took an effort not to draw his pistol and do the prudent thing.

'On that, I have no comment to make. Now, please go west.'

40

The job was tiresome, repetitive and, to the *oberwachtmeister* trusted with it, about the best task he could have been given on this strange, disturbing day.

He had been on the telephone for almost three hours now, working his way down the list of district police stations, taking returning street patrols' verbal reports on incidents on or near the line. Usually, these would of course be written up, collected and sent to Headquarters, but the force was a small one, and stretched so thinly today that no-one could be spared for usual things.

The small catalogue of arrests (almost all for disorderly behaviour) wasn't much reward for the time it had taken to compile, but he reminded himself that he was on his arse in the office, and several rations of almost-real coffee had helped to ease the boredom. His shift's end was almost in sight now, and tonight's supper – if his wife's foraging skills hadn't deserted her - was going to be *Königsberger klopse*, (she insisted on calling it that still), which was just about his favourite dish that wasn't a pudding. He could recall very many days that had gone worse than this.

He was making one of his last five calls, his mind wandering widely from police business, when a small ladle of dung spoiled the afternoon. He didn't know the voice on the other end of the line, but it sounded as if its day had been considerably busier than the *oberwachtmeister*'s. The man was flustered, ill-tempered, and, probably, on his own in a small station whose normal complement was officially, irreducibly, three.

'I have four arrests.'

'Charge?'

'One of them has false papers.'

'Damn, that's serious.'

'Look, we were told to watch for anyone trying to start trouble, and bad papers is trouble, isn't it?'

The *oberwachtmeister*, already tired of this conversation, sighed. 'I suppose so. What about the other three?'

'They were with him, so ...'

'Right. Names?'

'A male, Engelbrecht Preis, seventeen; a young female, Liesa Kästner, nineteen; a male, Kasper Schultz – he's the one with the crap papers, says he's twenty-three, it looks about right; and an older woman, Annaliese Beckendorp ...'

The name had been on the *oberwachtmeister*'s desk for several hours now, with *urgent* written over it and double-underlined. He had no idea who she was or what she'd done, but he could recall only two other occasions upon which an all-stations alert had been put out for named individuals, and both of those had been method-murderers.

He had clear instructions, allowing no latitude or initiative (which was how he preferred them), and the thought that his vigilance would be recognized was entirely soured by the certainty that he wouldn't be ending his shift on time. His only consolation was that the other fellow's already-crammed day was going to finish on an even busier note.

'I'm sending a squad to pick them up. Under no circumstances are you to release them. In fact, don't go into their cells until you have armed company.'

'Shit. What have they done?'

'I have no idea. But this comes straight from the Ministry.'

41

The return journey to Lichterfelde was relatively quick, followed bus
routes along which buses actually ran, and to Fischer and Kleiber
dragged no less than a failed pilgrimage. It was extended slightly –
and much against Fischer's will – by the other man's insistence that
he be present when the State of the Camera was explained to Herr
Grabner.

The proprietor and editor of the *Südwest-Berliner Zeitung* listened
silently while the entire tale of Kleiber's latest advance into Eastern
Europe was recounted, the narrative lingering on those brief but
violent episodes that explained the Contax's transformation from a
well-worn tool of photo-journalism to an attractive door-stop.
Having heard much previously of the gentleman's foul temper,
Fischer was surprised that this manifest of abject failure (unleavened
by a single recorded interview) was met with a sigh and a shrug.

'You did your best, Jonas. We'll, ah … we'll run with what RIAS
has been broadcasting today – at least their lies are officially cleared
beforehand. Then, do something on expectations for the flower
show, will you? Pull out what we wrote last time and waffle a bit
about standards getting higher each year. I'll make up a few quotes
for our good friend Anonymous.'

Kleiber saw Fischer out on to Curtius-Strasse. Despite his apparent
reprieve he was chewing his lip.

'I'm worried, Otto. He's never been like this. It's like there's no fight left in him.'

'Perhaps his wife hasn't come home one time too many. That, or there being not much in the way of news on a day that half of Germany's in turmoil.'

'You don't think he might be thinking of throwing it all up?'

'They say that newspapers need deep pockets and perseverance. Perhaps he's finally coming to his senses.'

'Shit. I can't start again – I'm almost twenty-three!'

'But you don't enjoy your work.'

'Who enjoys *any* work? It's not what it's for.'

Fischer left him brooding on the *Zeitung*'s front doorstep and went home. The tissue around his left eye (it had taken the brunt of the would-be assassin's head) was beginning to feel fuller than it should, and the rest of him ached proportionately to the day's uncommon exertions. He wanted to return to an empty shop and apartment, with no greater decision to make than whether to stay in for the evening or invest in a couple of *Spezial*s at his Schoss-Strasse bar. If the day were to continue on its present trajectory, he doubted that he'd be given the choice.

The big red Hansa was parked on the street this time, rather than in the alley, and the young man whose pride and joy it was sat at the wheel. The door to *Fischer's Timepiece Repairs* stood widely open, allowing the previously-discreet Holleman presence to advertise itself loudly from within. Reluctantly, he entered.

'Otto! For God's sake, where have you been? We almost missed you, and that wouldn't do, not at all.'

Freddie, babbling, was usually a positive sign, if a mixed blessing for his audience. Fischer opened his mouth, but the tide was unstoppable.

'It's alright, she's safe. The Nazis arrested her hours ago! You'd never have guessed ...'

Dietrich winced. The *Bundesgrenzschutz* uniform was largely a case of making do, the helmet a style of which the young Federal Republic had an embarrassing surplus. No doubt there were former National Socialists within their ranks, and the *stahlhelm* did nothing to discourage speculation in that regard. It was one of the few telling insults the East Germans could bring to bear on their richer cousins, so they took particular care to do so.

'... she used little Liesa to tempt Ulrich west, being as she is concerned about the baby. Did I tell you she was foaling? Anyway, he didn't get anywhere near a protest, but the silly bugger waved his new false papers at the Naz ... at the Border Police, and they took offence. Everyone's been sat in a western Berlin police station since about noon and all the time I was crawling up walls. It's mad!'

'Where are they now?'

'The *Rathaus*. They'll let me see her, but only for a hug. I'm off to Pullach this evening, to spill my secrets to the Gehlen Organization ...' Holleman drew breath and looked around. 'Shit. This is my last day in Berlin, ever.'

'You can come back and visit, Freddie. You're always welcome.'

'No, it's too dangerous. They won't forget what I've done. But then, that's what the Major said, and he's back ...'

'Who?'

A cough behind Fischer almost made him depart the floor. He turned, knowing already what the view was going to be.

'Hello, Major.'

'Hello, Major.'

Age hadn't withered the joke's witlessness, but Fischer was too surprised to improvise. He took the offered hand and despite himself noticed the watch – it looked expensive, as American baubles usually did. The suit was nice, too.

Acutely aware of Dietrich's presence and his particular business, the question Fischer really wanted to ask – the obvious one, of a man who had fled Germany only three years earlier with half the Red Army on his arse – remained unspoken. Yet Zarubin seemed relaxed and smiled easily, as someone who wasn't in deadly, present danger from several directions might.

'It's alright, Major. Herr Dietrich has been persuaded of my cause.'

'Which is?'

Dietrich coughed. 'We must be going. A 'plane's waiting at Tegel.'

Holleman beamed 'Here that, Otto? I'm airborne again, the first time since '40. They've found Kristin a little house in Neurried, so it isn't like we won't see each other. Can you believe that woman? The grief she's given me, who'd be a married man, eh?'

Fischer followed them out into the street and waited until the Hansa began to move. His hand was half-raised still when it stopped. Holleman's head poked out of the window.

'Get a girl, Otto! Really, you aren't good alone.'

'I'll think about it.'

Once more the Hansa rolled forward a few feet only. The head re-emerged.

'Where's Rolf?'

'We left him on Unter den Linden. I expect he's already across the line.'

'Good. Oh!'

'Christ! *What*, Freddie?'

'I forgot - you had a customer. Goodbye, Otto!'

When the car had disappeared into Drakenstrasse, Fischer returned to his new problem, who was quietly examining several of the tools that the premises had acquired from a clock maker's widow some months previously. He looked exactly the same as when they had last met, as if the tribulations of a new life had flowed around rather than over him. Together with his habitual air of self-satisfaction, Zarubin's seemingly eternal youthfulness was his least endearing quality.

'So you didn't warm to the United States of America?'

Zarubin laughed. 'Nor it to me. We were each over-sold to the other.'

'Was it the unavoidable pursuit of wealth? The tyranny of choices?'

'Strangely, I was comfortable with both, though I have no skills as a money-maker. It was the transience of it all, the sense that I was watching a nation passing through from nowhere to nowhere else. We Russians need our ancient bedrocks, as harsh as they are.'

'You're homesick? For what, a firing-post?'

'I've brought something that might push that prospect away.'

'Presumably, the latest uranium technologies? Anything less might not calm memories.'

'Ha! Not quite. In any case, delivering the atom bomb – in every sense - is Malenkov's brief. One doesn't want to step on toes.'

'Then given that you have no feel for anything other than putting a blade where it's least wanted, it's about the succession.'

Zarubin slapped the bench. 'I wonder what that says about me. That is, I should. And if I ever begin to worry about it, I will. You're right, yes.'

'There were three front-runners at the last count. And you intend to …?'

'Dig a divot. Put a *mickey in the mash.*'

'Eh?'

'Forgive me. It may take a while to lose the argot. I have very important information that isn't capable of being assessed for its accuracy – not that anyone who benefits from it would care to try.'

'And, these being high matters of State, the information is not of a sort that will raise anyone's reputation. Rather the reverse, I expect?'

For a few moments, Zarubin regarded his host carefully. 'Fischer, I swear that if ever you and I had worked together to the same end, we could have done considerable things. For an innocent, you have a beautifully *lateral* mind.'

'Who are the unlucky two?'

'It's just the one; but the information will force the second to make a hard choice. Really, I'll be doing my country a favour.'

'By simplifying things.'

'Yes. Three months of political paralysis is no great problem, if you're Italy. The Soviet Union can't afford the luxury.'

'And how will you do this?'

'That's the problem. I have the warhead and the intended target has been acquired; but the delivery system …'

'Is likely to end up somewhere quiet between here and Moscow, with a bullet in the back of its head?'

Zarubin pulled a face. 'You can't imagine the times I've pictured it – the ditch, or the woodlands; the ruins of a small hovel, perhaps, given time to say a quick prayer by some boy who misses his pious mother. One can get quite sentimental about life's last moments.'

'About wishing they weren't, you mean?'

'You must have done that yourself.'

Fischer rubbed the hairless side of his head. 'Actually, no. The only times I've had reason to consider the end it's been a matter of wishing it closer, not further away. Forgive me, but why are you *here*, particularly?'

'For a while, I've been assuming that I'd have time to work out a means of getting where I need to be. However, my American employers wanted me in Berlin today. It's a wonderful opportunity, but it's come too soon.' Zarubin glanced around and smiled. 'You're my stopped clock, if you like.'

'You want to stay *here*?'

'Only while I think through my next step.'

Despite the bad news, Fischer almost laughed, and Zarubin caught it. 'What?'

'You must be staring into the shit-pan, if I'm your first call.'

'They first and last, to be frank. I regret that I have few close relationships.'

'No Russian friends?'

'I had word last year that my uncle's housekeeper died. She was the last of my family, the only person to whom I ever felt close. Apart from Mother, obviously.'

'My condolences.'

'I miss her. As for company *per se*, I've never felt the need, though if I survive this I may invest in a dog. Emotionally, that is.'

Fischer had a spare bedroll, and adequate space on his sitting-room floor, and no polite reason to refuse the request of a man who had used him shamelessly several times and probably saved his life also. The *impolite* reasoning gave considerable weight to the possibility of one or several Intelligence agencies painting a bull's-eye on the premises' front window and then calling in artillery. On a day when his health had been risked already in the cause of good fellowship, it inclined him to be churlish.

'You're sure that Moscow itself won't be fatal, if you get that far?'

Zarubin shrugged. 'By no means. It will depend entirely upon whether the recipient of this information is grateful or merely Russian-grateful. If the former, I may yet have a future; if the latter, glasses will be raised fondly in memory of the tremendous favour I did him.'

'A gamble, then.'

'A very great one.'

'Yet you're committed to doing this?'

'I'm sure there are other paths. I just don't see my feet on them.'

'Alright.'

'I can stay here?''

'Tell me something first. A broad, deep red ribbon on a Red Army chest – what does that represent?'

Is it alone, or in company?'

'It's among others.'

'Then it signifies a Hero of the Soviet Union.'

'A high award.'

'There are none higher. Not many people get them.'

'In that case, no, you can't stay.'

'What?'

'You need to get to Unter den Linden, this evening.'

'For what purpose?'

'To stick out your thumb.'

A riddle thrown in Zarubin's direction never fell to ground. He frowned.

'Tell me.'

'On a day when examples are expected – in fact, directed - to be made, how would an officer strike you who refused to fire on protesters unless he had to?'

'I'd consider him … courageous.'

'Which we know already, because the broad, red ribbon lives on *his* chest. Would it also indicate a certain flexibility of mind – at least, a tendency to think about orders?'

'It might, yes.'

'At the least, it suggests a sheep that stands a little apart from the flock?'

'It does.'

'And if this man also gave an impression that he found air more breathable the further removed he was from political types?'

For almost a minute, Zarubin said nothing. The frown deepened and moved slightly as the permutations marched past, offering vistas of a dozen bad endings.

'I've known many men affect a distaste for politics. And every one of them became a politician.'

'It must be at least eight years since his heroism was recognized. He's only a lieutenant-colonel still. Hasn't he rather squandered the opportunity, if he ever thought of it that way?'

'Perhaps he's a fool.'

'He commands a Motor-Rifle Regiment. Is such a man likely to be a fool?'

'It's not unheard of.'

'His job was to clear East Berlin's streets today. It isn't one that Wünsdorf would have given to a fellow with free space between the ears.'

'But he doesn't know me.'

'With respect, that's a good thing. Because you're going to need to convince him of your honesty.'

Zarubin smiled. 'What a damn good, insufferable point. But really, how am I to convince the man?'

'You must have thought about this already. Tell as much of the truth as you can. You need to get to Moscow as quickly as possible – it's a matter of State security, of the highest importance. Tell him that men are trying to stop you – and emphasise that none of them are in uniform. Do you still have your MGB identification?'

'No, and it would be useless anyway. The Directorate was remerged with MVD – yet again - three months ago, and new papers issued.'

'Was it? I didn't know. Tell me what you have – I mean, the physical form of your information.'

'A CIA report.'

'Is it genuine?'

'The contents are my own invention. The medium is entirely genuine.'

'Good. Then you show it to him – I mean, wave it in his face. He can only conclude that whoever's trying to stop you doesn't want the Kremlin to have American intelligence.'

'And what will incline him to not immediately refer this up his chain of command? A good soldier would regard it as mandatory.'

'Hint at the real business - the power-struggle in Moscow. My feeling is that he's intelligent enough to get it. And if he asks why you chose him …'

'I say that the day has chosen the man. That in a city lacking all of its usual recourses, he's the only visible authority remaining. That I can't go to Karlshorst because certain people there may already be compromised. That I daren't simply push this up the line because I don't know who to trust, and therefore neither does he. That I must put this personally into the hands of a certain member of the Praesidium, or …'

'Or what?'

'Nothing. I leave it hanging.'

'May I make a suggestion?'

'Please.'

'If he helps, insist that he put you under guard on the way to the airfield, and keep you that way during the flight and after. It adds credibility.'

Zarubin nodded. 'And keeps me alive between Bykovo and the Kremlin. That's very good, but …'

'But?'

'I'm asking myself, why don't I just stay here and take my time? A rushed plan is usually a bad one.'

Fischer shrugged. 'A good one's still going to rely upon you finding someone to get you to Moscow. How many people in East Berlin do you know these days?'

'About three, if changes at Karlshorst haven't overtaken them.'

'And how many of those can you trust – I mean, *definitely* trust?'

'None.'

'So, how would you go about identifying the as-yet stranger who's going to get you safely to Moscow? It would take time – weeks, at least. All that while, the Americans would be looking for you, and however you persuaded Dietrich not to hand you over today, can you be sure his sense of duty wouldn't press too hard eventually? Worst of all, what if you *do* finally find someone who can be trusted and he manages to get you all the way to the Kremlin, but in the meanwhile the succession's been settled? Who wouldn't put a bullet in your head then?'

The Russian pulled his face but said nothing. Fischer had forensically laid out the holes in a scheme that relied upon far too many felicities that he couldn't influence, requiring a leap of faith rather than anticipation. He must have known it because he didn't speak, and a mute Zarubin wasn't commonly found in Nature. Fischer might have enjoyed his discomfort, had he not so sincerely wanted him to be convinced and then gone.

'Really, this man in Unter den Linden is the best chance you're going to get. It might have been wiser to conceive a more … *anonymous* means of returning.'

Zarubin sighed. 'There are no anonymous homecomings for traitors. This lieutenant-colonel – you have a strong feeling that he might be … persuadable?'

'As much as anyone might be. And he has a little army at his disposal, though it and he will probably be gone tomorrow.'

'What's his name?'

'Voloshyn.'

To Fischer's surprise, Zarubin brightened slightly. 'A Ukrainian?'

'Is that relevant?'

'More like fate.'

'You've become superstitious.'

'I never ceased to be. We were obliged to give up God, but not even the Party can loosen a Russian's sense that all things are ordained.' He stood and looked down at his suit. 'He won't think I'm too sleek?'

'A man who moves among Americans mustn't be noticed.'

'Ah, no. How much is a taxi fare to the line? I daren't risk the bus.'

'I don't know. This should be enough.'

Fischer gave him what he had in his pocket, and received a small bundle of dollars in return. He laughed. 'This is thirty times what I gave you.'

'I can't use it. If I ever return to Berlin you can repair a clock for me, gratis.'

'But you won't.'

'No, probably not.'

Fischer took the extended hand. 'Goodbye, then. Good luck.'

He recalled the message as Zarubin opened the door.

'Freddie said that I had a customer earlier.'

'Yes! A young man asked if you buy as well as mend and sell. We said we didn't know, so he's coming back later with his clock. I doubt that you'll want it, though.'

'Why not?'

'From the bullet hole in its face, I'd say it stopped sometime in May 1945.'

42

'He's awake, Comrade.'

For several moments, Voloshyn had to search his memory. For more than an hour now he had been inspecting his force's dispositions along the length of Unter den Linden, adjusting them where necessary (particularly around the Soviet Embassy) and deflecting respectful questions about what came next. All he could tell them was that they were going to remain where they were for the night, that darkness might encourage die-hard idiots to attempt something stupid, and that in consequence no-one was going to be getting much sleep. As for their relief, it would come when it came, or it wouldn't.

So, who was *awake* required a little thought. He had dismissed his prisoners in every sense, even the curious one who wore the mid-twentieth-century's trials so prominently, and he needed the good adjutant Pankov's nudge.

'The one who owns the gun. Allegedly.'

'Right. Where is he?'

Pankov had put him the back of one of their BTR-152s with a single guard. Voloshyn dismissed the latter and waited while the patient – or prisoner, depending on his answers – rubbed some awareness into his bloodied head. When their eyes met he saw no trepidation, no fear of what might come next.

The man nodded, and winced. 'Comrade *Podpolkovnik.*'

He was too young to be a veteran, so reading the tabs correctly answered most of Voloshyn's most urgent concerns. He turned to Pankov. 'Bring some tea.'

'Where's my gun?'

And forget Allegedly.

Voloshyn ignored the question. 'Who are you?'

'MfS.'

'Your papers say otherwise.'

'I was going west, across the line.'

'For what reason?'

The young man said nothing, but his eyes told Voloshyn to be serious.

'Alright. Were those three men your targets?'

'Not really.'

'But they were of interest?'

'They were … useful, or might have been. Where are they now?'

'Gone. I don't have time or the inclination to police minor affrays. They convinced me that the gun was yours, and you've just admitted that it is.'

The young man seemed to accept this philosophically, as one might the weather. He took the tin mug that Pankov offered, sipped the hot tea and gave the back of his head further, tender attention. Voloshyn had no direct experience of dealing with *Staatssichersheitsdienst*, and dreaded whatever form-filling this encounter was going to generate. At the moment, though, it was a distraction, to be flushed as easily as possible.

'Pankov, find his gun and return it, please.' He turned to the German, whose name he wasn't going to ask and certainly didn't wish to know.

'Obviously, I want you out of the area secured by my men.'

'Of course, Comrade. May I ask if you questioned the men before you released them?'

'I did, briefly.'

'An address? For any of them?'

Voloshyn stared at his guest. It required no great leap of imagination to understand the consequences of his answer. He might ask for a promise, a commitment; but that would be a waste of both their time and breath. In any case, it was not his job to care. The fact that he had felt a curious affinity for a broken-faced former enemy was irrelevant, a matter that his wounded sense of honour would deal with later. The probable sum of it was another dead German, the most debased of all human currencies.

He glanced at Pankov, who had returned with the Nagant. 'Not an address, no, but the one with the face repairs clocks. He has premises near the offices of …?'

'The *Südwest-Berliner Zeitung*, Comrade *Podpolkovnik*.'

The MfS man nodded. 'I'll find it. Thank you.'

The two officers watched him trot across Unter den Linden and into the waste ground between the ruined Comic Opera and Soviet Embassy. When he had disappeared Voloshyn turned to his adjutant. 'Did you check the magazine?'

'Yes, Comrade. It's full, twelve bullets.'

'Then I've signed some poor bastard's death certificate.'

'It's internal German business, Comrade. Not yours.'

'Yes, thank you, Pankov. Anything else?'

'Someone to see you, Comrade. He says it's urgent.'

'Christ! Can't a man make war in peace these days?'

'He's one of ours, a Russian, though I'm almost certain his suit isn't. He asked for you by name.'

43

Fischer took his time, examining each of the five bullets he had inherited with his venerable PRM-1892 with overly-critical care. Two of them represented a far greater threat to the hand that gripped the pistol than any intended recipient and were easily discarded. Of the others, a further two were an even bet and the third a lingering question mark. He (very) gently rubbed the latter's rim with glass-paper, but the corrosion was unwilling to part with any good that lay beneath, and it extended too far into the primer's face for him to judge whether powder had leaked. Eventually he convinced himself that two rounds would be enough. And if they weren't, a third probably wouldn't make a difference.

Since first moving into the premises he'd regretted the fact that his front window was north-facing. The sort of commercial lighting that got a display noticed was far beyond his means, so even in high summer the early evenings cast shadows that encouraged his potential consumer base to pass by without glancing in at what might otherwise seize their attention.

He felt very different about it now. Sat at his bench and lit by a single lamp, he was certain that no casual glances would notice the gun sat on the table before him. It had been stripped and oiled so many times that it looked like a display model (which was what it might be, of course, if he was wrong about the surviving ammunition). Holding it low, he placed the two possibly useful bullets in the cylinder, cocked the weapon and went to unlock the front door. He was hungry, having eaten nothing since his sparse breakfast that morning, and the hours between had stretched hugely. He thought of the cheese and bread in his small kitchenette but pushed away the urge. If he went to eat he might miss his next customer.

He felt the shop around him more than was usual, the comfort of familiar things pressing like a warm blanket - his first business adventure; the first home he had furnished without the help of a wife, a place in which he could take time to think. This evening it all felt more permanent than he could ever recall, and he wondered if that was a reaction to a sense of incipient loss. Perhaps he was grieving already, and hadn't seen it.

He resisted the temptation to check the back door and upstairs fire-window. They were secure, and though someone with the right experience would make nothing of their locks it would take too much time, and cause too much noise. Whatever was coming would come straight in, through the front door. It was what prospective customers did.

A small, distant part of Otto Fischer rebuked the rest. It would have taken no great effort to stand outside on the pavement and wait for a policeman to pass by. This was a busy street, close to the s-bahn, full of respectable, tax-paying traders who insisted on a visible presence to deter those elements who preferred not to pay for their acquisitions. He could then explain, in two or three sentences at most, what presently concerned him and then lock his front door, walk across to Schloss-Strasse and have his two *Spezials*, comforted by the knowledge that a stain was being wiped away as he sipped his beer and listened to the usual crap about the world's problems and how easily they could be righted. What was wrong with that? What failure would that represent, that he had dismissed the possibility out of hand? This wasn't his concern, and it certainly wasn't his fault, so why had he added yet again to the smothering mass of remorse he carried with him like Frau Siebert did – had - her bloody useless clock?

It's Otto being Otto Freddie Holleman would have said, and shaken his head wearily. *Otto's found another Deutsche Mark and worries who's lost it* Earl Kuhn might have laughed, and raised his eyes to Heaven. *Otto, darling, life's too short* Marie-Therese would sigh, and thrown him on to their too-small bed to prove her point magnificently. In this at least, all of them were profoundly wiser than he, and nothing make the slightest mark. He had what he had, a futile sense of duty around which no convenient path allowed a detour.

It wasn't even the last ember of police within him; rather, a refusal to take what had to be taken, preferably without complaint and lying down, the way that modern Germans did. It was sedition, in a way – Otto Fischer's bespoke little uprising, and no doubt as pointless as the day's greater broils. He didn't mind that; futility was something else that Germans had learned to live with.

It was darker now, almost ideal conditions for a transaction that needed not to be noticed. The young man might be circling, taking his time, giving it another few minutes to be sure. He wasn't too stupid, this one. The broken clock was a prop, obviously. It had no value, anyone could see that; but it was the legitimate means of getting him into a place that had a cash box guarded only by a badly wounded war veteran. After that small impediment had been dealt with he could take his time. Older men owned stuff; they were sentimental, and didn't care to part with their dead wives' jewellery, or their own medals, or the gilt-framed photographs of their fled children. Besides, a premises that repaired clocks probably had a stock of wristwatches also - and anything in gold, even faulty, was worth something. It would be a shame not to shop for the week, if the opportunity was there.

Fischer almost smiled. He wasn't at all bothered about his stock, or his few mementoes. This was upon a point of littering – of leaving elderly ladies with cut throats in inconvenient public places. Lichterfelde had seen quite enough of that sort of thing, and as a dutiful citizen he felt he couldn't just turn the blind eye.

He picked up the gun once more, noticing the weight of its two unreliably-filled chambers more than he should. In all his years in the police and Luftwaffe he had never known a misfire, so perhaps he was owed one. He began to hope that if one of them had to be bad it would be the second, but the thought drew out another, one that had been fermenting gently, hiding, not wanting to make its presence felt. The first one would discharge correctly or not, and that would be an end to it, one way or the other. But if all went well he had a further decision to make, and that was what to do with the second.

———————

Josef laid the body down carefully. The dropped clock he could have done nothing about, but it landed on soil, which muffled the clatter of its bowels slightly. It might have been heard, or not. It hardly mattered.

He assuaged any vestigial sense of regret by telling himself that civilians didn't lurk in alleys to the rear of commercial premises, straining their (now-broken) necks to see over fences; but he was relieved all the same when he found the cut-throat razor and two ladies' wedding bands in the same pocket. A fellow in the redistribution business had to expect bad days at the office.

Luckless had been reconnoitring the rear entrance, which is precisely what Josef himself intended. But even in the fading light he could see that the door was metal – do-able, certainly, but it would take too much time and not a little noise. The front door was wood and glass and of no great quality, so even if the hunched shape he had noticed sitting at a table behind it had thought to lock up, a shoulder would get him inside in a moment.

He had checked the Nagant soon after leaving Unter den Linden. He didn't trust the Ivans any more than he cared for their company, but they hadn't messed with the magazine's contents. It was just as well.

He suspected that, after squeezing and dealing with this fellow, he had an extremely busy night ahead.

Author's Note

The clashes of 17 June 1953 seemed briefly to threaten the existence of the German Democratic Republic, but their dangers were illusory, and fleeting. In total, some four hundred thousand workers and their supporters demonstrated in cities across the DDR, yet they represented no single grievance and had no central organization that might have directed them meaningfully. By nightfall, all but a small handful of protests had dissolved, leaving the streets to the Red Army and its paramilitary police allies. Estimates of the fatalities that they and their *Kasernierte* paramilitary allies inflicted vary; fifty-five deaths were confirmed and the victims identified, but it has been claimed that more than double this number died on the streets of Berlin and other East German cities during the course of the day.

Studies have since concluded that the vast majority of protesters wanted to make one or more of several points, and, having done so, went home thereafter, convinced for the most part that things wouldn't, or couldn't, change for the better. What had seemed to be a defining assault upon the Regime was rather an ill-coordinated criticism of its policies; yet ironically, the 'uprising' became the means by which Ulbricht's administration cemented its hold upon the institutions of State.

The day's winners were, unequivocally, Ulbricht himself and the fledgling security service, *Staatssicherheitsdienst* (though not, ironically, its Director, Wilhelm Zaisser). Beginning the following day, arrests occurred of Party officials who had criticised the undoubtedly disastrous economic policies implemented during the previous year. At the same time, the Government reaffirmed its commitment to earlier measures to relieve food shortages and confirmed the cancellation of the new work quotas. Defections of citizens to the BDR continued, but the root causes of the 17 June disturbances were sufficiently addressed to prevent further large scale protests against the Regime. Within weeks, Helmstadt and his ally Zaisser had been removed from office, though their expulsion from the Party took some months more to arrange. In the years that followed, the SSD grew from a core of some ten thousand personnel to become the largest, most pervasive internal security force in history, suborning vast numbers of the civilian population in the task of monitoring and controlling the behaviour and even opinions of their neighbours.

Distracted by its own preoccupations, the Kremlin reacted tardily to the rising. Little was committed to record, but it seems clear that Semyonov and the Soviet Control Commission in Berlin took the leading role in bringing Soviet units on to the streets, and that their decisions were ratified by Moscow only some hours later. However, in one respect, the events of 17 June exerted a powerful and direct influence upon the future history of the Soviet Union.

Nine days after the streets of Berlin were cleared by the Red Army, Krushchev confronted Lavrentiy Beria at a meeting of the Praesidium with damning 'evidence' of his secret negotiations with the Americans - during which, it was alleged, he had offered not to oppose the reunification of the two Germanies in return for massive US subsidies. Beria appealed for support to Malenkov, who hung his head and said nothing. At a pre-arranged signal, Marshal Zhukov burst into the room with several subordinates and arrested Beria. On 23 December that year, he and a number of his erstwhile subordinates were tried and convicted of treason. Curiously, the accusation regarding his dealings with the US – ostensibly, the most egregious of his alleged crimes - was not stated among the charges offered to the judges. He and his co-defendants were shot or hanged within an hour following the verdict. Beria's executioner, General Pavel Batitsky, later claimed that he had been obliged to stuff a cloth into the mouth of the man responsible for untold thousands of brutal, extra-judicial deaths in order to stifle his cries for mercy.

4124

Printed in Great Britain
by Amazon